CONCEIT AND CONSEQUENCE

'Legs apart,' Lucy chided, applying a gentle slap to the back of Lydia's tightly closed legs. 'It is important, I think, that a punished girl should be made to show what she has behind. Do you not agree?'

'No!' Lydia responded angrily. 'Is it not undignified enough that I should suffer a spanking, without you having to make it so rude!?'

'To the contrary,' Lucy replied happily. 'I like you to know that I can see your quim – or your cunt, to use the vulgar expression – and your bottom hole too. It amuses me. Now open your legs.'

CONCEIT AND CONSEQUENCE

Aishling Morgan

Nexus

This book is a work of fiction.
In real life, make sure you practise safe, sane and
consensual sex.

First published in 2005 by
Nexus
Thames Wharf Studios
Rainville Road
London W6 9HA

www.nexus-books.co.uk

Typeset by TW Typesetting, Plymouth, Devon

Printed and bound by
Clays Ltd, St Ives PLC

ISBN 0 352 33965 9

You'll notice that we have introduced a set of symbols onto our book jackets, so that you can tell at a glance what fetishes each of our brand new novels contains. Here's the key – enjoy!

cp (traditional)

cp (modern)

spanking

restraint/bondage

rope bondage/hojojutsu

latex/rubber/leather/enclosure

fem dom

willing captivity

medical

period setting

uniforms

sex rituals

One

Lucy tightened her grip in her cousin's hair.

'You will say,' she stated, 'these words – "I, Augusta Truscott, do solemnly avow that Lucy Truscott is quite the prettiest girl in the family."'

Augusta wriggled in Lucy's grip. Her face, set in a furious pout, was poised just inches above a broad, china chamberpot, so close that one or two of her elaborately coiffed curls of rich golden hair were already dangling in the deep pool of her night's pee. A cord of yellow silk, borrowed from her bedroom curtains, had been used to tie her wrists behind her back and another secured her ankles, making it impossible for her to rise from the kneeling position in which Lucy had placed her. One push and her face would be in the potty, but her lips remained firmly closed.

'Say it!' Lucy snapped, trying to sound commanding but quite unable to keep the mirth that was bubbling up inside her from her tone.

Augusta mumbled something unintelligible. Her head was forced down another inch, leaving the tip of her snub nose just touching the yellow liquid beneath.

'Say it! Do not doubt my intent, Augusta.'

'I shall scream!'

'As you wish. I wonder which servant would come first?'

There was no answer, but Augusta's expression grew more furious still, and her squirming more desperate. Lucy twisted her hand tighter as she spoke again.

1

'Do not be foolish, Augusta.'

Augusta squeaked in pain, and at last began to speak.

'Oh ... Oh very well! I, Augusta Truscott, do solemnly avow that Lucy Truscott is ... is ... is a conceited little pig who needs her sit-upon smacked, and ...'

There was a faint splash and her words gave way to a muffled bubbling sound as her face was abruptly immersed in the pee. She was held under, wriggling frantically but unable to break Lucy's grip.

'That is incorrect,' Lucy remarked, 'and if you're dictation is as poor for Miss Wescott, I imagine it will be you who has your sit-upon smacked. I am not spanked. I have never been spanked, and I never shall be spanked. For stating such an impossibility I will now punish you. Your face will be held in the piddle as I count to ten. One ... two ...'

Augusta continued to make bubbling noises as Lucy counted, and her feet began to drum on the floor in helpless, futile consternation. Lucy giggled and at last pulled up her victim's head. Augusta's pretty, freckled face was now shiny and wet, with pee dripping from the tip of her nose and her lips.

'These are the consequences of lying,' Lucy said. 'Now, who is the prettiest among us?'

Aside from a brief, angry spluttering, Augusta remained silent. Lucy waited a short moment, then pushed down once more, speaking as her cousin's face was once again immersed in the piddle.

'I see you are determined to be difficult. So be it.'

Keeping her grip firmly in Augusta's hair, she made short work of the long nightdress of embroidered linen that was her cousin's only garment, tugging it up to expose a little pale bottom, the cheeks quivering and well enough parted to show the tight, rose-pink anus between, and a puff of dark gold fur. Lucy spoke again as she lifted her cousin's head.

'Must I really spank you?'

Augusta didn't answer. Lucy sighed and began to slap at her cousin's bottom, making the little round cheeks wobble and quickly imparting a pink flush to the delicate skin. Augusta reacted with squeaks and gasps, until her face was once more immersed and her distress was reduced to the same odd bubbling sounds as before.

'This is most vexing,' Lucy remarked as she shuffled closer to improve her view of Augusta's rear end. 'Why can you not follow the example of your sisters? Lydia gave little difficulty, and Octavia none at all, yet both are as pretty as you, more so, perhaps. Why must you then be so stubborn? The answer is plain, is it not? It is vanity. Vanity and pride, a most unbecoming pride, for which punishment is the only suitable recourse.'

She began to spank harder, full across Augusta's rapidly reddening bottom, until her cousin's struggles had begun to grow truly desperate, with her feet drumming on the floor again, only now in a frantic rhythm. With a regretful shake of her head Lucy stopped and pulled Augusta's head up, waiting patiently until the gasping and spluttering had stopped before speaking again.

'Is your lesson learnt, Augusta?'

'You are a pig!' Augusta panted. 'A pig and . . .'

Once more she was blowing bubbles with her face well immersed in her own urine, while the slaps of Lucy's hand on her bottom flesh grew louder than ever.

'Do you never learn?' Lucy sighed. 'Must you always fight? I suppose you must, and yet you know I will have my answer, as surely as you know the truth of my assertion.'

Despite her rising distress Augusta managed a furious wriggle, which Lucy chose to take as denial. Reaching back, she pulled a silver-handled hairbrush from Augusta's dressing table and set to work with it, belabouring her cousin's now well flushed bottom. Augusta's

3

writing and kicking grew more desperate still, but Lucy paid no attention beyond allowing her mouth to curve up into a quiet smile. Only when panic had once more begun to set in did she stop.

'I do not wish to be cruel, Augusta . . .,' she began, only to change her mind. 'Indeed, I do, as it is a most enjoyable indulgence, both to spank your sit-upon and to put your face in your pot, but this is beside the point. Come, admit it. Say the words!'

Augusta was still gasping for breath, with the yellow pee dripping from her face and running down her golden curls to wet the carpet, and Lucy allowed her to recover herself before speaking again, punctuating her words with sharp slaps of the hairbrush to Augusta's bottom.

'Say it! "I . . . Augusta . . . Truscott . . . do . . . solemnly . . . avow . . . that . . . Lucy . . . Truscott . . . is . . . quite . . . the . . . prettiest . . . girl . . . in . . . the . . . family."'

On the last word she quickly dipped Augusta's head into the chamber pot, catching her unawares, so that she came up spitting piddle and blowing yellow bubbles from her nose. Lucy laughed, and with a defeated sob Augusta began to speak.

'Oh very well, if I must! "I, Augusta Truscott, do solemnly avow that Lucy Truscott is quite the prettiest girl in the family" – you wicked pig!'

'This is to be my command?' Lieutenant Fairbrother queried as he cast an appreciative eye over the sloop *Bull* where she lay riding placidly on the calm waters beside Bideford Quay.

'That's her,' the Commander answered.

'Ten guns, I see, sir.'

'A sufficiency, for your purposes.'

'Yes, sir. More than a sufficiency, I trust.'

Fairbrother nodded thoughtfully. She was small, and yet in a way that was all for the best. With a frigate,

4

which he had dreamt of but never dared hoped for, his task would have been easy, perhaps too easy. Even a small vessel of perhaps twenty-eight or thirty guns would have so easily overcome the smaller craft used by the smugglers he was supposed to apprehend that there would have been little honour in the deed. A simple cutter would never have done, too small to challenge the smugglers effectively, and generally unimpressive. With the *Bull* his task would be practical, yet require real courage, true resolution. Thus sufficient honour and reputation might be gained to impress his superiors, and perhaps even the beautiful, innocent, angelic Lucy Truscott.

At the thought of her his mouth set into a tight line, an expression compounded of determination, frustration and the powerful lust he found it impossible to contain every time he pictured her. She was fascinating, bewitching, at once so alluring, with her petite, pert figure, flame-red hair and vivacious ways, and so innocent and spiritual, far above such base, worldly lusts as came to afflict him, and yet they came, each time he thought of her, each time he saw her, the urge to tear her bodice wide and spill her little round breasts out into his hands, to turn her skirt up and rip away her petticoats, to drive his straining erection hard up into her virgin cunt . . .

Ashamed of such unworthy thoughts, he lowered his head in a brief prayer of self-condemnation. Lucy was worthy of a pure love, unsullied by the crude needs that came unbidden into his head, and yet it was impossible to hold them down. Just a glance at her face, so delicate, so fresh, was enough to set his heart hammering. She was always laughing and gay, her mirth setting her chest quivering in a most provocative manner, which invariably left his cock rock hard in his breeches.

The two weeks spent at the Truscotts' estate, Dricoll's, while waiting for his command in the

Preventative Waterguard[1] had at once been a delight and an agony of frustration. He had been smitten instantly, and yet her very gaiety made it impossible to judge whether his affection was returned, while their acquaintance had been far too short for propriety to allow him to make a declaration. Now, billeted in Bideford, his opportunities to call would be limited, and the more so for her father's somewhat grudging hospitality.

Henry Truscott had considerable reputation, it was true – fighting in the French wars, a string of duels in his youth, and a devil-may-care attitude in keeping with his family history. He was also among the richest and most influential men in the West Country, while his wife, Eloise, clearly regarded her daughter's place as elevated far above the rank to which the younger son of a squire might hope to aspire. Yet according to report, Eloise, herself the daughter of a French Count, had married Henry Truscott out of respect for his courage, so possibly there was hope . . .

'. . . and the Coppingers at Welcombe, although we've no proof and not a soul dare tell,' the Commander was saying, interrupting Fairbrother's daydream.

'Be assured that it will be my first duty to apprehend these persons,' Fairbrother answered quickly.

John Coppinger[2] gave a final tug on the strands of hemp and his wife was securely fastened to the bedpost. She was near naked, her full, pale buttocks bare between her woollen stockings and the heavily whaleboned corset that kept her waist in. Her big breasts were also bare, lolling heavily below her chest and heaving gently to the rhythm of her breathing. Coppinger laughed as he hefted the cat-o'nine-tails in his massive fist.

'Mother Mary!' he called. 'You'd be well to come upstairs.'

There was no answer beyond a soft whimper from his wife. Again he called out.

6

'Best come up, Mary, 'cause I'll flog her arse just the same.'

Still there was no response, and he hefted the cat, to bring it down with a heavy thwack across his wife's ample behind. Her scream rang out through the cottage, and he laughed as the white lines he'd laid across her fleshy bottom grew to a rich, angry red.

'Did you hear that, Mother Hamlyn?' he yelled out. 'Your eldest daughter's calling for you!'

'I did,' a voice answered from the doorway, and Coppinger turned to see the old woman standing there, her arms folded across her chest, her face set in a scowl as she looked up at him, her head barely reaching his neck. 'I suppose it's money you want?'

Coppinger laughed, nodded, and aimed a second cut at Annie's bottom, this time setting her screaming and making frantic treading motions with her toes to dull the pain. The old woman barely moved, her scowl merely deepening as her eyes moved to her daughter's whipped bottom and back.

'I told you it's gone,' she said. 'Every last penny, you've had.'

'And if I don't believe you?' Coppinger answered, shaking the cat out in preparation for another stroke.

'Give him what he wants, mother, I beg you!' Annie pleaded, twisting around in an attempt to meet the old woman's eyes.

'Can't give what I don't have,' Mary answered sullenly, and Annie screamed again as the cat was brought down on her bottom one more time.

'You've plenty,' Coppinger stated, 'and if you'd an ounce of mercy in your rotten old hide you'd give it up. What is it to you, mouldering in some hole out on the farm, like as not. I have need for it!'

As he finished he brought the cat down again, landing it across Annie's bottom with the full force of his brawny arm. She screamed and began to hop on her

7

toes as before, making her big breasts jiggle, to set him laughing before he gave his cock a reflective squeeze through his breeches. The old woman gave him a look of sour distaste and made to reply, only to be interrupted by a pounding on the door.

'Answer that,' Coppinger ordered, 'and tell them to go to hell, unless it's one of our own, or someone come to buy.'

Mary shuffled away with a last pitying glance for her daughter's buttocks. Coppinger listened for a moment, then shrugged and laid in another blow of the cat, setting Annie dancing and whimpering for mercy.

'No, John, not now! It can do no good, now!'

'Do no good?' he answered. 'It does me good, girl, reason or none.'

He laughed again and gave her another vicious cut, then turned to the door at the sound of voices, leaving Annie quivering and gasping for breath, with the first beads of sweat now running down over the discoloured skin of her buttocks. Mary's voice came again, the respectful tone very different from the grudging mumble with which she addressed him.

'Come in, come in do, Mr Truscott, sir,' she was saying. 'John's busy right this moment, but . . .'

'Not so busy I can't find time for my best customer!' Coppinger called out.

He gave Annie a last cut and turned for the door, to find his guest already approaching. As he saw the whipped woman, Henry Truscott allowed his eyes to move down her body before he gave an appreciative nod.

'Ah, there you are, Coppinger. Warming your bob tail? Afternoon, Annie, my dear.'

'Just a dose of what she deserves,' Coppinger answered as he threw the cat-o'nine-tails down on the bed. 'Thirsty work and all. Would you care to fire a slug?'

'I would,' Henry Truscott answered, 'but I've not come to make a purchase. I've news.'

'News?' Coppinger asked, with a curt nod to Mary, who promptly left the room. 'Good or ill?'

'Ill, after a fashion,' Henry answered him. 'The navy have finally set aside a ship, the sloop *Bull*, which is to be under a Lieutenant Fairbrother.'

Coppinger shrugged.

'The fellow you had at Driscoll's?'

'The very same,' Henry answered. 'Fancies himself a bit of a firebrand, does young Fairbrother, and the *Bull* carries ten guns.'

Coppinger nodded thoughtfully and sat down on the bed, gesturing towards the room's only chair as he did so. Henry Truscott sat after making a small adjustment to his chair so that his view of Annie's naked breasts and well whipped bottom was unobstructed. She turned a resentful pout to her husband, then spoke.

'John, should you not untie me? For my honour's sake if . . .'

'Hush, woman,' Coppinger interrupted. 'Your pardon, Mr Truscott, you were speaking of this Fairbrother?'

Henry made a languid gesture and continued.

'I was, and he's sure to be a thorn in your side.'

'Could he not be bought?'

'Not Fairbrother. He's an ass.'

'Killed then?'

'They'd merely appoint another in his place, but I've a thought. If I'm any judge, he's taken a rare liking to my Lucy, and a man's tongue's never so loose as when he has a woman to impress. Let him babble to Lucy, and I can tell when the *Bull* will be a danger to you, and the gist of his plans and orders, for a consideration, naturally.'

'Certain sure,' Coppinger replied, and laughed. 'But aren't you like to end up with an excise man for an in-law?'

9

'No risk there,' Henry answered, smiling. 'Mrs Truscott talks of Lords, and nothing less'll do. French, by preference, and not less than her own late father's rank. He was the Comte Saônois, you know, as Lucy has had impressed upon her since early childhood. No, she'll not marry Robert Fairbrother, but she'll flirt well enough, if only to vex her mother.'

Coppinger gave a gruff laugh and reached out to take a glass of pale tawny liquid from a tray offered by Mary Hamlyn. Henry had already taken his glass, and gave the contents an appreciative sniff as the old woman rounded on Coppinger with a question.

'Have you not the decency of a stoat?'

Puzzled for an instant, Coppinger hesitated, then realised that the old woman was remarking on her daughter's condition: Annie, tied in place, waiting in silence for the men to finish.

'I've not finished,' he growled, 'unless you've a mind to cease your lying and fetch what I need?'

'I tell you,' the old woman retorted, 'you've had every last farthing from me, and besides, with your brandy and your silks, haven't you money enough now?'

'I must invest!' Coppinger snapped back and turned to Henry again. 'Women! They understand nothing of business!'

Henry gave an understanding nod. Mary Hamlyn responded with a grunt.

'This is good,' Henry remarked as he swallowed his first sip of what was evidently a fine Cognac, 'and different to what you had before, unless I am mistaken?'

'New it is,' Coppinger answered, 'and I was hoping it would find your favour.'

'Mine and many others',' Henry assured him. 'The Stukeleys, I would think, and old Nat Addiscombe for certain, although I'm never sure if he drinks the stuff or feeds it to his damn tulips.'

'What of your brother?'

'Absolutely not. There is no more upright prig in England, and he would report you on the instant and put you on the gallows when the matter came before him as justice. Stay well clear of him, is my advice. Besides, the cellars at Beare are comfortably stocked and he barely touches a drop. What do you have in?'

'Twelve casks.'

'I'll take four, if the price is the same.'

'What of Fairbrother?'

'Pay me when I have some news of value,' Henry answered before taking a last, deep sniff at the contents of his glass and emptying it down his throat. 'I'll send Jack Gurney for it in two nights' time, but for now I must get back to Driscoll's.'

Coppinger gave an understanding nod and stood as Henry did, to show his guest to the door before returning to the task of flogging his wife.

Nathaniel Addiscombe frowned as he peered close to the tulip. It was a fine bloom, without question, and yet it was not black. There was a hint of black, yes, in the veins and at the base of each perfectly formed, velvet-textured petal, but the predominant colour was indisputably deep purple. He drew a sigh.

'Magnificent, Mr Addiscombe,' Stephen Truscott remarked, 'quite magnificent, a nonpareil. A credit to your perseverance and skill, also, I venture to suggest, to the Devon climate.'

'I thank you,' Addiscombe replied, 'and yet while I appreciate the tenor of your remarks, and that to a layman such words as "magnificent" and "nonpareil" are no more than justice, I am sure that you will likewise appreciate that to the horticulturist my efforts fall far short of perfection. A true, deep black is my endeavour, Mr Truscott, and no lesser shade will suffice.'

'A worthy aim, no doubt, but after some two hundred years of effort both by ourselves and the Dutch does it

11

not seem likely that a true black colour is an impossibility? After all, where in nature do we see black flowers of any species?'

'Nature may be moulded, Mr Truscott, and in truth it has only been in recent years that the black tulip has come to represent the acme of desire. The Dutch in the seventeenth century, for instance, prized variegation above all else, and while there is no question that my task is not an easy one, this knowledge only drives me on. After all, did Arthur's knights abandon the quest for the Holy Grail merely because it could not be found in the sideboard?'

He chuckled at his own wit, to which Stephen Truscott responded with a somewhat forced smile, then went on.

'No, they did not, and nor shall I. I am convinced that a true black is possible, and indeed, I believe I have discovered the key to achieving this.'

'And what is that, Mr Addiscombe?'

'A secret, naturally, a secret most dearly held, yet suffice to say that I have discovered that the answer lies as much in the soil as in the plant itself.'

He finished with a nervous cluck, as if feeling that he might already have said too much, then continued, changing the subject entirely.

'I trust I am to have the pleasure of Mrs Trucott's company this afternoon, and also of your charming daughters, and of Miss Lucy Truscott?'

'Absolutely,' Stephen assured him, 'Reuben has been instructed to drive them over from Beare in the landau. I trust so many will not be an inconvenience to you?'

'Not at all, not at all,' Addiscombe replied with enthusiasm. 'I need merely instruct Polly, which is no great task. Four young ladies? How delightful. I declare they almost put my flowers to shame. I shall have some pressed beef laid out as well as the ham, and perhaps some crystallised fruits, from my own orchards, you understand.'

'Nothing too rich, I trust?'

'Be assured of it, not rich, never rich, yet plentiful. I have always felt it important that young ladies should eat well, and maintain a proper diet, balanced between the meats and the staples, as I do myself.'

'Absolutely,' Stephen replied.

'I cannot imagine why Papa wishes us to visit Mr Addiscombe,' Octavia Truscott remarked, 'or at least why so frequently.'

'Possibly he intends to make a proposal of marriage to one or another of you,' Lucy responded.

Octavia began to colour and opened her mouth to give what might have been a sharp reply, only to think better of it. Lucy smiled and went on.

'You find the idea unsettling? I cannot imagine why. He is a gentleman, of sorts, and wealthy enough – although I believe his family to be of yeoman stock some three or four generations back – while you bring a respectable twenty thousand pounds. It is a union I imagine the world would find little to disapprove of, do you not think?'

Still Octavia didn't reply, pretending to adjust a honey blonde ringlet in the mirror of the dressing table at which she was sat. Lucy allowed herself a cool smile and then continued.

'Or are you saving yourself for better? If so, I advise against it. Your fortune, while adequate, is insufficient to tempt any of a titled family, save those who have fallen into poverty perhaps, while . . .'

'It is not a matter of the gulf that exists between Mr Addiscombe's status and my own,' Octavia interrupted suddenly, 'although I assure you it is greater than you seem to imagine, but of the gulf in our age. Besides, if you are so eager to find Mr Addiscombe a wife, why do you not put yourself forward?'

Lucy sniffed.

'An impossibility. Even Mr Addiscombe must be aware of this. You, on the other hand . . .'

'Mr Addiscombe is sixty-three years old, I believe, also portly, balding, and has a number of peculiar habits. To serve a large meal at noon, for example. How could one receive guests when forever having to excuse such eccentricities?'

'These things you must learn to put aside,' Lucy stated gravely, 'for if you seek perfection in a man you are like as not to end up with nothing at all. I say this, you understand, purely from a cousinly affection. You are pretty enough, I suppose, but your height is against you and if you wish to attract a man of sensibility you might do well to show a little less enthusiasm for dumplings, cream and so forth before the results begin to show on your hips and belly as well as your bust.'

Octavia's mouth was open in outrage and she failed to answer.

'My advice,' Lucy went on as she tied her bonnet, 'is to make yourself pleasant to Mr Addiscombe, and no doubt, in proper time, he will find an excuse to speak with you alone and, red faced and full of urgency, make a declaration of his passion. Perhaps I might even be able to expedite matters. Yes, why not? I shall assist you, within the bounds of propriety naturally.'

'Pray do not trouble yourself,' Octavia answered icily.

Lucy raised an eyebrow.

'Do not be pert, Octavia, or were the carriage not ready I might be tempted to take you across my knee and spank your little fat bottom. You would not like that, would you? Now come along, Augusta and Lydia will be wondering what has become of us.'

She left the room, Octavia following, tight lipped and sullen.

Lydia Truscott paused to adjust her parasol, allowing just enough time for her father and Mr Addiscombe to

enter the long glasshouse. Her mother and Lucy Truscott were already inside, admiring the long rows of
tulips, and her sisters had held back, but Mr Addiscombe paused to hold the door. With little choice but
to enter, she smiled politely and did so, her nose
wrinkling at the tang of manure. Mr Addiscombe
beckoned to Augusta and Octavia.

'Come in, my dears. I have something to show you,
which, I venture to hope, will come as something of an
honour.'

Both girls obeyed, Augusta with a smile every bit as polite
and every bit as decorous as Lydia's, Octavia struggling not
to pout as he motioned her through with a gentle touch to
the seat of her dress. Within the glasshouse many panes had
been lifted, allowing cool air through the netting intended to
deter insects, but it was still uncomfortably hot. She shared
a glance with Augusta, who returned the faintest of shrugs,
and together they were obliged to follow their father and Mr
Addiscombe to the far end of the aisle.

There were tulips to both sides, each in an individual
pot, and each carefully labelled. Many were in bloom,
showing a variety of colours: yellows, reds and oranges,
whites and pinks, a few variegated, fewer still rich, dark
shades, culminating in a group of blooms of intense
purple. Mr Addiscombe stopped beside them, beaming.

'My most recent cultivar,' he announced, extending a
hand to the darkest of the tulips.

'It is very beautiful, Mr Addiscombe,' Augusta stated
dutifully but with at least some genuine feeling. 'I
understand that the darker colours are the most prized?'

'You are not mistaken, Miss Augusta,' he responded,
'not mistaken at all, and while the ultimate goal, the
Holy Grail as it were, is to produce a tulip of perfect
black hue, the specimen you see before you must be
accounted a remarkable success by each and every
person of consequence within the field. But, my dear,
can you imagine what I have named it?'

15

'I would not dare to guess, Mr Addiscombe,' Augusta replied.

'No? Then it must be that your modesty equals your beauty, for this bloom is to be known to the world as Miss Augusta Truscott.'

He had made another flourish in the direction of the tulip as he spoke, and then put his hands behind his back, tucking up the tails of his black coat and beaming. Augusta's face was slightly flushed, and she gave the slightest of curtsies before responding.

'I am honoured, Mr Addiscombe, but if you are to bestow such a singular compliment, would it not have been more appropriate to select "Miss Truscott" as a name rather than my own in particular?'

'Ah ha,' Mr Addiscombe replied, 'your sense of propriety does you credit, my dear, but no. I have selected two fine cultivars for your sisters' names to honour: Miss Lydia, Miss Octavia, I refer to these, the crimson and this intermediate shade, which is of unusual richness. For Miss Lucy I have reserved the ultimate accolade – to have the world's first tulip of true black hue named after her.'

Lucy responded with a grudging smile and a nod of acquiescence. Lydia turned to inspect her own bloom, which she realised was labelled with her name. It was certainly unusual, a shade somewhere between the richest crimson and purple, with the veins darker still. She leaned close, only to draw back as the manure smell grew stronger.

'Quite beautiful, I thank you,' she remarked before sharing a concerned look with Octavia as Mr Addiscombe turned his back.

The elderly horticulturist continued to expand on the merits of his blooms, and Lydia listened politely as she grew slowly more uncomfortable in the heat. When they were finally able to leave the glasshouse the cool breeze blowing in from the west came as a profound relief, and she immediately proposed taking a turn of the grounds before going in. Mr Addiscombe responded enthusiastically.

'A splendid idea! It will improve your appetites for dinner, a meal which you will find conveniently announced by the next peal of church bells, at four o'clock. Sadly I am unable to join you, as I must see to affairs indoors, but I wish you the enjoyment of your walk.'

He was beaming, a perpetual expression in their presence, and he took his leave with a bow so exaggerated that Lydia found herself stifling a giggle. To her relief, both her parents and Lucy followed him towards the house, and she was left alone with her sisters for the first time that day. Augusta spoke the moment the other party were out of earshot.

'His presumption is extraordinary! To name his beastly flower after me, without so much as a by-your-leave, and I am sure he intends it as a prelude to making a declaration! On no account must either of you leave my side when we are in his company!'

'I am sure he intends to make a declaration, yes,' Lydia agreed. 'Why else would he be so persistent in inviting us here? But surely Lucy must be the object of his affections if he is intent on reserving the name of his precious black tulip to her?'

'You mistake his behaviour for that of a man in love,' Augusta responded, 'and therefore intent on the object of his desire to the exclusion of all others. Mr Addiscombe does not love, he lusts, and while it may be that Lucy is his favourite, I have no doubt that any one of us would suffice for his purposes.'

She gave a delicate shudder as she finished.

'At least he shows me no special sympathy,' Octavia said, 'for which I am profoundly grateful, while I find a most enjoyable irony in the prospect of his making a declaration to Lucy. Immediately before we came over,

17

she not only suggested that he favours me, but that I would be wise to accept!'

'Her behaviour is an outrage!' Lydia agreed with feeling. 'And so very vain! Why, only this morning she ... but no matter. Suffice to say that she is becoming intolerable.'

'This morning she demanded that I declare her the prettiest among us,' Octavia added, 'which I was obliged to do, for ... for she is horribly strong, and inclined to make threats ...'

'Threats she is quite capable of carrying through,' Lydia asserted, 'and I do not think her especially pretty. Much is made of her complexion, but it seems to me not so much pale as bloodless ...'

'Quite without colour.'

'A most unhealthy pallor, although typical of the red haired.'

'Her hair is not red, but orange, like a Dutch carrot.'[3]

'Also indicative of her temperament; cruel and irascible.'

'Her French blood, I imagine.'

'She has all of her mother's conceit, certainly.'

'Although in Lucy's case quite unwarranted.'

'Her mother's vanity also.'

'Again unwarranted.'

'And so immodest.'

'Positively vulgar.'

'And such grand airs!' Octavia stated. 'To suggest that I should accept Mr Addiscombe and yet that he is beneath her own notice, as if she were not my cousin, and of the junior line of family also!'

'Her conceit knows no bounds,' Lydia agreed, 'and I would give a great deal to see it pricked.'

Octavia laughed.

'Now if, from some turn of providence, she were obliged to marry Mr Addiscombe, that would be a conclusion both just and comic!'

Lydia laughed in turn.

'Just and comic indeed,' she answered, 'but I had imagined some other fate, more of the kind she chooses to inflict on us, perhaps . . .'

'No,' Octavia interrupted. 'She must marry Addiscombe. Imagine her kissing him, and those horrible hands, so white and fat, touching her!'

'And to be Mistress here,' Augusta added, 'and obliged to entertain his friends.'

'And to have that dreadful man always about,' Lydia put in. 'Mudge, who always seems to be somewhere in the background, and always watching!'

She shuddered at the image she had conjured up, but found herself smiling, the idea going at least some of the way to soothe her feelings at having had her arm twisted behind her back and her bottom exposed for a threatened spanking that morning. Octavia laughed too, and Augusta was smiling, but gave a cautious glance back along the path. Lydia followed suite, but there was nobody there.

'It could never be,' Augusta sighed. 'He will make a declaration, no doubt, but she would no more accept than Uncle Henry grant permission.'

'No,' Octavia agreed, 'she would not, and while it would sting her vanity for the declaration to be made, as a revenge for her behaviour it is perhaps somewhat abstract. I would prefer her to suffer a more palpable humiliation.'

Two

Henry Truscott eased his cock between Suki's fat brown thighs, drawing a pleased sigh from her as her quim filled. She was naked but for her stockings, boots and a corset that could barely contain her abundant curves. Certainly it could not contain her gigantic breasts, which hung naked and bulbous beneath her chest, quivering to Henry's thrusts as he fucked her. He took her hips, letting his fingers sink into her soft flesh, and began to pull himself in hard and deep, making her bottom wobble like a huge brown jelly. She was moaning deep in her throat and clutching at the dressing table over which he had bent her, enjoying herself every bit as much as he was. After a few quick thrusts he slowed his pace, intent on making her come before he did, only to twist around with an angry snarl as a knock sounded on the bedroom door.

'What is it, damn you, James!'

His footman's respectful voice replied.

'Mr Robert Fairbrother has arrived, sir.'

'I did say there was insufficient time,' Eloise remarked from where she had been watching Henry fuck her maid. 'So much better to wait for the evening, when we might have enjoyed ourselves at leisure.'

Henry's response was a grunt, Suki's a gasp as he jammed himself as deep into her as his cock would go. Digging his fingers into her flesh, he focused himself on the magnificent sight of her naked, quivering bottom, forcing all thoughts of Robert Fairbrother from his mind. She began to squeal as his pushes grew faster, rising to a pig-like crescendo which abruptly stilled when he whipped his cock from her quim to spray come across the velvet smooth skin of her upturned bottom and between her heaving cheeks.

As he sat back on the stool with a long and satisfied sigh, Suki had already begun to masturbate, her fingers working eagerly between the plump, fleshy lips of her quim. Henry watched as he recovered his breath, Eloise also, with her face set in a quiet smile, until once more Suki began to squeal, this time in orgasm as she took herself to climax. Henry gave her bottom a firm slap as her muscles began to go slack.

'My apologies, Suki, and rest assured that we'll take up where we left off just as soon as we've got rid of that puppy Fairbrother, who by good fortune is obliged to ride back to Bideford directly after dinner.'

He went to the washstand, while Suki moved to adjust the fall of Eloise's dress. Quickly washing his cock and pulling his breeches back up, he joined Eloise on the landing and they descended the stairs together. Lieutenant Fairbrother was in the hall, in full uniform and holding his hat across his chest as if uncertain what to do with it. Henry extended his hand as Eloise bobbed a curtsey and Fairbrother bowed.

'Ah, Mr Fairbrother, how d'you do?' Henry greeted the lieutenant. 'I am delighted that you could come, quite delighted. So, you are to be patrolling our northern coast after all, splendid. And the *Bull*, is she to your satisfaction?'

Lucy was standing in the doorway of the drawing room, and bobbed prettily, making the bare upper slopes of her breasts quiver and instantly setting Fairbrother's face scarlet. He began his reply as Henry ushered him towards the dining room.

'She is of the new Cherokee class,[4] and carries ten guns. Small, it is true, and in herself perhaps no more than a match for the smugglers, but with fortitude and courage . . .'

'Splendid, glad to hear it,' Henry interrupted. 'Sit yourself down. Cognac?'

'I'd be delighted, sir, thank you. Good afternoon, Miss Truscott.'

'Mr Fairbrother,' Lucy responded, with a coy glance apparently at the floor but in practice at the front of his breeches. 'A pleasure that you have been able to break away from your duties long enough to dine with us.'

'A pleasure indeed,' Fairbrother responded, 'but sadly a brief one. I must return to Bideford before sunset.'

'Not chasing around the coast at night, are you?' Henry enquired. 'Damn dangerous.'

'No, not at all,' he answered, and put his fingers together as he went on, only to have to disengage them to take the glass of Cognac being offered by James. 'Er . . . yes . . . I mean to say, no, not at night, no, but it has occurred to me that this may be precisely what is required.'

'Indeed?' Henry queried.

'Yes,' the younger man went on, full of enthusiasm, 'because I am convinced that it is the only way forward. Patrolling by day is of little use. These people know the coasts, every cove, every cliff path, every cave. The only way we'll ever catch them is to play them at their own game . . . Ah! Exquisite Cognac, Mr Truscott. You have broached a new cask, unless I am mistaken? Let me guess, an 'eighty-four?'

'An 'eighty-seven,' Henry lied, 'one of the last my father put down. Most of the stock is at Beare, of course, but we younger sons must make do with what is left us.'

Fairbrother gave an understanding nod and went on.

'The real devil of it is – begging your pardon, Ma'am, Miss Truscott – that we know who they are, at least the worst of them. There's a farm near Welcombe, Hamlyn's by name, where a man called Coppinger lives – you've heard the name, no doubt, Mr Truscott?'

'We do not number the local farmers among our acquaintance, Mr Fairbrother,' Eloise pointed out.

'Absolutely not, Mrs Truscott, of course,' Fairbrother responded, blushing scarlet, 'but he has the blackest of reputations, far and wide!'

'I have heard the name,' Henry admitted. 'He came ashore from a wreck, did he not?'

'So it is said,' Fairbrother continued. 'He is a Dane, or so he claims, others say Irish, and was the sole survivor, wading ashore through pounding surf as if stepping from a pond! More extraordinary still, if the story is to be believed, he went to Annie Hamlyn's horse where she was waiting on the beach to see what might be carried away, mounted up and rode to her farm, as bold as brass, with her on a halter behind him . . . er . . . though, naturally, that last detail can be no more than fabrication. In any event, he is now married to her, and the entire neighbourhood holds him in terror. I've not seen him, yet, but he is said to be a giant of a man, with the strength of ten . . . again, an exaggeration, no doubt.'

'A formidable foe,' Henry remarked before taking another admiring sniff of the Cognac Jack Gurney had brought over from Coppinger's that morning. It was reasonably mature, although undoubtedly not pre-war, and perhaps as good as the lesser examples among the stocks in his brother's cellars at Beare.

'Formidable indeed, Mr Truscott,' Fairbrother continued, 'and no fool either. I've posted men at every likely landing point from Tintagel to the Neck, and not a sign. My thought is he has his own men out on the cliffs at night to signal the boats in where it's safe,

23

perhaps at low tide beneath high cliffs, and we can't watch every yard of the coast.'

'You are likely correct,' Henry answered thoughtfully, and sat back to allow a bowl of soup to be served at his place.

'But what must you be thinking,' Fairbrother went on, 'with me troubling you with my own trivial difficulties when your own son is in Spain fighting the French ... um ... begging your pardon, Mrs Truscott. Do you have news?'

'Pray do not concern yourself,' Eloise responded. 'Since Llerena,[5] we have heard nothing from John, but we put our faith in God.'

'Quite so,' Fairbrother replied.

'He has a certain appeal,' Lucy Truscott mused, as much to herself as to her maid, Suki's daughter Hippolyta, 'but Papa is right to call him a puppy.'

Hippolyta continued to work on Lucy's hair, taking each bunch of flame-red curls carefully in her hand before running the brush through it. Lucy sighed, enjoying having her hair brushed, and also the memory of Lieutenant Fairbrother's attention. She was sure his cock had been hard as they stood together on the terrace after dinner, and he looked distinctly uncomfortable when mounting his horse. Her presence was the only possible reason for such a reaction and, while it amused her to think of his urgency and frustration, it was annoying to think that she had no more choice than he did in not indulging themselves in what was plainly possible in a physical sense if impossible in a social one.

For all her amusement at his hopeless desire for her, and her only partially pretended contempt for his masculinity, his company had left her slightly flustered, with her nipples annoyingly hard beneath her nightdress and an uncomfortably wet sensation between her thighs. That she should react to a man beneath her own station was annoying, and filled her with the need to take out her feelings on somebody else. As she rose to her feet with her hair now a cascade of red curls falling loose to the middle of her back, she was wondering if it would be soothing to find some pretext to spank Hippolyta.

The answer was undoubtedly yes, as turning the maid's coffee-coloured bottom the rich fox-red hue it became after punishment would assuage both her arousal and her sense of pique. Yet she hesitated, conscious that Hippolyta stood a head taller than her, and was quite capable of losing her temper, while the maid's position with the family was not open to negotiation. To watch her spanked was one thing, to do it another and, despite her determination to exert her will, she had a nasty feeling that in the event, it might be her, and not the maid, who ended up with a bare red bottom. Worse still, she might enjoy the aftermath. A less forthright approach was needed.

'Come,' she stated, patting the bed beside her, 'sit by me.'

Hippolyta responded, crossing from the dressing table with her languid, graceful walk. Her full mouth was set in a half-smile, indulgent, perhaps slightly mocking, which from any normal servant would have sent Lucy into furious indignation. As it was, she merely smiled back. Hippolyta spoke as she sat down.

'Well, Miss Lucy, what is it you want?'

'You know very well,' Lucy responded.

'Then perhaps I should lock the door?'

Lucy nodded, feeling more than a little chagrined but not entirely sure why as Hippolyta crossed to the door, turned the key in the lock and walked back. Both knew what was going to happen, and yet Lucy was blushing as she pulled her nightdress up and off, to leave herself stark naked, her pale skin smooth and lit yellow by the light of the candles. Hippolyta climbed back onto the bed as Lucy lay down, her chin resting on her folded arms, her eyes closed as the maid's long fingers pressed down on her shoulders. She sighed as Hippolyta began to stroke her neck, firm yet gentle, soothing Lucy's feelings but quickly increasing her need, until she had begun to want her quim touched.

Before long what little restraint Lucy sought to maintain had gone. As Hippolyta's caresses moved lower Lucy began to lift her bottom, offering herself to a more intimate touch. At first Hippolyta ignored the invitation, only to quickly move her position, kneeling up on the bed. Lucy's thighs were taken and eased apart. Hippolyta came to kneel behind her and Lucy's quim was showing, her own scent strong in the air. The maid's hands settled on Lucy's body once more, now lower, pressing onto the soft flesh in the dip of her back, caressing. Soon Lucy had begun to lift her bottom again, but with greater urgency, and higher, to make her cheeks open and invite a yet more intimate touch.

Lucy gave a shiver and a mew of frustration as Hippolyta's fingers once more began to work on the nape of her neck. Her hips were lifted, her quim offered to the maid's touch, but still Hippolyta held off, moving only slowly downwards, until at last she was caressing the fleshy cheeks of Lucy's bottom, moulding them and opening them to show off the tight, rose-pink anus between, then lower still, cupping Lucy's quim in one hand.

As Hippolyta began to masturbate her, Lucy's fingers locked in the sheets of her bed. It was done skilfully, with one long finger lying in the groove of her sex and the others holding the bulge of her quim, something that always filled her with a delicious sense of being held as well as the ecstasy of being brought to orgasm. Hippolyta's spare hand was on Lucy's bottom too, caressing her cheeks, teasing between them, tickling her anus, touching the tight ring of flesh which sealed off her virgin hole . . .

Lucy came, crying out her ecstasy into the bed as her body went into spasm after spasm with her quim jiggling under Hippolyta's fingers. Only when it was quite over did she move, rolling onto her back to take her maid into her arms and they were kissing and laughing together, but only briefly. After a moment Hippolyta had climbed off, to rise and peel her simple blue woollen dress over her head, taking her single loose shift with it. Naked but for her stockings and boots, she walked across to the candles, with Lucy's eyes fixed to her firm, coffee-coloured bottom and long, tapering legs.

Pausing only to remove her boots, Hippolyta snuffed out the candles, leaving the room in absolute darkness. Lucy climbed in under the covers and a moment later felt Hippolyta get in beside her, her flesh warm and smooth. Without a word, and only an instant of hesitation, she had burrowed down the bed, climbed between her maid's legs and buried her face in the warm, wet quim.

Robert Fairbrother knelt at the side of his bed, his hands folded in prayer although there was nothing reverent about the thoughts in his head, save in so far as his lust for Lucy Truscott had begun to border on worship. Thoughts of her crowded his mind at all hours, many of them unworthy, especially at night, when he had twice been forced to take his erection in his own hand to provide release from his own imaginings. Now, with his cock so stiff it hurt and his mind reeling with thoughts of how it would have been to simply pop her breasts from her bodice and make her fold them around it, what remained of his rationality was desperately seeking a more efficient means of relief.

Vaguely he was aware that some of the streets behind Bideford docks housed women willing to sell their bodies for a price, although it had never crossed his mind for an instant that he would need to use one. He had always condemned prostitution as an offence against God and against man, and yet as he adjusted his aching cock in his uniform breeches he had begun to see that to a bachelor it might be at worst a necessary evil. In any event it was clearly a choice between that and masturbation, which filled him with guilt and shame in any case.

For the best part of two hours he had been attempting to drive the wicked thoughts from his head by dint of prayer, as so many priests had advised as a panacea against all evil thoughts. It had done no good whatsoever, his mind lingering on Lucy's sweet curves with ever greater intensity and his cock remaining obstinately hard. Finally he gave up, said a final prayer to beg forgiveness for his intended sin, pulled on his cloak and made his way out of the barrack house.

Outside the moon was high and bright, the night remarkably warm. The *Bull* rode placidly at anchor, the watchman's lantern casting a dull yellow glow over her stern quarters. He hurried past, his collar pulled up to hide his face, and plunged into the tangle of alleys behind the docks. Some windows were illuminated, and in one a slatternly woman was looking out at the night, her painted face set in profound boredom and disinterest. He moved quickly on, unable to make himself speak to her, and as he turned the next corner he saw a man leave a house, an old man in a bottle-green coat, red faced and merry. Within the open door stood a woman, her cheerful, soft face framed in abundant black curls, her sole garment a nightdress under the front of which two large breasts made inviting balls.

If she had none of Lucy's pert delicacy or coy restraint it made no difference to his cock, which had grown stiffer still, to form an aching bar in his breeches. He was walking forward even as the other man merged with the darkness of an alley mouth, and as she saw him she gave a momentary start, then spoke in a soft, Irish

28

voice as he began to stammer out meaningless entrea-
ties.

'Sir! Hold a moment, give poor Molly a chance, will
you!'

Her initial shock had turned to giggles, and in a
moment he was inside, with the door shut behind him.
She took his hand, and he let himself be led up the
stairs, to a room hung with faded drapes. Unsure what
to do, he let her sit him down on the bed and proffered
a handful of coins in response to her arch look of
enquiry. She took them, still giggling, but now with
delight, and even through his fog of embarrassment and
arousal he realised he had overpaid.

It made no difference. His cock was harder than ever
and she was burrowing for his breeches flap, her heavy
scent intoxicating in his head, the feel of her soft flesh
against him impossibly alluring, too alluring, and even
as his cock came free into her hand he was coming, the
spunk erupting in a series of high jets across the
straining front of her nightdress and into her face as she
had bent with the intention of taking him in her mouth.

She squealed in shock, but was soon giggling again,
even as his desperate arousal died to give way to a guilt
of equal force. Red faced and babbling apologies and
snatches of prayer, he forced his still-hard cock back
into his breeches and fled, down the stairs and out into
the night. As he made his way back to the barrack house
he was burning with self-recrimination and guilt, yet
also filled with more zeal than ever to fulfil his duty, but
most particularly to bring each and every one of the
local smugglers to justice and thus make himself worthy
of Lucy Truscott, both in his own eyes and, with God's
blessing, in hers.

Henry Truscott rapped on the farmhouse door with his
walking stick. He had seen nobody since passing
through Meddon village, and there was a marked lack

of labourers on the Hamlyn farm. Both the open, grassy hilltops and the furze-covered slopes leading down to the rocky combe were empty of people, while the sea stretching away beyond the cliffs was equally empty but for distant sails in the channel and a pair of small fishing boats off Bude. He frowned as the door opened, then smiled and gave a bluff greeting to Mary Hamlyn, who ignored him. John Coppinger appeared behind her, towering over both of them, and as he entered Henry saw that there was another man standing at the parlour table, slim but broad shouldered, elegant in a fine coat of cherry-red cloth cut away at the hips, and holding a glass of amber fluid up to the light. Henry cast a questioning glance at his host as he threw his hat down on a chair.

'Monsieur de Cachaliere,' Coppinger explained, 'over to make certain arrangements. Monsieur, this gentleman is Henry Truscott, Squire to Driscoll's Estate and a name in these parts.'

'Citizen de Cachaliere, please,' the Frenchman answered, bowing stiffly. 'Mr Truscott.'

Henry gave a disapproving sniff but took the extended hand. The Frenchman's grip was bony and hard, suggesting strength and also control. Henry replied a little pressure in return and had the pleasure of seeing one corner of the man's mouth twitch up before he let go. De Cachaliere was evidently associated with Coppinger's Cognac suppliers, perhaps even the estate owner himself to judge by the expensive cut of his clothes. An open bottle stood on the sideboard. Henry poured himself a glass and took a sniff and a swallow before speaking again.

'I have news, no doubt of interest to both of you.'

'Spoken to your excise puppy, have you?' Coppinger asked.

'Puppy he may be,' Henry answered, 'but he's no fool, and he doesn't take you for one. He's had men watching the cliffs . . .'

'That I know.'

'. . . and has concluded that you signal the ships to come in, but no more than that, at least, not that I am aware.'

Coppinger nodded.

'He'll need better than that to catch John Coppinger. It would take a hundred men to cover my stretch of the coast, and we can sink rafts,[6] if needed.'

'No doubt,' Henry answered him, 'but you'd do well to be cautious, and it would be no bad thing to make the farm at least look as if it is worked as it should be.'

Again Coppinger nodded. The Frenchman gave a chuckle of amusement. Henry ignored the apparent slight for his caution and took another sip of brandy, which was warm and rich, with a faint scent of oranges. De Cachaliere was watching him sidelong with what might have been a sneer.

'You make excellent Cognac, Monsieur de Cachaliere,' Henry stated.

The Frenchman gave a precise nod of concurrence and buried his substantial nose in his own glass. Determined to be pleasant against all his instincts, Henry went on.

'How long do you keep it in barrel?'

'This one here, five years. In my *logis* at Beillant are casks dating back to the early part of last century. These last are reserved, naturally.'

'Indeed?' Henry queried with new interest. 'I would be willing to pay a not inconsiderable sum, if you would be prepared to release one or two.'

'No,' de Cachaliere replied, 'they are to me like children, and without intending insult, you do not possess the money to persuade me to give a single one.'

'Ten thousand pounds?' Henry suggested.

The Frenchman's eyebrows rose a trifle and he extracted his nose from the glass, where it had remained as they spoke.

31

'You would pay ten thousand pounds for a single cask of Cognac?'

'No,' Henry answered, 'I merely wished to establish whether they were genuinely not for sale.'

To his surprise the Frenchman smiled.

'Ah but yes, it is an old trick, no? In my youth I would play it upon the girls in Bordeaux, Paris too, but in Paris all but the youngest knew well what was intended.'

Henry laughed.

'Yes, the same is true in London, where one would think the bob tails took lessons in their art.'

'Bob tails?' de Cachaliere queried. 'Harlots?'

'Any woman who'll wiggle her backside your way,' Henry replied.

De Cachaliere laughed in turn and put down his glass before he spoke again.

'Then I am like your London bob tails, Mr Truscott, and will not be so easily caught. My oldest casks are not for sale, ever, and besides, much has gone to the angels, which makes for poor shipping, and yet I might be prepared to part with a little of the 'eighty-four, or perhaps the 'seventy-nine?'

'I'd be delighted to take either,' Henry responded, 'and as to price . . .'

The Frenchman made a gesture at once languid and dismissive.

'Discuss the matter with Mr Coppinger. I ask only that I am not openly cheated. And now, perhaps you would be so good as to advise me on where I might enjoy a little of your English "bob tail".'

'Advise you?' Henry responded. 'Damn it, I've better hospitality than that, I'd like to think. I'll join you. There's an Irish girl in Bideford, Molly Hynes, clean, and a dumpling shop the like of which you'll not see often in Paris, I'll warrant . . .'

* * *

Saul Mudge glanced up as a bell rang. It was one of a row in the Addiscombe pantry, each of which was marked with the name of the room in which he or Polly were needed. But the one which was ringing had no label, and Polly looked up from the cutlery she was polishing to throw him a look of deep disapproval as he got to his feet. He chuckled, and was still chuckling as he left the room, to peer cautiously out into the passage.

Nobody was visible, and he ducked quickly back, moving to a door off the parlour and into a small room flagged with slate and furnished with a single long table on which stood a number of pots, both china and earthenware. In one wall a square wooden door was set into the panelling and above this hung a picture, a crude watercolour of a moorland stream. Mudge moved close, eased the picture carefully aside and put his eye to the hole he had revealed.

His view was now of the interior of the privy, seen through an iron grill, in which Octavia Truscott was in the act of pulling up her skirts, exposing a fetchingly plump, pale bottom and a hint of the already slightly pouted ring of her anus as she sank into a squat. Mudge's mouth curved up into a sly grin and he squeezed his cock through his breeches. Watching Octavia on the privy with her skirts held high, he could still see the soft swell of her hips, the upper slopes of her bottom cheeks and just a hint of the deep crease between. He caught the hiss of her pee, then the heavy plop of a turd.

Octavia was his favourite, the youngest of the three sisters and the one with the fullest figure, her bottom a rounded, fleshy delight up which he yearned to push his cock every time he watched her at her business. Her open disdain for him made the pleasure all the greater, especially as she rose to take a piece of linen from the box provided to delicately pat her quim dry and wipe her anus clean. Only when she had dropped her skirts did he step away from the hole, rubbing his hands and chuckling with delight.

Another, briefer glance at the hole showed that she had left the privy. He quickly ducked down to open the hatch, extracted the pot she had used, tipped the contents into another which had the letter "O" worked into the glaze in a pale, bright green edged with gold, and replaced it with a clean one. His cock had grown half-hard as he watched her on the privy, and as he came back into the parlour he found Polly looking at him with an expression at once resentful and resigned.

'Not now, Saul,' she began, but there was no real hope in her voice and he was already undoing the buttons of his breeches as he answered.

'Oh yes, my pretty, now, right now, and be thankful the bell for the noon meal will be ringing soon, or it'd be going up that fine fat arse of yours, and not in your mouth. Now open up like a good girl.'

His cock was out, hot and damp in his hand as he peeled back his foreskin from the bulbous head within. She made a nervous motion, tucking one brown curl up under her mobcap, and her expression of resentment grew stronger still as the smell of his cock mixed with that of baking meat, but her mouth had come open. Mudge fed his cock to her, looking down to admire her full bust within her dress, and to enjoy the look of sullen distaste on her face as she began to suck him.

Pulling his balls from the flap of his breeches, he began to squeeze them as his cock grew in her mouth. Despite her disgust she had begun to mouth on his knob, trying to make him come as quickly as possible, but he was wise to the trick and took her firmly by the hair, forcing himself deep as soon as he was fully erect. Polly began to gag as her throat filled with swollen cock meat, and tried to shove him back. He only pushed harder, jamming his erection deep between her tonsils, ignoring her muffled protests and thoroughly enjoying her distress as he began to fuck in her throat.

Her face was going red and she had begun to bat at him with her hands, while her cheeks were blown out and her eyes wide. It was impossible not to laugh, and he did, a moment before he felt his orgasm start to rise up. Taking the struggling, frantic Polly hard by her ears, he forced himself deeper still, and as the muscles of her throat went into spasm, so did his balls, ejaculating a full four days' store of spunk down her neck. He groaned as he came, closing his eyes to picture Octavia Truscott wiping her bottom as gout after gout of come squirted into Polly's throat. Only when he was quite finished did he let go of her ears, to pull out and leave her gasping for breath, her face dark red and a runnel of mixed come and spit dribbling out over her lower lip.

For the first time in years Augusta Truscott found that being at Nathaniel Addiscombe's house was an experience more pleasant than otherwise. It had always been a pleasure in her childhood, with the beautiful flowers to admire and the wooded gully that separated his property from the Beare Estate to explore, but as she had grown older she had found first the attention of the servant Mudge and then of Mr Addiscombe himself unnerving.

Now, with her sisters busily engineering an amusing fate for Lucy, it was once more enjoyable, while Mr Addiscombe's obvious preference for her cousin went at least some way towards setting her mind at ease. His manner was still disconcerting, both his familiarity and the way he often seemed to be considering her and her sisters during quiet moments, as if they were not fellow human beings at all, but dainty curios of which he was considering the quality, or perhaps wondering whether or not to make a purchase.

Mudge was worse, yet she was never quite able to decide why his attention was so offensive. His very presence seemed to imply an insolent familiarity that made her skin crawl, and yet he seldom spoke to her and when he did it was in a suitably respectful tone. Wherever she was he seemed to be too, never close, never openly watching, yet always there. Time and again she had told herself that as Mr Addiscombe's man he had a perfect right to go about his business both in the house and around the grounds, but it did little to soothe her feelings.

As they took their leave she was smiling. An expedition had been arranged, an expedition which could hardly fail to provide an opportunity for Lucy's comprehensive humiliation. Everything had been carefully arranged, and they were certain of success, while the incident would hopefully leave the three of them with the appearance of innocence. All that remained was to issue the invitation to Lucy herself, and it seemed most unlikely that she would decline.

Yet her smile was nervous, and she was full of apprehension for what might happen if Lucy did discover their plot or, worse, if the plot was a success and she was not deceived. Lucy's cruelties had been growing slowly more inventive and more extreme in any case, and that without any real reason. With a reason she would really take trouble, and Augusta could guess that there were worse things than having her face dipped in the contents of her own chamberpot and having her bottom spanked, things which set her stomach fluttering and put a whole host of embarrassing and shameful thoughts into her head. Neither Lydia nor Octavia took the same view, as both were convinced that for them to fight back would mean the end of Lucy's wickedness.

'She will no longer dare,' Octavia was saying confidently as they picked their way along the lane towards Beare. 'Is this not the way with bullies?'

'She is no ordinary bully,' Augusta responded, 'but quite mad. Who knows how she might respond?'

'You are wrong, dear sister,' Lydia disagreed. 'I am sure of it.'

'I also,' Octavia put in. 'A show of resistance is all that is needed, and yet I am still tempted to encourage a declaration towards her from Mr Addiscombe. She will refuse, yes, but the mere fact of his presumption will put a heavy dent in her insufferable pride.'

'I imagine,' Lydia laughed, 'that by then her pride will be somewhat lessened. Perhaps she will even accept him!'

Octavia laughed, and Augusta found herself smiling too. It was a pleasant thought, although something deep within her rebelled at it, the same little voice that told her Lucy deserved the respect and praise she demanded, especially to be looked up to. It was not something she had admitted to her sisters, and nor was the reason that she always chose to resist Lucy and therefore bore the brunt of her cruelty.

Lydia and Octavia continued to talk and laugh together as they walked back to Beare, Augusta adding the occasional aside and responding to their open enthusiasm with affectionate smiles. Once back with their parents they were careful to behave as if there was nothing out of the ordinary, but their plan remained at the forefront of Augusta's thoughts, and Lucy.

By the time she was lying in the warmth and darkness of her bed, with just a sliver of bright moonlight coming in at a crack in the curtains, she was sure it would all go horribly wrong, and struggling against her own feelings for the consequences. Lucy would have her revenge, and it would be worse than anything before, far worse, undoubtedly adding a whole new chapter to Augusta's knowledge of how agonising personal humiliation could be, and what it did to her. Perhaps when it happened she would even prove unable to keep her feelings to herself . . .

Augusta closed her eyes as her hand went between her legs, to squeeze the soft mound of her quim through her nightdress. For a moment she tried to resist, but she knew she was going to do it, and a moment later had lifted her bottom to pull the nightdress up, first to her belly, and then to her neck, leaving her breasts naked, and everything below. With a gentle sob she allowed her hand to move back to her now bare mound, her skin sensitive beneath the thick bush of hair that hid her most intimate details, and lower, to the little split fig of flesh that was at once such an embarrassment and such a delight.

To have her nightdress up was bad enough, even in the darkness of the night with her covers to shield her body, but what Lucy did to her provoked feelings far, far stronger. As she began to stroke herself she thought back to how it had felt to have her nightdress lifted for her bottom to be smacked, how awful, and how wonderful, or her moment of terrified anticipation as her head was held over her own potty, about to be pushed in; her fear, her consternation, her dreadful sense of helplessness.

Then had come the moment, the moment her face had been pushed under and she'd been blowing bubbles in her own pee as her bottom was spanked, her bare bottom, with her quim sticking out behind, so utterly rude and so utterly vulnerable. It had hurt, and it had hurt more with the hairbrush, a stinging pain that had at last brought her to the point where she had yielded to Lucy's demand . . .

She gave a little shiver, tossing her head at the thought of what might have been, what might be in the future. Perhaps if she had resisted, Lucy might have taken the awful punishment further still, a harder spanking, or a cane brought up and applied to her bottom, mercilessly, until she screamed, until she wet herself in her pain and confusion, all over the carpet as Lucy laughed at her. It would have been so easy. With her hands and feet tied she'd been helpless. Lucy had done as she'd pleased, and could have done more, so much more.

Yes, she should have resisted for longer, until she'd been stripped naked, beaten with the hairbrush until she howled, made to drink her own pee, or worse. That was what Lucy should have done, really made her suffer, naked and tied, her bottom well spanked and her face well down in the pot as she gulped down the contents, all of it, then more, from Lucy's own pot, filled in front of her face. Perhaps that was what would happen next time. She'd be made to watch, close up, as the pee squirted from Lucy's quim into the chamber pot, then to drink it, every last drop until her belly was bulging and round with her own urine and her cousin's too.

She was squirming against her sheets, wriggling her bottom and tossing her head from side to side, her breasts jiggling wildly about, to rub her hard nipples on the upper sheet. Her thighs were wide, her fingers busy between them, pinching and rubbing at the little firm bump that was the focus of all her pleasure. As she started to come the last vestiges of her modesty and reserve broke, and she was biting her lip to stop herself from screaming as the vivid images in her mind came together.

Lucy wouldn't just beat her and humiliate her, she'd take it far further, making her strip naked, spanking her hard, making her drink her own pee, both their pee. Only when it came to drinking Lucy's pee, it wouldn't be from a pot, but hot from her cousin's body, quim to mouth, with what spilt out running down her bare chest and belly, over her own quim, but with plenty going down her throat, to fill her belly, and when Lucy was quite done, she, Augusta, would be made to kiss and lick at her cousin's quim until Lucy did in her face what she was now doing under her own, frantic fingers.

Three

Lucy Truscott smiled at James as she was helped down from the carriage. It was a perfect day for the year's first trip to Meldon Pool, the pretty, sheltered lake where the West Okement tumbled down from the heights of Dartmoor. It had been a favourite place for generations of Truscotts, and Henry now rented the land, ostensibly as a quarrying concession but in practice to ensure a privacy that had always been problematical.

As the north-western corner of Dartmoor lay roughly equidistant between Driscoll's and Beare, they had arranged to meet in Meldon village, where the servants would remain while the girls went to bathe. Lucy was looking forward to it, both for the pleasure of going naked in the cool water and the prospects it offered for tormenting her cousins. By good fortune both Mrs Caroline Truscott her maid were indisposed, meaning that Lucy, and Hippolyta, would be alone with the three girls, providing an opportunity to test a new humiliation she had long been considering.

Stephen Truscott's landau was already outside the inn, with Augusta and Lydia standing beside it, as bright as brimstone butterflies in their yellow summer dresses. Lucy approached them, leaving Hippolyta to deal with the hamper of provisions she had ordered. Both girls smiled in greeting, Lydia frank, Augusta delightfully nervous.

'Is it not a perfect day?' Lucy said, greeting her cousins. 'And not yet May. Where is Octavia?'

'She has a slight chill,' Augusta responded, 'and Mama would not allow her out for fear of its developing.'

'A shame!' Lucy went on. 'A very great shame. Nevertheless, we must endeavour to enjoy ourselves as best we may, and she will no doubt appreciate your descriptions of our day. Are you quite on your own?'

'Quite,' Lydia answered, 'but for Reuben.'

'Who can hardly accompany us,' Lucy responded. 'Have you brought nothing in the way of victuals?'

'We have a little smoked ham,' Augusta told her, 'a jar of pickles, hard-boiled eggs, a loaf of bread and two bottles of beer.'

'Then we have quite a repast,' Lucy said. 'I have a bottle of Hock, plovers' eggs, two different pastes, a little cheese, bread, and a flask of Cognac in case we feel the chill. Hippolyta, take Miss Trucott's packages.'

'Yes, Miss Lucy,' Hippolyta answered, and added the three parcels Augusta had taken from the carriage to her burden.

Lucy took Augusta's arm, and Augusta Lydia's as they set off up a lane which quickly turned into a steep track running between stone walls. Beyond the last cottages of the village they came into a wood of stunted trees, each hung with grey-green lichen, some with rough bark, others with clusters of orange berries. The path grew steeper, and increasingly rocky, making Lucy feel clumsy in her dress and petticoats, and eager to shed them.

At length they reached a place where the track turned sharply, to look down over the pool, an expanse of perfectly still water between the wooded slope and a cliff. Sunlight reflected from the surface, except in the shade of the rock, where it was so clear that the bottom could be seen as a jumble of pale shapes and shadows.

The air was hot and still, making the water seem cool and inviting. They descended the slope, stopping on an area of soft, flat grass beside the pool, a place familiar to all of them from earliest childhood.

Tall, ancient gorse bushes, still bright with yellow flowers, surrounded their space, providing shelter save for where the grey-green bulk of Langdon Hill rose towards the high moor. Nobody was visible, not even in the distance, and Lucy began to undress without fear of being overlooked, enjoying the warm air on her skin as she wriggled out of her dress and petticoats, passing each garment to Hippolyta, who folded them neatly on a rock. Both Augusta and Lydia showed considerably more embarrassment, to Lucy's amusement, and she was already peeling off her second stocking by the time they were out of their dresses.

Naked, she stretched in the sunlight, watching as the other girls, including Hippolyta, completed their strip. There was no doubt in her mind that she had the best figure, although there was a definite family resemblance between them. Both sisters had their mother's deep blonde hair and a little of her height, but all three of them were compact and pert, their breasts high and quite full without being heavy, their waists slender without undue exaggeration, their hips and bottoms womanly without excess flesh. With her height and sleek, muscular limbs, Hippolyta seemed a giant among them, and yet she too had pert, upright breasts and a rounded bottom.

Lucy waited until all four of them were naked before stepping into the water. It was cold, and it took a moment before she could pluck up the courage to plunge in. When she did it was a shock, and for a few seconds she was gasping and swimming as hard as she could in order to shake off the cold. By the time she had reached the middle of the pool Lydia had also entered the water, but not Augusta, who was hesitating on the brink with only one toe dipped cautiously in. Hippolyta was waiting politely in the background.

'Do not be a coward, Augusta!' Lucy called, 'or I shall have Hippolyta throw you in. How would that be?'

Augusta cast a single, extremely nervous glance at the maid, who grinned back, then jumped into the water, landing with a clumsy splash and disappearing for a moment beneath the surface. She came up spluttering and gasping, making Lucy laugh as she trod water in the middle of the pool.

For a while they swum and played, Lucy splashing the others and ducking both her cousins repeatedly, until she had begun to get cold. It was still short of noon, and not really time to eat, so she struck out for the far end of the pool. Where the cliff turned to the south a ledge of rock stuck out, dark slate worn smooth by the water and bathed in sunlight. They knew it well, as the perfect place to lie naked in the sun without the least chance of discovery, and Augusta was already hauling herself out of the water, her pale, wet skin glistening in the light as Lucy reached it. Augusta extended a hand and Lucy took it, pulling herself from the water. After a moment of hugging herself and jumping up and down on her toes she sat down on the warm slate, wondering if it would be a good time to indulge her new idea. It was, without question, and she signalled for Hippolyta to swim towards them. Lydia was already doing so, and soon all four girls were sitting naked on the rock, Lucy and Hippolyta in artless display, the sisters in more modest poses.

'If you are all quite dry and warm,' Lucy said after a while, 'we shall play a little game. It is called Choices.'

Both Augusta and Lydia gave her worried looks.

'The rules are as follows,' she went on happily. 'One among us, myself for example, presents one of the others with two choices, between which the one chosen must make a selection. Once she is done, it becomes her turn and she may choose somebody else.'

'What sort of choices did you have in mind?' Augusta asked cautiously.

'Oh, this and that,' Lucy responded with an airy gesture of her hand, 'whatever might amuse.'

'If you wish to be beastly to us, why not simply do so and have done with it?' Lydia asked in her most sulky tone. 'You know you can make us.'

'Do not be dull, Lydia!' Lucy chided. 'My game is ever so much more fun, and what is more, if you wish to be beastly to me in return, you need merely set me a choice when your turn comes. Is that not fair?'

Lydia's answer was a sulky pout, and she stayed silent. Augusta looked worried and thoughtful, apparently considering the possibilities of the game. Hippolyta had sat down a little way off, with her feet in the water, waiting to be instructed.

'If Lydia is going to be a baby about it, I shall present you with the first choices, Augusta,' Lucy stated, 'which are . . . let me see, yes, you must either pee in front of us, or come across my knee to have your bottom spanked. Which will it be?'

Augusta hesitated, blushing, glanced at her sister, then spoke, her voice cold but clearly forced.

'I would prefer not to do either. Must you always be so rude?'

'You misunderstand me,' Lucy answered, ignoring the question. 'Think of it this way if it is more in accord with your sense of modesty. If you do not pee in front of us, then I will spank you.'

Augusta had begun to pout, and once more glanced at her sister before replying in a barely audible voice.

'I . . . I am not ready to pee.'

'Then you shall be spanked!' Lucy crowed in delight, and quickly adjusted her position so her legs stuck out down the gentle slope of the rock. She patted her lap, but Augusta hesitated.

'Come,' Lucy said, her voice now firm and demanding, 'or I shall have Hippolyta do it, and how would that be, to be spanked by a maid!?'

Augusta had gone bright pink and quickly stood up, still pouting badly and also shaking somewhat as she came to lay herself across Lucy's lap, bottom up with her chin resting in her hands. Lucy rubbed her hands together in sheer glee as she admired the cheeky globes of female bottom flesh in front of her, and then set to work, spanking with both hands, one on each cheek, to set them wobbling and Augusta squealing in perfect time to each slap. Lucy was laughing, and continued to do so as she completed the spanking, giving Augusta two dozen firm slaps on each round little cheek, to leave them flushed deep pink.

'There, you are done, Augusta dear!' she declared as she delivered the final pair of smacks. 'And how comic you do look! Why, I am not sure which is the redder, your sit-upon or your face!'

Augusta got up as quickly as she could and scampered back to her place, rubbing her smacked bottom as she went. Lucy's smile was broader than ever as she tucked her legs underneath herself and spoke again.

'There we are, is it not the most amusing of pastimes? Now, Augusta, you may have a sore sit-upon, but it is your turn, and if it amuses you then you may inflict an equally horrid fate upon me, although you must remember that I am not spanked, not ever. Do you dare?'

Immediately Augusta was shaking her head.

'I had thought as much!' Lucy laughed. 'So then, you must present your sister with her choices, and be sure they are worthwhile. I will accept nothing that appears as an escape.'

Augusta hesitated, glancing to the scowling Lydia, then to Lucy. She spoke.

'It seems I must present you with a choice, Lydia dear. You must . . . you must either . . .'

She hesitated.

'Come, come,' Lucy chided, 'let us hear what it is to be.'

'She . . . you . . .,' Augusta went on, turning from one to the other, 'you must either bow down at Lucy's feet, or be spanked, as I was.'

'And if I refuse?' Lydia replied.

'I will have Hippolyta spank you,' Lucy assured her. 'Hard.'

Lydia hesitated, then moved position, rising to make a perfunctory bow towards Lucy.

'Not enough,' Lucy stated. 'You must grovel to me, on your knees, as you did the other night.'

'You made me!' Lydia retorted.

'And I shall make you again,' Lucy answered. 'On your knees, Lydia, this moment!'

Pouting more fiercely than ever, Lydia got down, kneeling and leaning forward.

'Kiss the ground,' Lucy demanded.

Lydia hesitated an instant before planting a gentle peck on the slate in front of Lucy, who burst out laughing.

'There, it is done, albeit with reluctance. So, Lydia, cousin dearest, do you have the courage your sister lacks, to force me to make some terrible choice?'

For a moment Lydia was going to speak, only to think better of it and sit down again, now with her arms crossed over her naked breasts. Lucy was shaking with laughter, and it took a moment before she could speak again.

'Have you no spirit at all, either of you! Come, I'll wager little Octavia would give me a choice, and a hard one. Won't you, Augusta? Think how I dipped your face in your pee pot, Augusta dear! Think of when I made you kiss old Orcombe's bulldog, Lydia, or strapped your behinds with Jack Gurney just outside the door! You squealed so prettily, just like two pigs! Do you not want to be revenged?'

'I fear your own revenge will be worse,' Augusta mumbled.

'Yes,' Lucy assured her, 'it will, be assured of it, because I am ever so much more clever and inventive, but is that not beside the point? Think, Lydia, you could give me the choice of kissing Hippolyta's sit-upon or your own, and in truth I am not sure which would be the more humiliating . . .'

'To kiss a maid, thus!' Lydia exclaimed, and then added quickly, 'or anybody at all, for that matter.'

'Now I have you! Now I have you well!' Lucy answered gleefully, now laughing so hard she was clutching her sides and had set her breasts quivering. 'Come now, make me choose, or you must forfeit your turn to me!'

'Not at all,' Lydia answered. 'I shall present my choices to Augusta.'

'As you wish,' Lucy chuckled. 'Would you care for some advice?'

'I am well able to make my own choices, thank you,' Lydia answered. 'Augusta, dear sister, if we must play this horrid game, I charge you either to . . . to stand upon your head, or to perform a cartwheel.'

Lucy gave a snort of deprecation.

'What sort of choices are those!? Hippolyta, spank her bottom for her and see if a pair of warm cheeks help to improve her imagination.'

'That will not be necessary,' Lydia said quickly as Hippolyta made to rise, 'but I will say this now, and you may do what you will to me. You have no sense of the proprieties at all, to suggest that I be punished, and in so ignominious a fashion, by your maid! I begin to wonder if you have not had the ill fortune to inherit something of that malaise which affected our mutual grandfather . . .'

'If old John Truscott was mad, at least he had spirit!' Lucy retorted. 'Now give Augusta her choices, and make them worthwhile, or I shall have Hippolyta spank you, and without further ado!'

Lydia had begun to pout again, but soon gave an answer.

'Very well, if I must I must. Begging your pardon, dear Augusta, but would ... would ... would you prefer to ... to pee for us, as Lucy so rudely suggested, or ... or to kiss her, as ... as a lover might?'

'That is more in the spirit of the game, much more, thank you, dear cousin!' Lucy chuckled. 'Come then, Augusta, which is it to be? Are you able to pee yet?'

'No!' Augusta answered, throwing Lydia a flustered look.

'Then you must kiss me,' Lucy declared, 'on my quim.'

'On your quim!' the sisters chorused in horror.

'Absolutely,' Lucy confirmed, 'that is how lovers kiss, at least, one of many ways.'

'What nonsense!' Lydia exclaimed. 'And how ... how base!'

'Oh do be quiet, Lydia! Come, Augusta, a kiss.'

She had opened her legs to show off her quim, which felt badly in need of a touch, and the thought of having Augusta kiss her there had set her stomach fluttering. Lydia was red faced and tight lipped, Hippolyta trying not to giggle. Augusta merely stared, and then she was crawling forward, on her hands and knees. She hesitated as she reached Lucy, speaking briefly to call her a pig, but then bent and kissed the soft, furry mound in front of her as Lydia gave a gasp of shock.

'Augusta, how could you!'

'You made the suggestion,' Augusta answered sullenly, rising.

'Not ... not like that! I meant upon the lips, as might one's betrothed!'

'Hardly suitable cousinly affection, even then,' Lucy chuckled. 'Now, Augusta, the game has passed to you again, and it would be poor sport to choose your sister. You must choose me, or Hippolyta and I shall spank you both, side by side, until your fat sit-upons are quite as pink as your faces. Come then.'

Augusta swallowed. She had sat back on her haunches, and her hands were shaking as she gave her sister a guilty glance. Lydia was scowling furiously, and looked away. Augusta hesitated. Lucy wagged a finger and raised an eyebrow towards Hippolyta.

'You are a beast!' Augusta retorted. 'To use us so, a wicked pig!'

'I do not understand,' Lucy answered. 'I am the one to be faced with the choice.'

Augusta made a face.

'If I must then. You ... you must choose that fate you threaten us with, to be given a spanking by Hippolyta, and ... and ... breaking your maidenhead, here and now!'

She had spat out the last words and as she finished the expression of her face had become one of stark terror. Lucy felt a flush of annoyance before she managed to respond with a now somewhat hollow laugh. The idea of Hippolyta spanking her was too close to home, a thought that brought agonising chagrin at any time, and was more than she could bear to think about with her cousins looking on. There was no choice but to refuse.

'Your choice is no choice!' she snapped back. 'Be sensible, Augusta, when I am merely playing. You know I am not spanked, not ever, and how can I be expected to break my own maidenhead? Provide sensible alternatives.'

Augusta made a face, but quickly stammered out an answer.

'You ... you must grovel at Lydia's feet then, as she did to you, or ... or pee for us, so that all may see.'

Lucy gave a satisfied nod and immediately pulled herself up into a rude squat, thoroughly enjoying showing herself off as she spread the lips of her quim open in full view. Augusta was staring, open-mouthed in horror, Lydia looking pointedly away, Hippolyta giggling behind her hand as a thick stream of pale golden pee squirted from Lucy's quim to splash on the rock beneath and trickle down the slope. Lydia was forced to move quickly aside to stop herself getting wet, setting Lucy shaking with laughter so that her pee started to come in little quirts instead of an even gush. Finally she lost her balance, to sit her bottom down in the little pool beneath her with a faint squelch, but still laughing as she struggled out her words.

'Look what you have made me do, Lydia! Oh, for that I must give you a proper choice, a choice you will struggle with!'

'How was this my fault!' Lydia gasped, now standing, and looking down at the little river of pee still flowing past her feet.

Lucy made a dismissive gesture and went on.

'Hush, Lydia, I must think. Hmm, perhaps as you are so conscious of your position, I . . .'

'I am conscious of my position? What of yourself!? What of this beastly game, where you make us perform lewd acts that any man coming onto the brow of Langdon Hill might observe! What if we are discovered!?'

'Any man carrying a ship's telescope and on the lookout, perhaps,' Lucy answered, 'but I see nobody. As to our game . . .'

'It would cause a scandal from Penzance to London, and beyond. You . . . you will promise not to reveal what Augusta and I have done today, will you not?'

'I give my promise, unconditionally,' Lucy stated. 'You will come to learn, Lydia, that an important difference exists between one's public behaviour and one's private. Naturally it would be unthinkable for such a game as this to be public knowledge, and yet among the three of us it is no more than an intimate and amusing diversion. Now . . .'

Lydia was left gaping as Lucy gave a thoughtful tug at her chin, then burst out laughing.

'I have it! You must kiss Augusta's quim, or Hippolyta's!'

'Kiss their . . . their . . . my . . . my own sister, or . . . or your maid!' Lydia answered in horror.

Lucy clapped her hands in delight as she replied.

'You see how clever my game is? Now you must choose between two dreadful improprieties, but which is the lesser, that is the question!'

'No!' Lydia answered. 'Never! Do what you will with me, if you must, but I will not submit to such impropriety, not willingly!'

'Come,' Lucy insisted, 'make your choice, I long to see!'

'No!'

'Lydia, do not spoil our sport!'

'Sport! You are a witch, Lucy Truscott, a mad witch, to suggest such impropriety, such cruelty, such . . .'

'Nonsense, dear cousin, it is but a game. Now come, make your choice.'

'Absolutely not!'

'Oh, spank her, Hippolyta, I am done with her bleating.'

Hippolyta began to rise, grinning, but Lydia threw herself into the water, striking out for the nearest shore.

'Catch her, and spank her well!' Lucy ordered, her voice now angry, but Hippolyta was already in the water, swimming out after Lydia.

There was never a moment's doubt who would reach the bank first. Hippolyta was far the better swimmer, and had pulled herself out onto the grass while Lydia was still in the deep part of the pool. Hippolyta stood,

51

her hands on her hips, her brown skin glistening wet, her full chest heaving. Lydia stopped, treading water as she looked first at Lucy and then at Hippolyta.

'Be kind, Lucy, dearest,' Augusta spoke suddenly. 'Leave poor Lydia and, if you feel you must give a spanking, then spank me instead, but yourself, not Hippolyta.'

'No,' Lucy answered with a stamp of her foot. 'I will not be flouted. Lydia, you are to be spanked, and spanked by Hippolyta, whether it is now, or after some time when you can no longer bear the cold of the water.'

Lydia gave her an angry glare.

'Come out,' Lucy ordered, 'or I will have her pick a birch wand and you shall have a proper thrashing!'

'You wouldn't dare! I shall tell Mama!'

'And what then?' Lucy laughed. 'She would come to know I had you whipped, and Uncle Stephen also, and so my father, and my mother, others too, perhaps. Your father is a man of stern principle, Lydia, he might even bring the matter to the bench. Everyone would look on you as the girl who was whipped by a maid!'

'More likely you would be whipped yourself!' Lydia stormed. 'And stupid Hippolyta dismissed!'

'I am never beaten, not ever,' Lucy answered, 'and Hippolyta will never be dismissed. Now you see how my little game mimics life. Make your choice, a playful spanking or the full consequences . . .'

She broke off, clapping delightedly as Lydia began to swim for the shore, directly towards the waiting Hippolyta, then calling out.

'Spank her well, Hippolyta, across your knees on that rock, but wait, I am coming over.'

As Hippolyta went to sit on the boulder Lucy had pointed to, Lydia reached the shore. Lucy waited, biting her lip in delicious pleasure as she watched her cousin climb out and walk to the maid with her face set in utter consternation, which grew stronger still as she was taken by the arm and laid down across the coloured girl's lap, bottom up in traditional spanking pose. Only then did Lucy slip into the water, swimming quickly across as Hippolyta waited to begin the punishment. Augusta followed.

Reaching the bank, Lucy climbed out, hugging herself against the cold as she stepped close to where Hippolyta was holding Lydia ready for spanking. It was a fine sight, with Lydia's wet curls hanging around her sulky face and drops of water on her nipples, which were hard. Behind, her knees were firmly together, but the rear of her quim could still be seen, with a split fig of furry flesh peeping out from between her thighs.

'How wonderful you look, Lydia!' Lucy chuckled. 'I declare that the pose suits you, to perfection. We must do this often, perhaps the three of you, one after another. Would that not be fun?'

Lydia shook her head in miserable denial, then gave a gasp as Hippolyta's hand settled on her bottom.

'A moment,' Lucy instructed, 'before you begin, let her consider her position, held naked across a maid's knee, about to have her sit-upon spanked for her wilfulness. Think upon it, Lydia, as you are punished, think how your pain and indignity might have been avoided by a simple kiss to your sister's quim.'

Lydia made a sudden, angry noise, but said nothing.

'Spank her,' Lucy ordered. Hippolyta tightened her grip around her victim's waist and it had begun.

As Lydia's bottom began to bounce to the firm smacks of the maid's hand Lucy was laughing immediately, and clapping her hands in glee. In no time Lydia had lost her reserve, and begun to squeak and beg for mercy, also to kick her legs so that the rude details of her quim were properly on show from the rear. Lucy scampered back and forth, laughing and clapping, unsure whether she preferred to watch the comic expressions on her cousin's face or the rude display of

virgin quim, puckered bottom hole and rapidly reddening cheeks from behind.

Hippolyta warmed to her task, grinning as Lydia's
squeals grew louder and her struggles more desperate,
but holding on easily. Augusta watched too, by the
water's edge, wide-eyed and biting her lip, but in a
position that gave her a full view of the thoroughly
immodest show Lydia was making of her rear end.
Soon Lydia's pleas for mercy had become an incoherent wailing, mixed with squeaks of pain as the slaps
landed. Her whole bottom was glowing red, with her
thighs pumping in her pain, and open, to show off her
quim, with the tiny pink hump of her hymen on plain
show, her flesh puffy, and wet. Lucy stopped her wild,
gleeful dance as she saw, and her hand went to her
mouth.

'I do believe!' she exclaimed. 'I do believe that our
little Lydia, our proper little Lydia, is really quite
excited. Hippolyta, enough spanking, you may stop.
Manipulate her instead.'

The spanking stopped and Lydia collapsed, gasping
and whimpering across Hippolyta's knee, only to let out
a pig-like squeal of shock as the maid's finger found her
sex. She began to fight, kicking wildly and beating her
fists on Hippolyta's legs, but the maid held her easily,
all the while rubbing at the fleshy split between her
well-spanked victim's thighs. Then Lydia had gained
some control over her outrage and her screams had
turned to words.

'No! Not there, you beastly girl! No! No! No!'

Hippolyta continued to rub, now pushing her thumb
in between Lydia's hot bottom cheeks so that it rubbed
on the slippery, sweaty little hole between. Again
Lydia's panic-stricken, furious pleading turned to wordless shrieks. Lucy had begun to jump up and down on
her toes in sheer delight, clapping and cackling with
joyful laughter, which grew louder and more delighted

still as Lydia's smacked bottom cheeks began to contract at the onset of orgasm.

'No! Leave me! Not there!' Lydia was yelling as she once more found her voice, only for it to break to a gasp of astonishment and ecstasy as she began to come under Hippolyta's busy fingers.

The maid was laughing as Lydia went through a squirming, wriggling orgasm, panting out her helpless pleasure and at the very peak even wiggling her bottom against Hippolyta's hand. Then it was over, and she'd been released, to tumble from the maid's lap and sit down hard in the grass, wide-eyed and shaking for a long moment before she remembered herself and her anger returned. Tight-lipped and clutching her spanked bottom, she stalked off towards where they had left their clothes.

'You see,' Lucy called after her, 'there is a great deal more dignity in simply accepting one or other choice without fuss.'

Lydia didn't answer, and Lucy turned to Hippolyta.

'Thank you, a job well done. I shall see that you receive an extra sixpence at the week's end. That was most enjoyable, was it not, Augusta, dear? Enough for now perhaps. I am hungry.'

Augusta didn't answer, but trailed after Lucy as they followed Lydia between the gorse bushes, picking their way carefully on the spaces of soft grass. There was a little gasp from Lydia, and as Lucy came out to where she could see their camp she realised why. Their clothes were gone, all of them, even down to their stockings, and Lydia stood with her hands to her face and her cheeks crimson, the spanking and every other indignity inflicted on her apparently forgotten as she turned to Lucy.

'Our clothes! Some rogue has stolen them, and . . . and they must have watched us bathe, and . . . and . . . your stupid game!'

Lucy looking around nervously, her hands going to her chest and quim by instinct as her heart began to hammer, imagining some man or men nearby, watching, perhaps waiting. Augusta had come up behind her, and she too gasped, looking around in perplexity. Lucy saw that their boots were still there and the picnic parcels lay where Hippolyta had left them. Relief welled up, but she kept her hands firmly where they were, her legs well crossed and her bottom towards a large gorse bush.

'What are we to do!?' Augusta wailed.

'This is no thief,' Lucy stated, fighting to sound calm, 'but some wicked prank. What rogue or gypsy would leave us our boots? He would take our bottles too, for certain.'

Augusta nodded but glanced around.

'You are right,' Lydia said, her voice shaking, 'but our clothes are gone, and a half-mile to Meldon village, where the servants wait and cannot fail to see us, villagers too!'

'One of us must go,' Augusta answered. 'What choice is there?'

'Not one alone, but two!' Lydia stated forcefully. 'What if some coarse fellow were to come upon just one of us?'

'You are right,' Augusta stated, swallowing. 'You and I shall go, Lydia, as it was we who suggested the excursion and therefore we who must accept the consequences of this catastrophe, however terrible . . .'

'Oh, nonsense!' Lucy broke in. 'You cannot go, neither of you. You are ladies!'

Lydia turned to her in surprise.

'Given your conduct, cousin Lucy, I would have thought the prospect of Augusta and me being forced to walk naked through the main street of Meldon would amuse you greatly.'

'Not at all,' Lucy responded. 'How can you think such a thing? As I believe I remarked earlier, there is a world of difference between what passes between us in private and what we may show the world. I would no more have you walk naked through Meldon village than do so myself. Hippolyta must go, it is plain, and for her modesty she must plait grass and ferns.'

Augusta made to speak but thought better of it and glanced at Lydia instead, who shrugged.

'Come, come,' Lucy went on, 'let us not allow this unseemly incident to spoil our excursion, or it will only provide greater amusement to the prankster. We will find a place in among the gorse to deny him the pleasure of peeping at us, and eat our picnic while Hippolyta goes to the village. Is this not the wisest course of action?'

Both Augusta and Lydia nodded an assent that struck Lucy as oddly reluctant.

Four

Henry Truscott looked around as the drawing room door crashed open. Eloise stormed in, her face set in an angry flush, and she was speaking before he could make an enquiry.

'What is this I hear from Suki? That Lucy was abandoned naked at Meldon Pool, her clothes stolen by some villain!?'

'Yes, just this morning,' Henry laughed. 'That will teach her not to set somebody to mind her things, eh?'

'This is not the moment for levity, Henry, anything might have happened to her!'

'At Meldon Pool?' Henry queried. 'And besides, who would dare, in these parts?'

'The same insolent whelp who stole her clothes!'

'You exaggerate, Eloise, my dear. There is a great gulf between a boyish prank and an act of violation. Doubtless some lustful ploughboy followed the girls up to peep at them and when the opportunity presented itself, stole their clothes for a prank. Why, I recall doing the same myself, when Aunt Rachel used to bathe naked in the Cherrybrook.'

Eloise gave an angry sniff.

'You must speak with Lieutenant Fairbrother!'

'Fairbrother? Whatever for? It's hardly an excise matter, after all. I mean, nobody could accuse Lucy of carrying above her tonnage, and nothing she has could be considered contraband, although one might argue that her personal attributes . . .'

'Henry!'

'Well, she's a fine looking girl. If she weren't my daughter . . .'

'Henry! This is a serious matter, and this man must be brought to proper justice for his insolence!'

'Insolence does not fall within the remit of customs, although who knows what they'll put a tax on next? Besides, I hardly think Lucy would thank us for letting young Fairbrother know she's been running around in the nude, and it would give him a seizure, like as not. Best to let things lie, I believe.'

'Let things lie! How can you say such a thing, when your own daughter has been forced to endure public disgrace!? Stephen is a justice of the peace. He must have the local population flogged and we will soon discover the culprit!'

'We're not in France now, dear, and her disgrace was hardly public.'

'Well, something must be done!'

'To the contrary, it is for the best that nothing whatsoever is done. If we do discover the culprit I suppose I will be obliged to take a horsewhip to the fellow, or perhaps have Gurney do it, just for the sake of good form, but no harm has been done . . .'

'No harm!'

'. . . beyond a dent in Lucy's pride, of which she possesses an ample sufficiency.'

'She has been degraded, made a laughing stock!'

'Hardly that. At worst some fellow will have a happy memory of her to tug his cock over. And besides, she'll get over it. You always did. The servants may gossip for a time, but they are inclined to do so anyway, and most among them have seen worse and know better than to open their mouths to outsiders. No, Eloise, these things do a girl good, help her to realise her place in the world. Remember the first time I spanked you, eh?'

59

He laughed and Eloise stamped her foot in fury before making a hasty exit from the room. Still chuckling, Henry turned to where a decanter of de Cachaliere's Cognac stood on the sideboard.

As Lucy Truscott walked slowly down towards the lake she made the very picture of genteel English womanhood, in her white summer dress with her red curls artlessly framing her face beneath her bonnet and her parasol open to save her delicate skin from the effects of the sun.

The thoughts going through her mind were somewhat less than genteel, and her intentions would have given John Coppinger pause for thought. Somewhere in the grounds, either by the lake or more likely in the woods of Burley Down beyond, was her cousin Octavia. Octavia had come over to take a lesson in watercolours from Miss Wescott, who had been their governess and still taught painting and music to supplement her income. Fondly believing Lucy to be in Okehampton with her mother, Octavia had taken a walk in the grounds after the lesson.

Lucy's face was set in a purposeful frown as she crossed the ornamental bridge over the lake. The woods rose steeply beyond, up a north-facing slope which remained in cool shadow for a good part of even the longest summer day. At the top was a little folly, which marked the southern boundary of the estate, and from which one could look back over the house and grounds and beyond, to where the hills finally gave way to sea in the grey distance. To the east rose the great sweep of Dartmoor, now green with spring growth save for where the rocky tors broke the skyline.

Passing the door to the ice house, she started up the long zigzag of pressed gravel path which had been cut into the hillside when she was a little girl. The woods had already been familiar then, and she knew every twist and turn of the track, walking swiftly until she had reached the crest of the hill. As she had expected, Octavia had also chosen to ascend to the very top, and the hem of her pale blue dress was visible where she was sitting on the steps of the folly, also her boots, but with the rest of her hidden behind a pillar. Lucy stepped onto the verge and approached quickly, speaking only when she reached the folly itself.

'Quite the prettiest view in Devon, is it not?'

Octavia jerked around, her mouth open as she saw who it was, and a look of fear and perhaps guilt passed across her face before she managed to compose herself.

'Cousin Lucy!' she exclaimed. 'You quite startled me. I thought myself quite alone.'

'So you are, save for myself,' Lucy responded. 'Mama is in Okehampton, buying gloves, I believe, as are James and Suki. Papa and Jack Gurney have ridden out somewhere or other. Cook alone remains in the house, so yes, we are quite alone.'

'Why are you telling me this?' Octavia asked nervously.

'In case you should feel the need to scream,' Lucy answered.

'Why . . . why should I wish to scream?' Octavia queried, rising and backing away.

Lucy made a swift grab and caught first one of the elaborate bows that decorated Octavia's dress, which tore, but then an arm, which she twisted up hard. Octavia gave a cry of pain, and was struggling frantically as Lucy frogmarched her into the interior of the folly, but to no avail. She was still struggling as Lucy tore the ruined bow free, but a slap to her face quietened her and she was led gasping to a pillar. Lucy spoke as she pushed Octavia against the cool marble.

'I wish the truth,' she stated, 'the full truth.'

'What truth!?' Octavia panted. 'What truth do you mean! Let me go, Lucy, you beast, you are hurting!'

'That is my intention,' Lucy responded, 'because I

know that otherwise you will lie to me. Hold still or it will go the worse for you!'

Octavia obeyed, sobbing as her arms were taken behind the pillar. Lucy continued talking.

'What I wish to know, cousin, is the full story of what occurred at Meldon Pool last week.'

'What would I know of it?' Octavia wailed as her wrists were tied off behind the pillar. 'I was not there!'

'I do not believe you,' Lucy responded.

'I had a chill! I remained at Beare! You know this!'

'Far from it. I know only that it is a peculiar thief who would take our clothes but leave our picnic, and even our boots!'

'I . . . I can only imagine clothes are easier to sell!' Octavia squealed. 'How would I know the ways of such rogues in any event? Or anything else! I was not even there!'

'No?' Lucy queried. 'I rather think you were. Strange that your mother knew nothing of your chill, and stranger still that when your sisters thought a man had stolen her clothes, a man who might well have still been about, neither thought to shield her body, and both seemed more concerned with the impropriety of being nude than what such a man might do to them. Moreover, both were suspiciously fast to volunteer to walk stark naked to Meldon village for inevitable public exposure. What of these facts?'

'I . . . they . . . I . . .,' Octavia babbled. 'How would I know? I was not there! I was not! Why ask me? Ask Augusta, or Lydia! How could I know!?'

'I think,' Lucy stated, 'that you were on the path, just out of sight, with their clothes, so that they could come to you, dress as quickly as they might, and leave poor Hippolyta and me naked by the pool to find our own way back to the carriage.'

'No!'

'Yes, Octavia.'

'No! It was not so! What . . . what are you going to do to me, Lucy?'

'Well,' Lucy stated, standing back and smiling happily as she admired Octavia's tightly bound wrists, 'that will depend. Should you admit to your wicked little scheme, and I shall untie you, place you across my knee, lay you bare and spank your fat little sit-upon until you are unable to sit for a week. I happen to have brought my favourite hairbrush too, which as you know is well suited to such a task.'

Octavia responded with a bitter sob, then spoke again, her lower lip quivering in fear.

'But I did not steal your clothes, Lucy. What then? Will you release me?'

'That rather depends,' Lucy responded. 'First, I shall have the truth from you . . .'

'You have the truth, you do!' Octavia squealed. 'I promise!'

'Well,' Lucy said archly, 'if you are not to be spanked for your attempt to humiliate me, you must certainly be spanked for lying.'

'I am not lying! I did not steal your clothes!'

Lucy shook her head. She had come round in front of Octavia, whose chest was heaving in her distress, her rounded breasts rising and falling in her bodice.

'A pretty dress,' Lucy remarked. 'You full-chested, plump girls are perhaps fortunate in the fashion, a high waist making the most of your bust while concealing your belly.'

Octavia responded with a look of consternation which changed to shock as Lucy reached out and gripped her dress. One hard jerk and Octavia's bodice had been ripped down, the front of her light undergown with it, to spill out her puppy-fat breasts. They were quivering in her fear, and Lucy gave a light laugh as she stood back again.

'What . . . what are you going to do?' Octavia asked again.

'As I said, silly, to gain the truth,' Lucy answered over her shoulder as she jumped down from the lowest of the folly steps to the grass.

She quickly saw what she was looking for, a clump of fresh green stinging nettles growing against the stone of the folly wall. Octavia's eyes had followed, and she gave a gasp of distress as Lucy squatted down and gingerly extended a gloved hand.

'No! Not nettles!' Octavia begged.

'I must speak to Papa about it,' Lucy stated. 'He is too easy a master, and the men are inclined to abuse his trust. Why, somebody might get stung!'

'No, please!' Octavia begged. 'That is too cruel a fate, Lucy, too cruel! Not nettles, Lucy, not on my chest.'

'Not nettles, no.'

'Oh, thank you, Lucy, thank you . . .'

'A single nettle should suffice.'

'No!'

'Now, perhaps we shall have the truth,' Lucy remarked as she plucked a single young stinging nettle from the edge of a clump.

'I have told you the truth!' Octavia squealed. 'I have!'

Lucy rose and advanced on Octavia, holding the nettle up, her mouth twitching in a delighted grin as she watched the fear in her cousin's face and the way the two fat little breasts quivered naked in the sunlight. Coming to stand directly in front of Octavia, she stopped, holding the nettle up as she spoke.

'You have my word, cousin dearest, that if you confess to your sin you will avoid the nettle, and all the pain it brings. If you do not . . .'

'I didn't do it!' Octavia wailed.

Lucy sighed and shook her head, moved the nettle forward and brushed it lightly across the plump upper curves of her cousin's breasts. For an instant Octavia didn't react, and then she was screaming and jerking in her bonds. Lucy laughed to see the comic expressions on her cousin's face, then applied the nettle again, across Octavia's nipples, to set her screaming in earnest and bring both fleshy little buds to straining erection in moments. Lucy raised a thoughtful eyebrow.

'How droll,' she said, tapping the nettle against one hard nipple to evoke a little shriek. 'I wonder if your quim is wet?'

Octavia merely stared at her, trembling, then shrieking as Lucy once more wiped the nettle back and forth across her exposed breast flesh. Lucy giggled, smiling happily as she began to stroke the nettle from side to side in even, regular movements, as if putting the wash on a watercolour. Octavia's screams rang out louder than before, echoing back from the interior of the folly, and she had begun to squirm desperately in her bonds, wriggling her body in a futile effort to escape the nettle, which only made Lucy laugh the more.

'Indeed,' Lucy mused after a while, 'I do wonder if by careful application you might be induced to attain the same peculiar reaction as Lydia did after her spanking?'

She had stopped using the nettle, and Octavia hung gasping where she was tied, her face flushed and sweaty, her lower lip trembling uncontrollably, the smooth pale skin of her breasts angry with nettle rash, her chest heaving, her nipples stiff and swollen. Lucy went on, her voice calm, with just a hint of laughter.

'I do not know what it is called, if indeed anything so indelicate might have a name at all, but it comes about by rubbing one's quim, quite briskly, and apparently all the better for a good spanking. Perhaps if I were to apply my little green friend to your quim?'

'No!'

'Then tell me the truth, Octavia. Were you at Meldon Pool?'

Octavia's answer was a great flood of tears. Lucy clicked her tongue in vexation and stepped back to select a fresh nettle.

* * *

Reaching the open top of Burley Down, Robert Fairbrother urged his horse into a canter. His trip to Tavistock had not been successful, the row of casks hidden among timber behind a coaching inn having proved to contain tar, but there was no denying it had been a pleasant ride. The day was glorious, the heavens a vault of even blue, the air fresh, all of nature rejoicing in the spring.

He had hurried down, rising before dawn and following the toll roads to reach Tavistock in best time. Yet he had fully expected to spend the rest of the day on official business, confiscating and guarding the contraband, making the orders necessary to have the men involved taken into custody, securing the relevant documents from the magistrates, and a dozen other tasks. Instead he had found himself with the day clear ahead of him, and after a brief flush of guilt for his duty, he had chosen to ride back slowly, and not by the toll road but through the lanes leading north across the ducal estates, a route he knew would inevitably take him out along Burley Down. Having reached Burley Down, it would be impolite not to pay a call on the Truscotts at Driscoll's.

As the canter picked up to a full gallop his mind was firmly fixed on Lucy and what pleasantries he might exchange with her, whether she would flirt, and whether her dress would be more or less demure – light, pleasant thoughts greatly at odds with the screams that came to him on the wind as he breasted the rise to look down on the Driscoll's Estate. Immediately he was tugging on the reins, to force his path towards the little building. The screams stopped, began again, and he was throwing himself from his saddle and clutching for his sword even as he rounded the corner of the folly, to stand frozen at the sight which met his eyes.

Octavia Truscott stood against one of the pillars, her arms pulled back behind it. Her face was red, her expression a mask of fear, her chest bare and shaking, her naked breasts strangely discoloured, the skin lumpy, the nipples swollen to what seemed an impossible size. At the bottom of the steps was Lucy herself, her angelic features contorted in shock for her cousin's fate, her eyes wide in fear.

'Who has done this?' Fairbrother demanded, turning quickly to spare Octavia's modesty.

'A . . . a man! Some man!' Lucy answered after an instant. 'I . . . came here . . . I heard screams! Oh, my poor Octavia, what has he done to you?'

Octavia's answer was incoherent, but Lieutenant Fairbrother was already scanning the wooded slope below for signs of whatever vile rogue had tried to violate Octavia. Nobody was visible, and he began to rush towards the trees, only to realise that his first duty lay in protecting the girls. Lucy had already covered Octavia's chest, and he went to them, quickly cutting the strip of ribbon that had been used to bind Octavia's hands and setting her free. She collapsed, helpless in his arms, her soft flesh against his and her body so vital as she clung to his arm that his cock began to stiffen in response. Cursing himself for such an unworthy reaction to her distress, he helped her into the folly and to a bench. Lucy followed, speaking quickly as she came to hug her cousin to her chest.

'He is gone, Octavia, do not be afraid. I am here now, and good Mr Fairbrother, who will see us safe.'

Octavia said something that was muffled by Lucy's chest and Fairbrother stood back.

'Rest assured of that!' he stated. 'And also that I shall have whoever did this brought to justice be it the last thing I do upon this earth!'

'Well spoken!' Lucy answered. 'But I pray you, return with us to the house, and please, Mr Fairbrother, think also of the scandal if what has happened here were to become generally known. For Octavia's sake, say nothing save to those most intimately involved. Should the full facts of this matter become publicly known, great harm will be done. Is that not so, Octavia?'

'Lucy is right,' Henry stated, 'far better that this remain within the family.'

'When some fiend is at large in the countryside?' Stephen objected. 'This is a public matter, and plainly so.'

'On the face of it, yes,' Henry admitted. 'But would you have your daughter's shame paraded before the county?'

Stephen paused before answering, his face set and black with anger.

'Duty is duty, brother. Whoever it was, I'll see him on the gallows . . .'

'Which will do nothing to restore Octavia's honour,' Henry responded. 'Rumours will circulate, Stephen, inevitably, to the distress of us all. Think, man, what people would say!'

Again Stephen paused.

'There is always fertile ground for malice,' Henry went on quickly. 'Her prospects would be ruined, or at best greatly reduced. Only ask Caroline . . .'

Stephen raised a hand, and was going to speak again when the door opened to admit Lucy, arm in arm with Octavia, whose chest was plainly bandaged beneath her dress. Both looked pale, their faces racked with emotion, and Octavia was looking at the carpet as she was led to a sofa. Worried eyes followed them, then turned to Eloise as she came in.

'Octavia shows great resilience,' she said. 'I have applied a poultice, but no real harm is done. She is now ready to be interviewed, as is Lucy.'

'You are strong, my dear child,' Stephen responded, 'but if you do not wish . . .'

Octavia shook her head.

'Brave girl!' Henry added. 'A Truscott through and through.'

Lucy gave a wan smile and passed the bottle of salts she was holding to Octavia, who inhaled deeply. Henry waited, doing his best to look stern and serious while searching the girls' faces. Both had given the same story, that Octavia had been accosted while out walking, tied to a pillar of the folly with a piece of her torn dress and tortured with stinging nettles. It seemed an odd thing for even the most deranged of villains to do when he had a beautiful and helpless girl at his disposal. He glanced at Eloise, who nodded and then spoke.

'She is intact, may the Lord be thanked.'

Stephen tried to hide a sigh of relief. Henry frowned but refrained from commenting. Robert Fairbrother, who had been standing in the corner of the room looking serious but saying nothing, had gone pink. Stephen spoke.

'Let us then attempt to turn our minds to the practicalities of this situation. Octavia, dear child, I will understand if you are too fraught to answer my questions, but what of this man? Was he known to you? If not, could you describe him?'

'He . . . a terrible man . . . tall and . . .'

'He wore a mask,' Lucy supplied, 'and was tall, but not unusually so.'

'As tall as Jack Gurney?'

'Yes,' Octavia answered.

'No,' Lucy said, 'I think, dear cousin, you are perhaps mistaken in your fear . . .'

'But you saw him only from a distance, Lucy?' Stephen asked.

'Yes, er . . . perhaps forty yards,' Lucy responded, 'and as he heard the approach of our good Mr Fairbrother he started towards me. As he ran I could see him clearly.'

'A man of roughly Jack's height, we must allow,' Henry stated, trying to stop the corners of his mouth from twitching up into a grin, 'which leaves us few enough in the district. What of his build?'

Both girls began to speak at once, but Octavia went quiet, allowing Lucy to go on.

'Middling, Papa, poor beside Jack Gurney, if he is to be our yardstick.'

'And this mask?' Stephen queried.

'Quite absurd,' Lucy answered quickly, 'with a foolish grin. Like those of the mummers we saw at Okehampton last year, chequered in red and white. I imagine him to have been some wandering rogue, and now long fled.'

'A mummer's mask?' Henry queried. 'This is not a common item. How did he speak, Octavia, if he spoke at all?'

Lucy made to answer but thought better of it, and Henry once again forced back a smile. Octavia glanced at Lucy before she answered.

'Little, and then with coarse curses and harsh words.'

'Words you did not understand?' Henry asked.

Octavia nodded.

'He spoke in cant, I suspect,' Henry stated. 'And what of his clothes? Bright yet shabby, I venture?'

'Yes,' Lucy answered, 'a coat of blue . . . powder blue, yet stained and ill fitting, breeches, and boots of worn leather . . .'

'A cockade of green pheasant feathers in his hat,' Octavia added.

Henry nodded.

'Lucy is right, Stephen, this is no labourer, but some wandering rogue, and doubtless well away . . .'

He stopped, holding back the dismissive remark he had intended to make. When he did speak it was with an earnest gravity that made him sound like his brother.

'Lieutenant Fairbrother, you have your duty, and I would not ask this were it not both of the utmost delicacy and the utmost necessity. Such a man as this does not travel unnoticed, and his description may doubtless be obtained in inns and villages. As I am sure Stephen will come to realise, this matter is best kept from the public knowledge, and you are ideally placed to do this, it being well within your task as a preventative officer to enquire after singular rogues seen going about the country. Also, I approach my fiftieth year, Stephen his sixtieth, but you are a young man, with a young man's energy and zeal. May I ask you to take this task in hand, for the sake of my family's honour and that of poor Octavia?'

Fairbrother's response was immediate, a sharp nod of the head, and his face was set in an expression both severe and earnest as he replied, first addressing Stephen.

'Mr Truscott, Mr Henry Truscott, ladies, pray be assured that I would hold my honour cheap indeed if I did not rise to this call. You may be confident of both my assistance and my discretion.'

He gave a stiff bow. Henry finally allowed his smile to come to the surface.

Lieutenant Fairbrother drew a heavy sigh as he began to pull his boots off. Since the previous day only two matters had exercised his mind, neither related to his work as a preventative officer. First and foremost had been the matter of bringing whatever vile rogue had dared to accost Octavia Truscott to justice, and not the justice of the law, as Stephen Truscott had wanted, but more immediate and forthright justice, as advocated by Henry Truscott.

He had also learnt of the incident at Meldon Pool, and was certain that the two were connected. Some man was at large, a callous, mocking villain, the sort of man who refused to acknowledge his place in the great scheme of things, but laughed in the face of all that was just and godly, yet in his heart burned with jealousy and hate towards those born to high station. A man who thought it amusing to steal the girls' clothes while they bathed at Meldon Pool, and took lustful pleasure in Octavia's pain and degradation, a man who would undoubtedly have violated her, and perhaps Lucy too, had he himself not chanced upon the scene.

There was no doubt of it. The man had to be a gypsy, or some such individual, one of those rogues who set themselves outside the boundaries of society, beggars and thieves, the "canting crew"[7] as Henry Truscott had termed them. No other human being could have fallen so low, to watch girls naked as they bathed, to tie and strip the daughter of a man such as Stephen Truscott, to dare to think of inserting his vile member into her body, as the villain no doubt had . . .

Second in his thoughts had been his own feelings, and burning jealousy had been added to his righteous indignation at the thought of the man seeing the three girls bathing naked, Lucy's maid Hippolyta also, and yet more at what had been done to Octavia. He was grinding his teeth with anger as he began to work on his second boot, his fists clenched tight as he imagined what he would do to the man who had dared to do what he himself was struggling to resist so hard. Henry Truscott was right, hanging was too good. The man deserved to be run through and left to die in a ditch.

Every night he struggled with his own lusts, often forced to take relief either in his hand or with Molly Hynes. Never would he have spied on the girls, let alone forced his attentions on them, and yet the ghastly creature had done both. It was unthinkable that it should go further, that another man, any other man, let alone some canting gypsy thief, should have those pleasures he so longed for. He shook his head at the sudden image of Octavia Truscott's breasts, heaving in

72

agitation, her skin puffy with nettle rash, her nipples so swollen it had seemed they might burst . . .

He cursed and kicked out hard at his reluctant boot, which flew free to crash into the opposite wall, leaving a dent in the plaster. Since the incident it had been impossible to get Octavia's body out of his mind, and specifically her chest. His love for Lucy was pure, he knew, or he had thought he'd known, and he found himself gritting his teeth in agitation. Thoughts of Octavia called into question his devotion to Lucy, and he forced himself to think of her instead.

Her bust would surely prove no less glorious, if only he could see it bare. She was a little smaller, perhaps, but no doubt as round, no doubt as pale, paler still indeed, but with a scattering of freckles in the gentle valley between them, the valley in which he longed to bury his face, to rub his cock, with her pretty hands folding the little balls of joy around it and her giggling and licking at his knob as it popped up and down in her cleavage . . .

He stifled a shameful oath as he swung his legs off the bed again. Molly Hynes might be a poor substitute for Lucy, and indeed Octavia, at least so far as youth and breeding were concerned, but her breasts where bigger by far, and more importantly she was willing to fold them around his cock and let him fuck between them for an outlay of a shilling and thre'pence. With a fresh sigh he began to pull his boots on again.

Molly smiled as de Cachaliere entered the room and bowed to her. It was his third visit, and while his requests had been a little peculiar he had asked nothing she had not be able to put down to his being French. He had also paid well, although she was unsure whether he was naturally generous, or if this was simply because rates were higher in France. In any event, he was clearly a customer to be flattered, and all the more so for having been introduced by Henry Truscott and being associated with John Coppinger.

'May I offer you a drink, sir?' she asked as he carefully placed his hat on the back of her chair.

'Thank you, but no,' he answered. 'I have a flask, should I require a restorative.'

'As you wish, sir.' Molly giggled as he began to remove his fine peacock blue coat. 'Pleasure first, is it to be?'

'It is,' he answered, 'and today, I am of a mind to enjoy that splendid backside. Lift your skirts.'

Molly obeyed promptly, giggling and looking back as she threw up her dress and petticoat to show off her rear view with her back pulled well in to make the best of her ample curves. De Cachaliere chuckled and lifted an eyebrow. He had taken from his pocket a small glass jar, beautifully painted with a design of foxes pursuing geese, and placed it beside her on the bed before his fingers went to the flap of his breeches. Sure her quim would not be ready, Molly opened her mouth in invitation. De Cachaliere nodded, climbed onto the bed, and in one smooth motion pulled his cock from his breeches and into her mouth.

She began to suck, doing her best to enjoy what was her fourth cock of the day and wondering if she should apply a little lard to her quim. It did feel good to have a man's penis in her mouth, and he was at least clean and considerate, not trying to choke her the way some men did, but allowing her to control the sucking as his erection grew slowly to full size. Before he was ready she had pulled her bodice open to spill out her breasts, and when he withdrew she decided she wouldn't be needing the lard after all.

He had a fine cock, pale and straight and long, like the rest of him, and from the taste she was sure he had even applied a little powder. She wiggled her bottom encouragingly. He had been stroking her cheeks as she sucked him, and tickling between them, on her bottom hole, to make her wonder what he intended, but as he got into position he simply slid his cock deep in up her quim. She was whimpering with pleasure as he began to fuck her with long, slow strokes, and it was not entirely fake. Nor was her gasp as something cold and slippery touched her anus.

Twisting around, she realised that he had the little pot open on the bed, and that he had scooped out some thick, yellowish grease, which he was now rubbing on her bottom hole with his thumb even as he fucked her. Realising that she was to be buggered after all, she allowed herself a little sob, wondering if he would prefer acquiescence or resistance to having her anus penetrated. Some men, like John Coppinger, liked her to fight and pretend to hate it. Others, like Henry Truscott, simply enjoyed the tightness of her bottom hole and assumed she would enjoy a cock up it in the same way.

'Be easy, I'd not hurt you,' de Cachaliere grunted as her anus opened to his thumb and Molly sighed again, this time in relief at not having to act.

De Cachaliere chuckled, pushing his thumb deep in up her bottom and wiggling it inside her, as all the while his cock moved evenly in and out of her quim. Her anus had soon begun to open, and when his thumb pulled free to be wiped clean on her petticoats she was left gaping and ready. His cock eased out from her quim and up into the crease of her bottom, rubbing briefly between her plump cheeks before the head was put to her anus.

She closed her eyes, moaning as her bottom hole stretched wide, and his cock was in her, slowly easing up into her slippery passage. He pushed the full length in, until the taut, wrinkly fleshy of his balls met her empty quim, and began to bugger her with the same deep, even strokes he had used before. She was panting and moaning for real as his pushes grew faster, to make

75

her breasts swing against the cover of the bed, rubbing her nipples, while his front was slapping against her upturned bottom.

By the time he started to get urgent she was ready herself, and put her face in the bed, praying he wouldn't object when she began to rub at her quim. He didn't, but laughed and slapped her bottom, calling her a jolly Irish slut, and then came, deep in her gut, even as she went into her own climax, her buggered anus contracting over and over on his hard cock as he pumped sperm into her body. She was still coming as he finished, and he pulled out straight away, to leave her sighing and gasping on the bed with her anus still in spasm and bubbling sperm down over her quim. He watched, and gave a little laugh as she finally collapsed on the bed.

'You bugger well, *mon petit chou*, so well I shall add a little extra something.'

'Thank you, sir,' she managed, still gasping as he wiped his cock on the hem of her petticoats.

'Magnificent, in fact,' he went on, musing. 'Indeed, with experience I am becoming convinced that the bigger a girl's bottom, the better she buggers.'

Molly managed a smile as she began to rearrange herself, wishing that being buggered didn't leave her bottom hole quite so sore but grateful that he had taken the trouble to lubricate her properly first. He also dressed, spending some time adjusting the set of his clothes in front of her mirror before removing a silver hip flask from the pocket of his coat and pouring a measure of the golden spirit it contained into the cap. With a nod to Molly he drained the contents before returning the flask to his pocket and placing a coin on the mantelpiece.

'You may rest assured of my custom in any event,' he remarked as he made for the door, 'but I would be obliged if for our next *rendezvous* you were to rouge your nipples and cunt.'

Not waiting for her reply, he gave a stiff inclination of his head and left. Molly stood up, to discover that the coin he had placed so discreetly on her mantelpiece was not a shilling, but a crown, a sum she would not dare to have requested even for the service provided. With a contented nod she placed the coin in her pocket before removing her soiled petticoat and putting on another. No sooner had she done so and opened her curtains to indicate that she was once more able to receive customers that she heard the door bang below. She composed herself hastily, applied several generous dabs of perfume to her body, called out, and was able to open the door just as the newcomer reached the landing.

'Good evening, Mr Fairbrother, sir, and how d'you?'

His answer was an embarrassed glance back down the stairs, as if he expected to find somebody following him.

Lieutenant Fairbrother had become a little less nervous with each of his visits to Molly Hynes, but as she ushered him into her room he felt less at ease than ever. Even being there felt a terrible betrayal after what had happened to Octavia, in that he was giving in to those same base lusts which had driven the fiend in human shape who had accosted her. Yet there was no resisting, and just to watch the way her huge breasts bounced as she bobbed a curtsey made his cock begin to stiffen in his breeches.

The room reeked of cheap scent, and something else, roast meat perhaps, which he put down to the open window. Molly had gone to sit on the bed and patted a space beside her. Fairbrother noted that the covers were rumpled, and with a fresh flush of shame for his own needs wondered if she had just that moment entertained another man. Certainly there had been somebody in the alley as he turned into it, a tall man in a blue coat who had kept his face hidden beneath his hat and had hurried quickly into the foggy darkness of the night.

'Like before, sir?' Molly asked.

Fairbrother tried to answer, but could only manage a guttural grunt.

'No call not to be at ease, sir, not with me,' she went on. 'How about you take them out yourself, sir? Wouldn't that be a pleasure?'

He nodded earnestly and at once began to fumble with the laces of her bodice, clumsy and over eager, but quickly getting it loose enough to spill out her breasts. He gave a low moan at the sight of them, and took them in hand immediately, his eyes popping as his fingers worked on her flesh, to set her giggling.

'Now go easy,' she advised, 'and don't go rushing your pleasure.'

Fairbrother nodded, but he was already rummaging for his cock, and when he had pulled his breeches flap wide it sprang out, already erect, with the tip wet as Molly folded her breasts around his shaft. He closed his eyes, muttering a prayer as he began to fuck in her cleavage, rubbing up and down as urgently as ever. Molly shut her eyes, just in time as he erupted in her face, spattering her with his usual large quantity of thick come, across her chin and lips, over one eye and even in her hair.

He gave a pleased grunt as Molly released him from between her breasts, an instant before a great wave of shame hit him for his behaviour, and the fact that as he had come his mind had filled with an image of Octavia Truscott tied to the pillar with her round little breasts pink with nettle rash and her nipples straining upwards as if fit to burst. Shaking his head, he sat down at Molly's dressing table.

'You'll have a drink,' she stated, her tone more the mother than the harlot. 'You look fit for the sexton, you do, sir, begging your pardon.'

'A drink, yes,' he sighed, wishing he could tell her of the agonies he was suffering but sure she would never understand.

78

'I've only gin,' she went on, 'not fit for a gentleman like yourself, perhaps, but strong.'

'That will do well enough, thank you, Molly,' he answered her as she stood to pour a cup from an earthenware flagon. 'I don't suppose you have many gentlemen calling on you?'

He managed a weak laugh, and was surprised to hear a slightly hurt tone in her response.

'Not at all, sir, many fine gentlemen come to visit me. Not that I would be naming names, but some of the most respected names in the district have been in this very room, they have.'

'Oh, nonsense,' he replied, offended in turn but taking the cup in any case.

'It's God's own truth,' she answered. 'Why, my very last, he . . .'

She paused, perhaps stopping an instant before giving the man's name. Fairbrother stifled a wry laugh, both at her and at himself as he thought of how far above her station a sea captain or a prosperous merchant would seem. To Molly the man might be a gentleman, but he knew otherwise. She went on.

'. . . a fine gentleman indeed, very elegant in his ways he was. Put a crown upon the mantelpiece, he did.'

'A crown?' Fairbrother asked in surprise.

'A full crown,' Molly confirmed before taking a swallow of her own gin.

Fairbrother tried a swallow and immediately found his eyes watering. Compared to what he was used to, let alone the fine Cognac served by the Truscotts at Driscoll's, it was barely drinkable. He forced himself, knowing how hard it would be to sleep without it. Curious despite himself, he put another question.

'A crown seems a great deal?'

'As I say,' she answered, 'he was a fine gentleman, a peculiar gentleman and all, mark you, one of those sorts, makes me wonder if he wouldn't have preferred a boy, if you know what I mean.'

Fairbrother gave her a puzzled look, then coloured up at the implication of what she was saying.

'A boy? He was a sodomite?'

'That and more. It's often the gentlemen what have the peculiar tastes, it is.'

Fairbrother found himself blushing harder still as the realisation that she undoubtedly included his preference for coming between her ample breasts under the heading of "peculiar tastes". He swallowed the rest of his gin, intent on leaving, but only succeeded in provoking a coughing fit. She went on, suddenly apologetic.

'Mind with that, it's not water, it's not, and please don't go thinking I mind what you like. It's a pleasure to have a visit from a young gentleman such as yourself, and I'm happy to serve as best I may, and whatever you've a mind for, just you ask.'

Fairbrother nodded and made to rise, only to pause.

'Pardon my curiosity,' he asked, 'and please, if the gentleman is respected in the neighbourhood then say nothing, but could you describe this man?'

'Not respected in the neighbourhood, no,' Molly confirmed. 'Fact is I've never seen him before in my life. Off a ship, no doubt. He was a gentleman though, and no mistake, fancy coat, hat with a plume . . .'

'A blue coat? Pale blue?'

'Right enough.'

'Thank you, Molly,' Fairbrother answered her, 'you have provided a greater service this night than you can know.'

'I give of my best, always,' Molly answered as he carefully placed two shillings on the mantelpiece.

Robert Fairbrother nodded thoughtfully. A fancily dressed man unfamiliar to the district, tall and wearing a blue coat, who paid a crown for unusual pleasures with Molly. There could only be one.

Five

Saul Mudge sipped thoughtfully at his beer as Polly sucked at his erect cock. She was half under the table, her hair twisted into his hand as he forced her to take him good and deep, the way he liked it, but his mind was only half on his pleasure. She had been over to Beare on an errand, where she had spoken to the coachman, Reuben, and had come back with a strange story. It seemed that while three of the Truscott girls had been bathing at Meldon Pool somebody had stolen their clothes. The dark-skinned maid who served Lucy Truscott had been made to go for help, wearing nothing but a few leaves sewn together with grass to cover her modesty. That alone had been enough to leave his cock hard, but there was more, if less certain. Octavia Truscott, and perhaps Lucy Truscott as well, had been caught out on Burley Down and forced to what could only have been a lewd act.

Some man was trying his luck, some man who would no doubt end up caught and hanged if not worse. Only a fool would behave in such a way, and yet it opened possibilities. Nobody would be blaming him, not when he'd been driving the master to Exeter on the day the girls had been at Meldon, and nowhere near Driscoll's or Burley Down for months. Nothing that happened until the man was caught would be blamed on Saul Mudge, and so Saul Mudge might well be able to put

81

into practice some of those ideas he had stored up since he'd been collecting the girls' soil and watching them at their toilet. All that mattered was that he should not be recognised.

As he swallowed the last of his beer and tightened his grip in Polly's hair he let his imagination roam. Just let him get access to the girls and he'd really show the precious little bitches what life was about. He'd make them suck his cock, just as Polly did, and spunk down their throats. Maybe he'd even fuck them, tie them down, all four in a line, and fuck their little cunts one by one, maybe with their prim little arses turned up. That way he could whip them first and then take them, bursting their precious maidenheads and fucking in their virgin blood . . .

As he pressed the head of his cock deeper down Polly's gullet he could easily imagine it was one of the girls' cunts, her hole tight around his cock, slippery with the blood running from her torn hymen. Perhaps pretty little Octavia, so coy and so innocent, or Lydia, who looked at him as if he were dirt, or Augusta, who always seemed scared of him . . . no, best would be Lucy, who never so much as noticed his existence.

He took Polly firmly by her ears and began to fuck her head, forcing his erection deep into the tight constriction of her throat. She began to gag, and he moaned in pleasure at the feeling, but his eyes were shut and his mind fixed firmly on what he'd like to do to the Truscott girls, and most of all Lucy. First he'd tie them up, their hands behind their backs, then strap them down on trestles, arses high. He'd strip their bottoms and whip them well, pull out their tits and piss on them, in their faces too, and their hair. He'd fuck their cunts, one at a time, making each beg for mercy before he burst her hymen. He'd fuck their arseholes and make them suck his cock after he'd been up each pert little bottom. He'd use them for hours, but the one he'd spunk up would be Lucy, and he'd do it in her cunt, to leave the high and mighty little bitch with a servant's bastard in her belly . . .

At the thought he came, full down Polly's throat, holding himself deep as she writhed on his penis, gagging and choking, with bubbles of spunk and mucus frothing from her nose, then sick as her stomach finally gave in to the agonies of her body. He pushed her back, cursing, to leave her puking on the floor as he milked the last of his spunk out into her hair, then stood up to refill his flagon with his slimy cock still hanging from his open breeches.

Once he had come down from the heights of ecstasy, his mind turned to practicality rather than fantasy. It would no doubt prove impossible to do what he had imagined and get away with it. The girls were sure to be well guarded, and few chances would present themselves, while there was no denying that to do anything was running a terrible risk.

He thought back to the stories his father had told him, of how old John Truscott had hunted men down with dogs for far less. True, it had been years before, and Stephen Truscott was not the man his father had been, although he was quick enough to put a man at the end of the hangman's rope. If half the stories were to be believed, then Henry Truscott was himself thoroughly debauched, but that didn't mean he would turn a blind eye to having his daughter molested.

Snapping an order at Polly to clean up her mess, he pushed his cock back into his clothes, not troubling to do up the buttons as he went to sit on an old chair in the yard, to look out over Dartmoor as he considered what might be done.

Lucy Truscott closed one eye to peer through her perspective grid, considering the sweep of Dartmoor before her. Ideally, she considered, Brattor should be taller and craggier, while Arms Tor should be smaller, thus allowing the rocky crown of Great Links Tor to be seen beyond. There were also too many shades of green and brown but not enough colour. Still, with a little thought she could shrink Arms Tor and pretend that more of the slope was heather clad, also add a few extra gorse bushes and crags.

Taking her pencil, she began to sketch, ignoring the grid in favour of her own interpretation of nature. To her left Augusta had already applied her wash, over delicate pencil lines that exactly followed reality. It was impossible to see either Lydia or Octavia's paintings, but both appeared intent on their grids and still held pencils. Shaking her head for her cousins' lack of imagination, Lucy began to sketch in a half-ruinous shepherd's cottage, which wasn't there, but should have been.

A shepherd's cottage implied a shepherd, and presumably some sheep. The sheep could appear as specks on the face of the moor, but the shepherd presented interesting possibilities. Jack Gurney sat a little way to the side, his heavily muscled arms folded lightly across his chest, there to ensure that the four girls were not ravished by the non-existent fiend. Not for the first time Lucy found herself marvelling at how handsome he was, and wishing any one of the various men who considered themselves of her own station was even half as fine. He also made an excellent study for a romantic shepherd.

'Jack,' she called, waving at him, 'be a good fellow and sit on that rock there, the flat one, yes.'

Gurney nodded and sauntered across to the rock she had indicated in the same casual manner he had always adopted since they had been children together. He sat down, facing her, then in profile as she waved her hand again, a pose that gave the impression he was thinking deep thoughts as he looked out across the hills. As she began to sketch him in she was wondering if he was in fact thinking about her, and whether it was as his master's daughter or simply as a woman. With a touch of irritation she began to wonder why it was reasonable for her father to indulge himself with the servants while she couldn't, when she was interrupted by Augusta.

'Lucy, dearest, there is no cottage there.'

'Then there should be,' Lucy replied. 'Where else would my shepherd live?'

'I really don't know,' Augusta answered, 'but having Gurney sit there quite spoils my composition.'

'Be grateful for his presence,' Lucy answered, 'or I might suggest a break for a game of choices.'

Augusta blushed but said nothing, attending to her paints for a moment before speaking again.

'You only have yourself to blame, with your beastliness. Poor Octavia!'

'Yes, a pity, when she was just starting to enjoy it . . .'

'She was not!'

'Indeed she was. I suspect that with a little care I might have put her into raptures, as Hippolyta did to Lydia. Anyway, I wanted the truth of your scheme at Meldon Pool.'

'Now you have it,' Augusta answered with satisfaction, 'and although at some cost, the result is all that I might have hoped for.'

'How so, cousin?'

'Is it not plain? We are escorted everywhere, and so you are no longer able to torment us.'

Lucy smiled to herself. Without doubt Augusta's tone was tinged with regret.

'Do you think so?' she replied. 'I might at the very least find some pretext for spanking you.'

'What pretext!?' Augusta demanded. 'You have no right to spank us, none at all!'

'Would Jack Gurney question it if I were to take you behind the gorse for a good bare bottom spanking?'

'He . . . I . . . no,' Augusta answered, now blushing scarlet, 'but . . . but he might mention it to your Papa, who in turn would speak to mine. Then you would be sorry!'

'Hardly that,' Lucy replied, 'although I suppose a little effort might be needed to explain my action.'

'A little!? A great deal! We are of an age, and of like station. What gives you the right to punish me, or my sisters?'

Lucy merely shrugged and went back to her painting. Augusta, she was convinced, had been learning to enjoy her sessions of spanking and humiliation. It was not something Lucy wished to give up.

Henry Truscott sat at ease on his terrace, looking out over the estate and the land beyond, a glass of Cognac in his hand. With the girls painting on Dartmoor it was tempting to indulge himself in a little vicious amusement, perhaps having Eloise whip Suki in front of him before he fucked one or the other, perhaps both, perhaps Hippolyta also, although the girl had spirit and it was taking a while to get her used to the idea of being whipped for pleasure. He began to ponder the question, wondering if it was better to tell Hippolyta she was being punished for some imagined crime, or simply that it was natural for women to become excited under a man's whip. Both possibilities had their advantages, and he was beginning to lean towards being frank with her when his daydream was interrupted by a red-faced and gasping Lieutenant Fairbrother.

'There is news?' Henry demanded.

'A great deal,' Fairbrother answered, to Henry's surprise. 'I have ridden hard from Bideford to bring it. The man was there just two nights after the outrage . . .'

'Man? What man?'

'The violator . . . the fiend . . .'

'Indeed!? How do you know this?'

'I . . . I . . . I have men in my pay. It was him, beyond doubt, a tall man in tawdry finery, a coat of pale blue with a cockade in his hat, and a stranger to the district. Could there be another?'

'In Bideford? Possibly, very possibly,' Henry reasoned. 'Ships from Bideford sail far and wide.'

'I think not, sir,' Fairbrother replied, 'for I also have reason to believe this man is of amoral character.'

'You do?'

'I, er . . . I have my little bandobust, sir. He is amoral indeed, just the sort who would think nothing of inflicting his lewd desires upon a woman, be she of high birth or otherwise.'

'Perhaps it is he,' Henry admitted, with an uncharacteristic twinge of conscience for whoever Fairbrother had decided was the fiend. 'So then, do you plan an arrest? At the least I would have you bring him before my brother, rather than simply dumping him off the side of your sloop with chains on his feet, or whatever it is you excise fellows do.'

For a moment Fairbrother looked shocked, before giving a nervous laugh.

'You joke, of course, Mr Truscott. He shall be brought here, rest assured, the moment I have laid him by his heels.'

'You do not know his whereabouts, then?'

'No, but I know a great deal. For one thing, he rides a horse. He must do to have travelled from Driscoll's to Bideford in so short a space of time.'

Henry nodded in agreement as Fairbrother went on.

'And he is a man of at least some means, ill-gotten means.'

'Indeed?'

'Yes. I have made other enquiries. There is little to go on, and nobody I have spoken to admits to having seen him, but that in itself tells us much.'

'It does?'

'It does. A tall man in a fine but travel-worn coat of pale blue riding a horse. Who would not notice him pass?'

'Few, I imagine.'

'None, unless they are blind. More likely they prefer not to answer questions of a man in the service of the Preventative Waterguard!'

'Your position is a drawback, I can see.'

'A drawback which can easily be turned on its head, Mr Truscott! Do you not see? The reason they will not speak to me of him is fear, and they are afraid because he is one of those I am set against. A smuggler.'

'A smuggler, you say?'

'Without question! Each detail fits. He is a base rogue, who cares for neither man nor God, but with money for fine clothes and a horse. No gypsy, nor pedlar, nor common thief could do this, and none of these would be sheltered by the populace, but a smuggler could, and would.'

'You could be right,' Henry admitted. 'Present your compliments to Mrs Truscott, then join me that we may discuss the matter.'

Fairbrother bowed and walked into the house. Henry put his hand to his chin, frowning as he tried to work out what, if any, advantage could be taken from Fairbrother's flight of fancy. None was obvious, rather the reverse. He had hoped Fairbrother would begin his search in nearby towns such as Okehampton and Launceston, wasting ever more time as he searched for a man who Henry was certain did not exist.

For one thing, Lucy, and even Octavia, had been far too calm for women genuinely accosted by a depraved maniac. The incident at Meldon Pool bore all the hallmarks of a prank played on Lucy, and that at the folly of her revenge. Her behaviour concerned him not at all, but the idea of it becoming common knowledge did, while it had been convenient to have Fairbrother searching the countryside for a fiend he could never hope to catch. Unfortunately it now looked as if there would be more pressure on John Coppinger and his colleagues rather than less, although just possibly Fairbrother might be distracted. Clearly he would have to speak to Lucy.

Lucy Truscott was smiling as she reined in her pony on the summit of Langdon Hill. It was impossible not to, both for the pleasure in being taken into her father's confidence and the comic nature of what he intended. Certainly the object she held in her hand was comic, the head of a puppet in red and white harlequin mounted on a yard-long stick, its face subtly altered from a happy smile to a crazed grin.

The plan was simple, and foolproof. She and Jack Gurney would ride out onto the moor together, intending a picnic on Cawsand Hill with its magnificent views and ancient monuments. Gurney's horse would go lame, but she, being a headstrong girl, would insist on riding on alone. He would follow on foot, coming up with her just in time to save her from the cruel embraces of the fiend, from whom she would snatch the peculiar trophy she now held, and which had been hastily manufactured from some of her childhood toys that very morning.

Fairbrother could then be alerted and informed that while the fiend might have been in Bideford, he was not a smuggler but a travelling mummer, and a comprehensively demented one at that. Only her cousins might guess that the truth was something different, but they would not dare speak out, especially when the incident would further reduce her chances of revenging herself on Augusta and Lydia for the theft of her clothes at Meldon Pool. That was the sole drawback, yet her time would come, if not outdoors, then in.

Jack Gurney had held back, and was on foot, leading his horse, just in case anybody might witness her riding across the moor. Langdon Hill was open to the whole Vale of Okehampton, and beyond, but among the sharp gullies where the East Okement flowed down past West

Mill Tor, her little charade could be completed without risk of discovery. She rode on, moving her pony up into a canter across the short, firm turf of the hilltop. It was a ride she knew well, and had enjoyed many times, always with thoughts of the romantic tales of how her grandfather had won her grandmother to add spice, and to make her wish that any man of her acquaintance would behave in such a way to her.

It was a fine thought, having somebody to simply decide that she was his and come and take her in the face of all opposition, and the more opposition the better. Obviously it would have to be the right man, somebody young, handsome, full of laughter and good humour, in short, a man like her father or grandfather. Sadly, nobody came close, save Jack Gurney, who as the son of her father's mine captain was out of the question as a match. Among the others, only Lieutenant Fairbrother showed any real gallantry, and he was an impossible prig.

She reined in, slowing her pony as they reached the rocky slope where the hill began to fall towards the river. It was a glorious day, a day for Meldon Pool, or possibly some lonely river out on the high moor, where she could go naked with impunity. Unfortunately, with Jack Gurney likely to stumble on her . . .

Then again, why not? It would at the very least be amusing to let him see her naked, something to rub her quim over once she was back in the privacy of her own bed, and no doubt something for him to grow aroused over as well. Perhaps he would even dare to make an advance, suggesting some delicious impropriety, not to break her maidenhead, obviously, but there would be other things.

It was a bold plan, and too delightful not to go through with. Some of the pools beneath West Mill Tor were big enough to swim in, and entirely sheltered, where the river ran between huge boulders and little cliffs of granite, with plenty of rowan, hawthorn and stunted oak for added concealment. All she needed to do was tether Rose where Jack Gurney would see her, and recognise her among the moor ponies, and he would be sure to come. Yet it would look quite accidental.

Her smile had widened to a grin of pure mischief as she made her way down the slope as fast as she dared, with Rose's hooves slipping on the steep grass. Before long she was at the bottom of the valley, and riding up the river to find the perfect pool. She passed three before making her selection, not the deepest, but quite the prettiest, with a little waterfall where a stream came in from the side and several great boulders half submerged, which would be ideal to disport herself on for best advantage.

She tethered Rose to a suitable rowan, far enough up the slope to make sure Jack Gurney saw without simply passing by. Walking back to the pool, she began to undress, her heart fluttering at the thought of stripping for a man, even as she pulled off her gloves. Her half-boots followed, and her stockings, each peeled slowly down and off with considerable pleasure as her legs came bare. Slipping her dress from her shoulders was nicer still, and as she stepped free of it to stand in just her petticoat and chemise her stomach was full of butterflies. Two light garments and she would be naked, which was what she needed, without delay.

Her fingers were trembling as she unlaced her chemise, and shook harder as she fumbled with the tie of her petticoat. With both open she made herself pause a moment, enjoying what she was about to do, and then she had shrugged the chemise off and pushed the petticoat down, to stand nude and alone in the warm spring sunlight, her skin tingling, her nipples hard and her quim already urgent. Slowly and carefully, she folded her clothes, placing each garment on top of the next where they were unlikely to get splashed. Even doing something so ordinary when naked and with the prospect of being seen by Jack Gurney felt deliciously naughty, and by the time she was finished and had poked a toe gingerly into the water she was wondering whether to swim or rub at her quim to bring herself to rapture before he arrived.

It was certainly tempting. She needed it, and wanted to make the best of her deliciously naughty mood, perhaps even be rude with herself in ways she had never tried before. For one thing the puppet stick was intriguing, thicker than her thumb, smooth and rounded, just right for insertion into her body. Not that she could risk her maidenhead, but just possibly the tight little hole which felt so nice when she wiped her bottom might be investigated . . .

She was giggling as she slid herself into the water, then spent a moment gasping and splashing until she could cope with the cold. If she was going to do anything so rude she would have to be quick, because while the thought of Jack Gurney catching her naked and in some suitably elegant pose was a delight, it would hardly do to be discovered with a puppet stick up her bottom while she rubbed her quim. It would also make it rather difficult to feign shock and surprise at being caught.

Yet she needed to be a little more aroused before she could be so bold, and she began to swim and play in the water, deliberately adopting teasing or vulnerable poses as she wondered how it would feel to take Jack Gurney's manhood in her hand, perhaps in her mouth, as Hippolyta had said she did for Papa, or even where she planned to put the puppet stick, up her bottom hole . . .

No, it was too much, too rude, and besides, from what she had learnt by touching with a finger, and from Hippolyta's descriptions of men's pricks, it seemed highly unlikely that it would fit. Better to take it in her mouth, and perhaps to rub at her quim as she did it, a delight Hippolyta had described in vivid detail only the previous night, immediately before they had taken each other to mutual ecstasy.

At the thought of Hippolyta's warm, soft flesh she decided that she could do it, then and there. Hauling herself from the water, she lay down on a rock, spread-eagled in the sunlight, her heart beating fast for what she was about to do. The rock was worn smooth, and as comfortable as she was going to get. Solid granite or dense bushes hid her from every side bar one, and there empty moorland stretched down the valley to a distant line of trees. She was alone, and there was no excuse.

Her jaw was trembling hard as she stuck a finger into her mouth, sucking as her legs came up and open. With her other hand she reached down, to feel the soft swell where her bottom cheeks pushed out below her quim and the deep groove between. She sighed deeply as she touched her anus, tickling the little knot of flesh to make it twitch and tighten before placing a finger to either side and stretching it wide for penetration. Her finger left her mouth, wet with spit, and went down between her legs. For a long moment she held it poised above her anus, delighting in how dirty she was being with herself, and then she was touching, probing, letting the little hole open to her finger.

Lucy sighed again as she pushed deep, her eyes closed in pleasure as she began to finger her bottom, probing deep into the hot, mushy cavity. It felt glorious, and she put her thumb to her quim, stroking her lips and wriggling it in the little wet valley between, then touching her maidenhead and wishing she could insert a finger the way some man would one day insert his prick. Her bottom hole had begun to feel slippery and loose, and it was time for the puppet stick.

She reached out for it, giggling, then began sucking on the smooth, rounded end, to wet it for her bottom. Her legs came higher, rolled right up to her chest but open, spreading herself wide to the warm sunlight. The stick went down, her eyes closed, and she was imagining it was a man, Jack Gurney, his prick as hard as wood as he put it to the soft, wet mouth of her bottom hole, pushed, and slid it deep up into her body. She had suited actions to thought, penetrating herself with the puppet stick, and with the handle now deep in her rectum she began to bugger herself, sliding it in and out to create a sensation so wonderful it left her mouth open in raw bliss.

For a while she continued to ease the puppet stick in and out of her bottom, until her sense of naughtiness at last overcame simple physical pleasure. Giggling and grinning, she turned over onto her knees, sticking her bottom up and looking back over her shoulder as she wiggled it, to make the puppet head jiggle and the little bells on its hat ring. It made her laugh, and she did it again, thinking how funny it would be to do the same to Augusta, or perhaps Lydia, who would really hate it.

Again she reached back, to grip the puppet stick and ease it in and out of her bottom hole a few times. She was loose, deliciously loose, and after a while she took the stick out, to penetrate herself again, purring with pleasure at the feel of her anus opening to the rounded tip and wondering if perhaps she might be able to accommodate a man's cock after all. First, of course, she would have to find just how big they really were or, more exactly, how big Jack Gurney's was, as she had no intention of investigating any other men.

Her bottom felt wonderfully full, and as she went back to buggering herself she was imagining just how much fuller she would feel with a good-sized prick in the same place, and whether the feeling was greatly different in her quim. She shut her eyes again, thinking of how

Jack would take her, his huge, powerful hands on her bottom, opening her, his cock, newly withdrawn from her eager mouth, put to her slippery little bottom hole, and up, deep up, until his balls touched her virgin quim.

He would bugger her, long and slow, bringing her to the same exquisite ecstasy she felt with the puppet stick moving in her rectum, only a hundred times more, a thousand times more. As he buggered her she would rub herself, yielding utterly, nothing hidden, as she brought herself to a state of rapture with his prick deep up her bottom. Vaguely she knew that he would do something similar, as horses did, and bulls, squirting out a great quantity of thick white seed, deep up her bottom as she shook in ecstasy.

She was going to do it, her hand was already back, stroking her quim as she began to ease the puppet stick in and out of her anus with increasing speed, penetrating herself and pushing it deep, again and again, all the while thinking of Jack Gurney's cock in the same willing orifice, hot and hard in her rectum. As her climax hit her she began to gasp, crying out her ecstasy with her dangling titties jiggling and slapping on the smooth rock, her bottom hole pulling in and out on the puppet stick, her fingers working furiously in the wet crease of her quim. Her screams rang out across the moor as the climax built, her whole body shaking in uncontrollable ecstasy, the puppet stick held deep up her bottom hole, her legs and cheeks in frantic contraction, as was her anus, just as she had imagined it would be with Jack Gurney's prick in her instead of a toy.

For a long while she stayed as she was, whimpering softly with her eyes closed, before carefully extracting the puppet stick from her bottom. It had felt good, astonishingly good, and she was determined to do it again, to herself, to at least Augusta, and perhaps she would even permit Jack Gurney to do it for real. She was bright eyed and giggling as she slipped back into the water, wondering how long he would be and if she would really dare offer herself, or if he was man enough to simply take her because she was nude and he could.

After washing she scrambled out onto the biggest of the partially submerged boulders, sitting in an apparently casual pose designed to show off her breasts, legs and the curve of her hips to best advantage. It was hard to judge how long she'd been playing with herself, or how fast Jack Gurney would have come up behind her, but it seemed safe to assume he would now be close by.

No more than a few minutes had passed when she heard Rose whinny, and an answering whinny from further away. A quick adjustment of her hair and she was posed as if without a care in the world, enjoying the sun, as naked as the day she was born, and without a thought for anything but her own idle pleasure. She heard a rustle in the heather a little way down the slope, then the chink of metal on stone, and suddenly her heart was hammering fast and one hand began shaking uncontrollably.

Nothing happened, and after a moment she turned her face towards the direction from which she imagined he would be coming, then stood, still attempting to look casual as she scanned the hillside above her. Gurney was there, but only halfway down, moving quickly among the rocks towards where Rose was tethered. Suddenly she felt intensely exposed, and as her hands went to cover her breasts and quim she was wondering what on earth she was doing, stripping off for the amusement of a servant.

Unfortunately she was stuck, unable to get to her clothes without getting wet, and unable to dress while wet without looking very silly indeed. For a moment she stood in indecision, biting her lip and wondering if she could jump from the rock to the edge. Gurney's voice rang out and she decided she had to, braced herself, leapt, slipped on the moss of the bank and fell backwards, disappearing beneath the water and rising be-draggled and gasping just in time to find a grinning Jack Gurney looking down on her from above.

'Nice day for it, Miss Lucy,' he called out, obviously fighting back his laughter.

Lucy spat out her mouthful of water, struggling for words as he jumped easily down to the rock beside her clothes and extended a hand. She ignored it, still shielding her chest and sex, also pouting angrily as she scrambled out, and at last finding her voice.

'You should not be here!' she remonstrated. 'Have you neither sense of decency nor place?'

'I've seen you bare in the lake often enough, haven't I?' he answered, laughing even as his eyes moved down her body with unconcealed admiration.

'Yes, when we were children!' she snapped.

'Not a child anymore, are you?' he stated. 'Not a child at all.'

She gave an angry grunt and turned around, only to realise that in doing so she was exhibiting exactly that part of her body she had been thinking of him enjoying. Then her mouth had come open in a squeak of shock and outrage as he planted a firm slap on one wet cheek.

'Not a child at all,' he repeated, grinning as he went to sit on a rock, evidently intending to watch her dress.

'I am wet,' she pointed out, 'pray . . .'

'So I see.'

'Then pray be good enough to take yourself some-where else so that I can dry, or at the very least turn your back!'

He laughed, but swung his legs around so that he was side on to her. Still pouting, Lucy tried to fight down her own feelings, only to realise that in doing so she was being a coward. In an equivalent position, it was impossible to imagine her father, let alone her grand-father, being anything other than forward. Gurney had begun to fill a pipe, which suddenly seemed insultingly casual. She went to stand in the full sun, gingerly lowering an arm so that both her hands were shielding her quim. He paid no attention, concentrating on packing the tobacco into place. Her mouth set into an angry line.

'I . . . I suppose you'll expect to take advantage of me now?' she managed.

'What, and lose my place? Not to mention having your father try and belt seven shades of hell out of my arse.'

'What . . . what if I was too mortified to report your behaviour?'

He half turned his head and raised an eyebrow.

'Who can say?' she went on. 'I might well find the disgrace of having been . . . been made to perform some lewd act upon you, too much to bear, and keep it to myself.'

'You would, eh?' he answered grinning.

'I might,' she went on, tilting her head up a little, 'although not, of course, had I lost my virtue.'

He chuckled, and to Lucy's fury went back to his pipe.

'I would have imagined,' she stated, 'that any man worthy of the name, finding himself alone with a beautiful lady of a social station to which he could not hope to aspire, and her naked, would have some difficulty in restraining his base feelings.'

Jack Gurney nodded, put the pipe down, pulled open the flap of his breeches and extracted a long, thick and very hard cock.

'How's that for not restraining my base feelings?' he said. 'Now seeing as you're determined on playing the slut, I suppose you'd better come and get your mouth around it.'

Lucy stood gaping, a huge lump in her throat, outraged by his words, his tone of voice, his whole attitude, but desperately wanting to take the big cock protruding from his breeches in her hand, and her mouth, as she had been offered, ordered almost.

'It . . . it seems I have little choice but to do as you demand,' she managed, struggling to sound offended.

He merely shrugged and swung his legs around, leaving them well apart, so that there was an area of flat rock between his feet while his cock and balls were easily available. She realised she was going to have to kneel at his feet to do it, but the urge was overwhelming and she got down, her head full of chagrin even as she opened her mouth wide and for the first time in her life took a man's cock inside.

Jack Gurney gave a pleased sigh as Lucy began to suck his erection. With the taste and feel of him in her mouth the last of her reserve was quickly fading, and she was soon sucking eagerly, her head bobbing up and down on the shaft, her knees wide. He winced as her teeth grazed his taut skin, and took her gently by the hair, to slow her down and control her sucking. Being held and having her mouth gently fucked made her feelings yet more exquisite, and with a last flush of embarrassment she stole her hand down to her quim.

As she began to rub herself he was moaning with pleasure, his cock rock hard and well in, pushing into her throat as he began to grow urgent. She sucked as best she could, wanting to come before she got her mouthful of white stuff, as she was sure to. Her quim felt wonderfully sensitive, as did her anus, and as her ecstasy began to rise she was wondering if he would turn her over and jam the fat, hot cock currently in her mouth rudely up her bottom hole . . .

She came, sucking urgently on his cock as her body shook and shivered, all the time wishing she was bent over, with his lovely erection well up her bottom, buggering her in the warm spring sunshine, her in the nude on her knees, stripped and sucking cock, stripped and buggered. Maybe he would even spank her first, for her insolence, spank her well. As the thought of being spanked and buggered by a servant hit home, her pleasure rose to a yet higher peak. An instant later a jolt of angry self-recrimination followed, but too late. She had thought the impossible.

At the same moment he came, full down her throat and into her mouth, to make her cheeks bulge and her eyes pop in surprise. She tried to pull back as her own climax faded, but was held firmly in place and made to swallow her mouthful, making her sense of chagrin stronger still.

Six

Saul Mudge let go of his cock. It was red raw, too painful to touch anymore. He'd had so many orgasms he'd lost count – in his hand, Polly's mouth, between her breasts and lastly up her bottom. She had complained bitterly about being buggered, even threatening to tell Mr Addiscombe, but he had ignored her, imagining it was Lucy Truscott's neat little rear end in which his cock was sheathed rather than Polly's big white one. She'd still been complaining after he'd spunked up her bottom, but a couple of slaps had shut her up and encouraged her to take his cock in her mouth to suck it clean.

It had been good, but it had done nothing to quench the burning lust he'd had ever since watching Lucy Truscott on the moor. He had been making up the composts, to Mr Addiscombe's exact specifications, when he'd seen a distant figure on horseback, far across the valley and well above him on the slope of Langdon Hill. A white dress and the pony she'd been on had made him sure it was Lucy, and she had been alone.

With Mr Addiscombe in Okehampton it had been the work of a moment to saddle the other horse, snatch the cloth mask he'd made, and ride hard up the valley, following a path that could not fail to intersect her route. Sure enough, he had arrived at the edge of the moor to find her pony tethered some way up the slope, and where her pony was, she was sure to be too.

Sneaking close, he'd wondered how far he dared go; to tie her up and enjoy a leisurely feel of her body, to spunk in her face, to force her to suck his cock, to torture her a little, to bugger her, even to take his pleasure up her virgin cunt . . .

By the time he came in sight of her he was determined to fuck her and have done with it, but the reality of her appearance had dulled his nerve. She had been naked, swimming, but before he could find the courage to accost her she had climbed out, after which her behaviour had been unexpected, odd, and very dirty. Never could he have imagined that such a well bred and aloof young lady would push a puppeteer's stick up her bottom, let alone play with her cunt while it was in. Lucy had, not only penetrating herself, but waggling her bottom to make the bells on the puppet's hat ring, adopting a series of poses to make herself look as lewd as possible, and finally giving herself a thorough buggering while she masturbated.

His cock had been hard in his hand by the time she came, and he'd been determined that it would shortly be in that same soft, hot cavity in which she'd stuck the puppet toy she'd been playing with. She'd be loose, he knew, and easy to bugger, but even as he'd started for her he caught sight of Jack Gurney riding towards them across the moor. Cursing his luck and wishing he'd acted sooner, he'd slunk back into his hiding place, expecting to enjoy Lucy's shocked reaction at being caught bathing naked by her father's man.

The encounter between Lucy and Jack had been very different to what he'd been expecting. It had been impossible to hear the conversation, but Lucy had been coy only briefly, and had seemed only too eager to do what he himself was obliged to force from Polly, sucking cock on her knees and swallowing the spunk. By then Saul Mudge had come in his hand, and was seething with jealousy and frustration.

He knew full well that had it been him in place of Jack Gurney her reaction would have been very different. She was a slut, that much was obvious, but she would not be a slut for him, and he hated both of them for it. Rather than a brief pretence of modesty before going down on his cock, she would have screamed and fought with all her strength. She'd still have ended up with a cock in her mouth, and if her resistance would have provided an extra edge to his pleasure, that in no way diluted his resentment.

Also, while it was clear that she and Gurney had an arrangement to keep what they'd done a secret, he knew full well that Lucy would have run screaming for help the moment he had released her. What Jack Gurney had enjoyed so easily would mean prison or the rope for Saul Mudge, perhaps worse if the Truscotts' reputation had much truth in it. Yet he had seen her, he knew what she was, and just possibly that might be turned to his advantage. Certainly she would not want her family to know she had indulged herself with a mere servant.

'It would seem then,' Henry Truscott stated, 'that if Mr Fairbrother will not come to us, we must go to Mr Fairbrother. You and I, I think, Jack, and we can take the puppet with us.'

'Pray be sure not to lose my puppet, Papa,' Lucy put in. 'It is a favourite toy.'

'You only made it a few days ago,' Henry pointed out, 'but as you wish. With luck a look at it should be sufficient to convince Fairbrother that we are dealing with a deranged mummer and not a smuggler. Jack, if you'd give James a hand with the horses?'

Jack Gurney nodded and made for the door, the front door, earning reproving looks to his back from both Lucy, and Eloise, who had entered the hall. Henry paid no attention, but continued, addressing Eloise.

'The French smuggler, de Cachaliere, has his boat in tonight, and he'll be back to France. I've persuaded him to bring in some of his better stock, also some claret, so the last thing we need is to have Fairbrother haunting the coast. I'll try to bring him down to dinner, on the pretext of discussing this supposed fiend perhaps. Make him welcome, and above all make sure he stays here for the night.'

Lucy nodded obediently. Eloise sighed.

'We must not too greatly encourage his attentions, Henry dearest,' she said, 'and he is quite the bore at dinner.'

'Needs must when the devil drives,' Henry answered. Then he kissed her, and gave her bottom a slap. 'Now for Bideford, where I will likely remain, and bring Fairbrother back tomorrow.'

He kissed Lucy and made for the door, while both women returned to the drawing room. A heavy overcast was blowing in from the north-west, cool and fresh, ideal conditions for a long ride, and he drew in a deep breath of air as he began to walk towards the stables. A figure caught his eye as he reached the corner of the drive, a tall man in a cutaway coat of peacock blue, walking with a cane. He recognised de Cachaliere and changed direction, greeting the Frenchman with a friendly handshake.

'I had thought to pay my respects before my departure,' de Cachaliere stated. 'I trust that this is not inconvenient?'

'No . . . no, you are very welcome,' Henry responded. 'Although I have business in Bideford which must be attended to, it can be delayed at least long enough for us to share a glass of your excellent Cognac.'

'A pleasure,' de Cachaliere said. 'So few Englishmen have a proper appreciation. One day, with fortune, and when our countries finish this foolish squabble, you must visit my *logis*, and I will have the opportunity to demonstrate to you true glory.'

'I look forward to it,' Henry answered, glancing at de Cachaliere's coat. 'Pray be assured that I intend no offence, but may I ask if you have been wearing that – quite splendid – coat abroad?'

'I have,' de Cachaliere answered, 'and I take no offence. Clearly you are concerned that I will be recognised, but there are, I venture to suggest, a sufficient number of *émigrés* in your country for my presence not to excite undue curiosity.'

'Not, perhaps, in north-west Devon,' Henry responded, 'but no matter. You leave tomorrow night and the matter will no longer be of importance. Do you plan to return shortly?'

'I do not. I have reached agreement with Mr Coppinger and must return to the Charentais.'

'A pity. Good company is rare in these parts. Perhaps you would care to take a turn around the grounds while I instruct my groom?'

De Cachaliere responded with a polite bow of acquiescence.

Lucy Truscott stepped out onto the terrace, her happy smile breaking momentarily at the look of the sky, but quickly returning. Matters had gone better than she could possibly have expected. The news of her supposed lucky escape on the moors had sent her uncle Stephen into a rare fury and aunt Caroline into a fit of the vapours. The girls had evidently been doubtful, but had said nothing, and all had agreed that Jack Gurney, as a servant of life-long standing, was the ideal person to escort them. Lucy had only been able to hide her laughter with the greatest of difficulty.

Having enjoyed her on the moor, Jack Gurney would now do as she told him, at least, so long as it suited him. With Jack Gurney's compliance the possibilities were limitless. Since he was her father's man and their trusted chaperon, the cousins would suspect nothing until it was too late. Once alone, with the secret they now shared, they would have no choice but to bend to her will. She could spank them as he watched, with their bottoms quite bare, naturally. If she felt so inclined she could suggest bathing and have them strip nude in front of him. When he grew excited and his prick began to swell, she could make them suck it and swallow down the unpleasant-tasting white substance which emerged . . .

Her smile had grown to a maniacal grin at the picture of the three girls naked on their knees as they sucked and licked at Jack Gurney's prick and balls, but faded a little. All together, in front of each other, the suggestion would no doubt prove too much, and the girls would risk their father's wrath rather than do it. Alone was a different matter. Augusta would doubtless enjoy the experience, for all her feigned distaste, and could no doubt be made to do it. Lydia would hate it, and yet grow aroused despite herself, a prospect Lucy found particularly amusing. Octavia was less predictable, but could probably be made to do it when the alternative was a smacked bottom. A little Cognac might facilitate matters.

She nodded to herself. It was all a question of balance, and of personality. Papa had guessed, and now knew the full story. He had merely laughed, his reaction to every mischievous folly she had ever committed. Mama, when she had learnt the truth in turn, had given her little indulgent smile. Stephen Truscott's reaction to his own daughters would be very different: the application of his belt to three soft, round bottoms, all in a line, along with a lecture on honesty, modesty and doubtless a wide selection of other dull things. Nothing Lucy could think of to do, short of having her maidenhead broken, would induce Augusta to face her father. Lydia might, if pushed far enough. Octavia always took the path of least pain and so could be safely humiliated, although her reaction to being made to perform for a

106

man was less certain. First, then, would be her revenge on Augusta, then Lydia, and with all three girls thus suitably chastened for their prank at Meldon Pool she could go back to amusing herself with them when she pleased, only now with Jack Gurney to add to the fun.

Deciding to take a turn around the lake, she started down the path, only to stop short before she had walked ten paces. A man was coming around the corner of the house, a tall man in a blue coat, elegant, with a face she had last seen on a painting of the devil in a particularly lurid religious tract. He approached, and her knees went weak at the thought that her sins had caught up with her and an incarnation of the imaginary fiend had been sent to punish her, perhaps to ravish her then and there, on the lawn. Only when he gave a courteous bow and spoke to her in French-accented English did she manage to recover herself.

'Pray forgive me, *demoiselle*, for the intrusion, as we have not been introduced. I am de Cachaliere, an associate, a friend indeed, of your father, who I take the further liberty of assuming to be Mr Henry Truscott?'

Lucy managed a curtsey, still unable to speak for her visions of being put on her back and summarily fucked.

'For who but Miss Lucy Truscott could present such exquisite beauty?' he went on.

'I am Miss Lucy Truscott, yes,' Lucy managed, and as he extended an arm she took it without thought for the proprieties.

'You enjoy a most pleasing aspect,' he remarked as they started down the path. 'A blend of the most modern fancies and the mature.'

'Much of the estate is newly landscaped,' Lucy admitted, 'but the property is old.'

'So I am given to understand,' de Cachaliere went on. 'Your father is a man of great worth, to have achieved so much. A younger brother, and yet this magnificent estate, a beautiful wife and a yet more beautiful daughter.'

'You flatter me,' Lucy answered, blushing, but unable to feel offended by the intimacy of his remarks.

There was an easy strength in his arm, and her heart was still beating fast from her initial shock, while her nipples were uncomfortably stiff within her chemise. She had recognised his name as that of the French smuggler from whom her father had been buying Cognac through some low sort on the Cornish coast, but he was quite evidently a gentleman. She thought again of being ravished as they walked down towards the lake, wishing it could be done without consequences.

John Coppinger stood looking out from Knap's Long-peak into the blackness of the night, his eyes narrowed to slits. He had stood for an hour, barely moving save to operate the shutter of the dark lantern he held in one hand. At last there came what he had been expecting, a signal in return, the same burst of three short flashes he had given.

'She's out there,' he stated as he once more operated the shutter, sending a new signal, to indicate that the French cutter that rode the waves somewhere out in the darkness was safe to send a boat in on the same bearing.

'Shall we go down?' de Cachaliere enquired.

'We've a while yet,' Coppinger answered. 'You'll be glad to get back to France?'

'To return, yes,' de Cachaliere said thoughtfully, 'although England has its charms, one of whom I met yesterday, young Lucy Truscott.'

'Fine mort that. D'you aim to have her?'

'Not if it means losing her father's trade, but by God I am sorely tempted!' de Cachaliere joked.

Coppinger gave a cruel laugh, drawing a cluck of rebuke from Annie, who stood behind them. Ignoring her, Coppinger went on.

'She'll go to waste, like as not, that one. The mother's proud, daughter to some French Count, and she'll have nothing less than a man of noble rank, but the Truscotts haven't quite the style. Old John was quite mad, for one, and Henry's money's from mining, which'll not do at all.'

'Sheer foolishness,' de Cachaliere answered. 'You should rid yourself of the lot of them, as we did.'

'There's many enough think that way,' Coppinger admitted, 'but not Eloise, Mrs Henry Truscott, who'd rather have her daughter an ape-leader than wife to a titleless man.'

'What is a title?' de Cachaliere snorted in irritation. 'It is the deed that makes a man. I've money, and property too, and in France there are no titles!'

'Cross you won't be pricking little Lucy's cunt?' Coppinger enquired with a laugh. 'You didn't take a last ball with Molly either, eh?'

'No,' de Cachaliere admitted, 'I hadn't time.'

'Four days at sea and not a sniff of cunt!' Coppinger laughed. 'A sorry shame!'

De Cachaliere gave a grunt. Coppinger laughed again and slapped his companion on the back.

'Have at my Annie, if you've a mind. She's a rare biter once there's a cock in her hole.'

'John!' Annie protested immediately.

'Quiet yourself, woman,' Coppinger answered her. 'Have you no sense of hospitality? My friend here has a mind to wet his cock before he leaves, so take up your skirts and show us your arse.'

'I have no wish . . .,' de Cachaliere began, only to be interrupted by Coppinger.

'Nonsense, man. You're in need of tail and you shall have it, or what sort of a host would I be?'

Coppinger turned and opened the shutter on the lantern, revealing Annie, only her face visible within her cape, her expression set in accusation.

'Show us your arse, I said,' Coppinger growled, 'unless you've a mind for belting and buggering instead?'

Annie scowled, but said nothing, and after a moment turned about, to throw up her cape and the skirt of her dress beneath. For a moment she was fumbling with her petticoat before the dull yellow light shone on her full, well rounded bottom, pale but marked with bruising.

'Now that,' Coppinger said with pride, 'is a woman's arse. Go on, man, make the best of what's on offer.'

'I . . .,' de Cachaliere began, stopped, and began again. 'How can I refuse such an offer, and my prick has no mind to, for certain.'

'Have her then!' Coppinger laughed. 'With my blessing, and if you take a penny a cask off the price of my brandy I'll count you a generous man. Take her down by the hedge, and do as you please.'

De Cachaliere gave a slight bow and stepped towards Annie, who was looking back over her shoulder, her bottom still bare, scowling, but as the Frenchman approached she extended a hand. He took it, and Coppinger laughed as she was led away into the shadows.

'Not in her cunt, mind,' Coppinger called out as he turned back towards the sea.

'But naturally,' de Cachaliere replied from the darkness.

Once more Coppinger gave the clear signal, which was promptly answered, then squatted down on his haunches. Low voices sounded behind him, then the wet smacking of de Cachaliere's cock being sucked. Coppinger squeezed his crotch through his breeches, thinking of how he'd belt Annie for being such a slut and giving in to his demands so easily, then fuck her. Presently the noises behind him changed, a gasp from Annie, then a low moan and Coppinger realised she had been entered.

'Not in her cunt, didn't I say!?' he growled, starting to rise.

'Nor am I!' de Cachaliere answered, laughing.

Annie gave a low sob and Coppinger sank down again, grinning quietly to himself as he listened to the moans and grunts of his wife being buggered. It was a pleasing thought, and his cock had begun to grow, ready for her cunt. Deciding not to wait until they were back at the cottage, he unbuttoned himself and freed it into his hand. Tugging gently at his erection, he listened as the noises from behind him grew more heated, de Cachaliere grunting and puffing, Annie moaning, then crying out in pain and begging the Frenchman to go gently. De Cachaliere gave a low curse, Annie a broken sob, there was silence, and Coppinger realised the Frenchman had come up his wife's bottom.

'Leave her there!' he called, striding across the grass, cock in hand.

He opened the lantern as he drew close, to find de Cachaliere doing up his breeches and Annie bent down across a cattle trough, her skirts and cape on her back and her bottom high. Her face was slack in reaction to her buggering, with a thread of spittle hanging from her lower lip. Her expression changed little as he pushed his cock into her mouth to fuck between her lips for a moment before going behind her.

'Not again, John, please!' she gasped as he laid his cock into the slippery crease between her bottom cheeks.

Coppinger merely laughed, but put his cock head to her quim and pushed it up, the full length sliding easily into her wet, ready hole. He took her hips and began to fuck her, holding her bottom wide with his thumbs. She began to moan, and to call out his name, low and plaintive as his cock drove again and again into her body. He laughed and called her a slut, first near to orgasm, then there, pulling out at the last instant to prod the head of his erection into her slimy, easy bottom hole and spunk in it, drawing a gasp from her, then a last, low moan.

He pulled out, to wipe his cock on her bottom before letting her up and sitting down on the edge of the big stone trough to get his breath back. Annie said nothing, rearranging her clothes in silence and remaining by the trough until Coppinger stood once more, to point the lantern beam down the slope.

'Enough sport,' he stated. 'We should go down.'

De Cachaliere had stood a little way apart, watching as Annie was fucked, and joined them as Coppinger started down the narrow, concealed path, through a thick scrub of thorn and gorse above a deep gully with the murmur of a stream in the blackness beneath them. Before long they had come out onto the beach at a tiny cove with the lantern illuminating yellow sand and the froth of the breakers which crashed towards them in the dark.

Coppinger used the lantern to make a signal, which was returned from a little way to the north. A minute's walk and they reached the longboat as it was being pulled ashore. A man stood in the bows with a lantern held high. Few words were exchanged, with Coppinger and de Cachaliere making a final review of their bargain and clasping hands before the latter stepped into the boat. Coppinger and Annie helped to push it off, then turned back for the path.

Dawn was not far off, with the cliff top now visible as a black line against deep grey. As they climbed slowly up the path it grew lighter, until by the time they had reached the top the scene was suffused with a pearly light and the sea was visible far below, leaden grey with the breakers crashing onto a broad stretch of golden sand, a beach that vanished completely when the tide was in, to leave the cliff rising vertically from among jagged rocks.

The sails of de Cachaliere's cutter were still visible, far out to sea, and Coppinger paused to watch, Annie also, standing with her arms folded against the fresh breeze. He glanced north, to where Lundy Island had become a dim bulk rising from the sea. No other sails were visible,

112

to his relief, as he was not at all sure that de Cachaliere's vessel would be able to outrun the *Bull*.

At length, with the cutter's sail no more than a speck on the western horizon, he turned back across the field. Annie fell into step behind him, not saying a word as they made their way across the dewy grass towards the farm, in one window of which a light already shone.

'We have it all then?' he asked suddenly.

'Every last farthing,' his wife assured him.

'You're sure of this?'

'Certain sure.'

Coppinger nodded and grinned. With his mother-in-law's full fortune in hand he could afford to bring in cargoes that would see him set for life within a few years, enough to buy an estate, perhaps a good-sized estate, and to turn respectable, or at least, as respectable as Henry Truscott, who seemed to get away with the most outrageous behaviour, and never a word spoken against him.

The only thorn in his side was Fairbrother, who had proved every bit as incorruptible as Henry Truscott had suggested. Nor was blackmail a realistic option, with Fairbrother's admittedly frequent visits to Molly Hynes insufficient to provide the leverage that would be needed. For all Henry Truscott's efforts, Fairbrother remained a risk, as did the *Bull*, and as he turned his attention back to the ragged sea his mind had begun to turn to a way in which he could be rid of both man and boat in one fell swoop.

Determined to avoid a *tête-à-tête* with Mr Addiscombe, Augusta Truscott had ducked into the glasshouse, only to find Lucy already there, admiring a display of luxurious butter-yellow tulips. Lucy gave her a look rich with feeling.

'Where is he?' she demanded.

'He has gone to order tea,' Augusta replied. 'Lydia

113

and Octavia are with Mama, and I was sure he intended a declaration.'

'I also,' Lucy admitted with a shudder, 'but in your case, should he do so, you must ... no, you must not. It is amusing to punish you, and to tease you, but that is beyond reason. Besides, the opportunity to spank Mrs Addiscombe would be unlikely to present itself.'

Augusta managed a weak smile.

'I would never accept,' she stated firmly, 'not if you were to ... were to ... to do what you did to Octavia, or worse.'

'I would not expect you to,' Lucy answered, 'nor your sisters. I would not inflict him upon anybody. Did you see how he stared at my chest as he suggested a nosegay?'

'I did. Quite horrid. And the way his eyes bulge ...'

'Yes, as they follow our bottoms as we walk!'

'The remarks he passes on our figures!'

'Every aspect of his conduct! It is intolerable that he should even think himself suitable, and yet he does, I sense it.'

'I also.'

'If only Papa did not think so highly of him.'

'Indeed.'

There was a moment's silence, both girls admiring the tulips, Augusta wanting to ask about Lucy's encounter on the moor, a story she was convinced was false, but unsure how to begin. Lucy spoke first.

'A great shame Jack Gurney is in Bideford.'

'Reuben, no doubt, serves as well,' Augusta answered.

'Not so well as Jack,' Lucy answered her.

'Your gratitude is understandable,' Augusta replied, 'given your horrid encounter upon the moor. Were you very frightened?'

'I am not much given to fear,' Lucy answered.

'You seem remarkably composed, for certain.'

'Too composed, perhaps?' Lucy laughed. 'You are right to doubt me, Augusta. There was no more a fiend

114

upon the moor than at Burley Down, nor Meldon Pool, but no doubt you see the importance of maintaining our little deception?'

'I see little choice, if that is what you mean,' Augusta answered with a delicate shudder. 'Papa would be furious. But why a fresh incident, when our being constantly chaperoned is perhaps to your disadvantage?'

'It is not a simple matter,' Lucy answered, 'but you may be sure that the situation will not prevent you receiving your just punishment, Augusta dearest.'

'Just punishment?' Augusta asked. 'Why should I deserve to be punished?'

'For your part in the theft of my clothes, naturally,' Lucy responded.

'A small thing, intended to teach you a lesson in humility,' Augusta answered, and immediately regretted her choice of words as Lucy raised her chin.

'You will learn,' Lucy stated, 'that I am not to be trifled with. Octavia has had her punishment. You shall have yours, and so shall Lydia, be sure of it.'

Augusta felt herself starting to pout, and also to feel the now familiar trembling at the thought of what Lucy might do to her.

'If you must,' she mumbled.

Lucy laughed.

'Oh, I must, cousin dear, we both know that, do we not?'

'Know what?'

'Know that you crave what I give, perhaps more than I crave to give it.'

'No! Absolutely not!' Augusta exclaimed. 'It is horrid, quite horrid, and yet what choice do you give me? You are a pig, Lucy, a beast!'

'A beast, you say? Perhaps there is a little of the beast in me, yes, if by that you mean I have some spirit. As to choice, at Meldon Pool you seemed strangely eager for your fate, and perhaps a little jealous when it was Lydia I had spanked by my maid and not yourself.'

'Pure fancy!'

'Pure fancy, you say? Could you not have peed a little, when first given your choices, and thus avoided a spanking in front of both your sister and my maid?'

'It is no less humiliating to be watched as I pee.'

'Perhaps not, and yet you gave no great resistance to kissing my quim.'

Augusta's answer was a sulky look and silence. Lucy laughed.

'Why so coy? Think of the pleasure we might take together, you and I. You might lick my quim properly, perhaps after a good spanking to warm your bottom, and a dozen other delights. How would you like to be at my feet, in the nude, to kiss them, to kiss my bottom . . .'

Suddenly Augusta was babbling.

'Lucy, I beg you! What you say is . . . perhaps, true, but this is something I hardly dare acknowledge to myself, let alone speak of!'

'Oh what nonsense! Yes, we must keep these things to ourselves, but between us, what harm can there be?'

'I . . . I do not know! But surely it is against God, to take pleasure in one's own degradation, just as it is against God to take pleasure in degrading others, Lucy Truscott!'

Lucy gave a shrug of indifference and went on.

'In any event, you must be punished for the wicked trick the three of you sought to play on me, and severely. If you refuse to admit the pleasure you take in that punishment, that is your concern, but rest assured that I shall take my pleasure with you, and with neither concealment, nor guilt.'

She swung her hand in a mocking bow as she spoke and hit a tulip, one of those named after Augusta herself, whose hand went straight to her mouth as the thick green stem sagged further instead of springing back up.

'Lucy! See what you have done!'

Lucy gave a petulant shrug as she bent to examine the damage. The stem was not broken, but was badly bent, leaving the beautiful bloom lying at a forlorn angle. Frowning, Lucy took hold of the stem and set it upright once more, but it slowly toppled over and she began to giggle.

'What will Mr Addiscombe say?' Augusta gasped.

'A curse on Mr Addiscombe.'

'He will be furious! Who knows what he might do?'

'Nothing,' Lucy said with certainty. 'He would not dare, but he would be angry, yes, and is sure to tell our fathers. We must conceal the damage.'

'Conceal it? How?' Augusta answered, glancing around the immaculate greenhouse. 'If we leave here, he will see us, and he is sure to come in shortly.'

'Then we must be quick,' Lucy stated. 'If we rearrange the pots perhaps he will not notice that one is missing. The broken flower must ... must ... pull up your skirts, Augusta, and stick out your bottom.'

'My skirts? Why ...'

'Do as I say, Augusta, and quickly!'

'You are going to spank me? Now!'

'No, you silly girl, I am going to conceal the flower.'

'In the top of my stocking? A clever thought ...'

'No, Augusta,' Lucy giggled, 'not in the top of your stocking. This is to be your punishment. Now be quick, or I will spank you, in front of Mr Addiscombe and that man Mudge! That I know you would truly hate, and I mean what I say, Augusta.'

Augusta was already lifting her skirts, her petticoats too, blushing furiously as her bottom came bare, but sticking it out as ordered, as if waiting to have it smacked. Lucy was giggling uncontrollably as she snapped off the tulip and stepped close. Augusta's mouth came open in shock as Lucy's finger was pushed in between her cheeks and up the bottom hole, and wider still as the tulip stem followed. She was gasping in outrage as it was inserted deep up her bottom, to leave just the flower showing between her cheeks. The leaves followed, pushed down her stocking tops and into her garters. Lucy stood back.

'Stay a moment,' she ordered, 'I want to see. How pretty you do look, Augusta, and how comic, with a tulip at the centre of your sit-upon! Yes, most becoming, although a posy might perhaps be better still! You may drop your skirts.'

Lucy glanced around the glasshouse again as Augusta hastily covered herself. She could feel the stem of the tulip in her bottom hole, and the flower at the back of her thighs, but only imagine how she would have looked from the rear. Intense chagrin filled her, but the effect was inevitable, a desire to be further humiliated that only the immediate risk kept down.

'What of the pot, and the soil?' she asked.

'The pot may go among a stack,' Lucy answered, her voice still full of wicked laughter. 'The soil . . . the soil you must eat!'

'Eat!?' Augusta demanded in outrage, even as her quim tightened in response to the horrible suggestion. 'I cannot eat soil!'

'Why ever not?' Lucy answered. 'There is no harm in good, honest earth. Now eat it, before Mr Addiscombe comes in!'

'I . . . I don't think I could,' Augusta managed, glancing as the moist black earth from which the tulip had been pulled. 'Could you not simply share it among the other pots?'

'Do not be dull!' Lucy answered her. 'Eat it, Augusta, I want to watch you!'

Augusta swallowed, but nodded. Pouting furiously, half-hating herself for what she was about to do but unable to resist, she lifted the pot and an old spoon, green with verdigris, which Mr Addiscombe had been using. Lucy watched, eyes glittering with pleasure, as Augusta gingerly dug the spoon into the dark soil and put it to her lips with a heavy sob. Her nipples were stiff and her quim tingling in her humiliation, but the instant the soil was in her mouth and she caught the thick, acrid taste her stomach revolted, forcing her to pull the spoon out and quickly swallow down her own sick.

'Eat up, cousin dearest,' Lucy chided.

'I can't, Lucy,' Augusta gasped. 'I really can't. It is ... I think it is dung, or some substance equally vile.'

Lucy laughed.

'What of it? Indeed, I can think of few things more comic than watching you eat dung. You will do as you are told.'

Augusta shook her head.

'No, Lucy, I can't! I shall be sick.'

Lucy clicked her tongue in disapproval.

'Eat it, Augusta!'

'No, I beg you, Lucy, not that!'

'I have told you, Augusta. I do not believe your protests.'

'No, Lucy, I am in earnest!'

'On this occasion?'

Augusta hung her head, defeated.

'On this occasion, yes, Lucy.'

Lucy gave a triumphant chuckle.

'Oh very well, seeing as you have chosen to be truthful. Spoon it out among the other pots, evenly mind you. But you are to accept another punishment of my choosing.'

'Yes, Lucy. Thank you, Lucy.'

'And you are to be my plaything?'

Augusta paused, fighting with her own feelings, but only for a moment.

'Yes, Lucy.'

Seven

A week passed, and a second, with Lucy growing slowly more frustrated. Stephen Truscott had decided that Reuben and also an older woman, a Mrs Hawkes, should accompany his daughters at all times. Lucy was frequently in their company, but no further opportunities presented themselves, either to let her play with Augusta, or to revenge herself on Lydia. Mrs Hawkes had been hired from Beare village, and took immense pride in her role, shepherding the three girls like so many ducklings, usually with Lucy straggling at the back.

Even her opportunities to indulge herself with Jack Gurney were severely restricted, and she only once had an opportunity to take his prick in her mouth, or rather had it put in hers, as he had wasted no time. He had also ejaculated down her throat before she had become sufficiently aroused to want her own pleasure, leaving her to seek solace in Hippolyta's arms that evening. As usual that had meant being masturbated as she lay face down on her bed and then licking her maid's quim, an arrangement she would have preferred to reverse.

Safe moments were rarer still because Lieutenant Fairbrother was likely to turn up at any moment and there were frequent invitations to Mr Addiscombe's house, few of which she was able to refuse. At first each appearance by Fairbrother would put her into a near panic, as he seemed to be working himself up towards making a declaration, which she would have been forced to refuse, and therefore cause all sorts of complications and awkwardness.

Her response was to spend more time with her cousins, even seeking out the company of the huge and motherly Mrs Hawkes to ensure that neither he, nor Mr Addiscombe, was presented with an opportunity to speak to her alone. The technique worked admirably, which made it all the more irritating when she realised from various hints among the gallant remarks and understated boasting that he did not intend to make a proposal until the fiend had been brought to book. On finding herself briefly alone with Augusta while the group were walking on the lawn at Driscoll's, she remarked on his behaviour.

'I like to imagine him spending the remainder of his days combing the country for a crazed mummer who does not exist, growing steadily more and single minded and steadily more eccentric, until at last he comes to be regarded as a harmless lunatic best humoured with a glass of ale or a piece of cheese.'

'I feel you are harsh on Mr Fairbrother,' Augusta responded. 'He is a fine young man, and would, I imagine, make a most attentive husband.'

'You marry him then. He lacks any real fire, not when it comes to accosting smugglers, perhaps, but in so far as women are concerned. Were he a real man, he would have ravished me long ago.'

'Lucy! What a thing to say! Were he to behave so he would be no better than the fiend!'

'Nonsense, not if I wanted him to ravish me. Any man should know, by all sort of hints and signs, whether his affection is returned. Having determined this, he should then sweep her up on his horse, carry her off to some sylvan grove and ravish her thoroughly.'

'Oh what nonsense! Better a magnificent declaration made on a moonlit meadow, or perhaps in an orchard,

121

with the apple blossom sprinkling the grass and our hair . . .'

'Then once you have accepted he can ravish you on the grass, with petals drifting down on your naked bodies as his prick fills your quim!'

'Lucy! You are an outrage in itself! What if you were overheard using such words?'

'By whom? Your sisters? Hardly of consequence. Jack Gurney? He would laugh. That old mother hen Mrs Hawkes? She would cluck and bluster, perhaps even make some clumsy remark to Mama, who would merely lift her nose and give a single, delicate sniff.'

Lucy suited action to words, imitating Eloise's manner so exactly that Augusta burst into giggles. After a moment of walking in silence, their arms linked and their parasols tilted to make the best of the shade, Augusta spoke again.

'You would refuse Mr Fairbrother then, even if your parents had no objection?'

'Absolutely,' Lucy responded. 'He has his virtues, but I do not want a man with virtues. Also, Mr Fairbrother manages to be extraordinarily trying without making the least effort. He is not for me.'

Augusta nodded, and spoke again, softly.

'You would not then be offended should another accept him?'

Lucy looked at her wide eyed before replying.

'No, Augusta! Do not consider this, I pray! What of our friendship, what of . . .'

'You mistake me, Lucy dear. I have no interest in Mr Fairbrother, if only because one whom I hold very dear is already in love with him.'

'Lydia, or Octavia!?' Lucy demanded. 'There can be no others!'

'I am not at liberty to say,' Augusta answered her.

'Tell me!'

'I cannot.'

122

'You would tell me soon enough with a pink sit-upon and the prospect of my hairbrush handle up between those fat cheeks!'

'Lucy!'

'It is what I would do to you . . .'

'I know.'

There was a yielding look in Augusta's eyes as they exchanged a glance, which set Lucy itching for her pleasure.

'It is what I yearn to do to you, Augusta,' she breathed, 'that and a thousand other things! Let us loop back to the house, and . . .'

'We will be caught! Your mother is in the drawing room! The servants . . .'

'Hippolyta? She . . . no matter, she is safe, and Suki also. The remainder will be in their wing or outdoors. Come!'

The others, Lydia, Octavia and Mrs Hawkes, were some way ahead, on the little bridge that crossed the lake, while Lucy and Augusta had paused at a junction of paths halfway between lake and house. Augusta cast them a look, only half wishful, and as she allowed herself to be steered onto the path that led back towards the house Lucy could feel the trembling in her arm.

Not another word was spoken until they were indoors. Eloise was visible in the drawing room, sitting by the window that looked out across the terrace and beyond. She could not fail to see them, but continued her embroidery with no more than a passing smile as they started up the stairs. once at the top, Lucy hurried into her room, pulling Augusta behind her, only to find Hippolyta folding sheets.

'Put those aside,' Lucy instructed her maid, 'and go to the door. I intend to teach my cousin a lesson and you will need to watch out for us.'

Hippolyta bobbed a curtsey, and was trying to hide a

knowing smile as she went to the door, closing it behind her.

Augusta's eyes followed the departing maid, and she was biting her lip as she turned to Lucy.

'She will know!'

'Then it is all the better for your sense of humiliation, cousin dearest. Now is an ideal moment, and you will not escape. Quickly, before we are missed. First I shall spank you, and then, when I have had my pleasure with your bottom, you shall have yours with mine.'

'How ... how do you mean? Do you wish to be spanked yourself?'

'Absolutely not! As you know well, I am not spanked, not ever. Such punishment would hardly be suitable for myself, however appropriate it is for you and your sisters. No, Augusta, I intend to sit my bottom on your face, quite naked.'

Augusta swallowed hard.

'Must you, here and now?'

'I must,' Lucy assured her, 'and I will have no protests, Augusta. Now, come across my lap, and we shall soon have your pretty bottom bare and blushing.'

With considerable trepidation, Augusta stepped forward, to lay herself down across Lucy's knees, her sense of humiliation rising hard at putting herself into such an ignominious position, and stronger than ever, because it was by choice. She steadied herself on the floor, pouting as she studied the design of the carpet just inches in front of her face. Lucy took hold of her dress and she felt it being pulled up and piled onto her back. Her petticoat followed and she was bare, her bottom naked in a froth of lace and silk, exposed for punishment as Lucy went on gaily.

'There, quite ready, and so pretty. I am sorry, Augusta dearest, if I have called your bottom fat before. You are not fat in the least, merely pleasantly plump, a joy to behold and a joy to spank. Now come, stick it up a little. I like to see your quim as she peeps out from between your thighs.'

Augusta obeyed with a fresh rush of humiliation. Lucy gave a little purr of pleasure and her hand settled on Augusta's bottom, stroking and squeezing gently as she continued to talk.

'No doubt your husband will spank you like this, when you are married, and no doubt he will enjoy your bottom every bit as much as I do. You are not to marry out of the district, Augusta, so that I may visit, and when privacy allows I will take you over my knee, for it is a pleasure I never wish to lose. To work then.'

Augusta made to reply, but her words came out as a gasp of shock and pain as Lucy's hand landed hard across her naked bottom. The spanking had begun, and as Augusta began to wriggle and kick in her pain Lucy was laughing, high and clear. Each slap stung furiously, and brought Augusta's resentment of what was being done to her higher still, until at last it broke to a glorious warmth and with a final sob she abandoned herself.

Lucy sensed the change, and began to spank harder still, and no longer across the full expanse of Augusta's bottom, but right on the fleshy swell over her quim. In no time Augusta was moaning and sticking her bottom up, utterly surrendered to the joy of being thoroughly spanked, then wiggling and squirming herself on Lucy's knee as she began to beg.

'Harder, my darling Lucy, harder. Use your hairbrush on me, Lucy, and pay no mind to my cries!'

The spanking stopped, only to start again an instant later, now with Lucy's hairbrush applied hard and fast to Augusta's bouncing, quivering bottom. For a moment the pain was intolerable, and Augusta was screaming, before she was in ecstasy once more, gasping out her pleasure with her bottom stuck high to take the smacks. Lucy's laughter had become nearly hysterical, and grew yet more so as Augusta began to babble again.

'I . . . I am going to do it, Lucy, I am going to do it! Beat me harder!'

Lucy obliged, clutching onto Augusta's squirming body as she spanked with all her strength, smack after furious smack laid in, hard and even. Augusta's cries grew broken, and then she was screaming again, only not in pain, but ecstasy, as the muscles of her legs and bottom and quim went tight in frantic contraction. Brought to ecstasy by her punishment, she was wriggling herself on Lucy's lap, in a wanton ecstasy that needed only the least touch to her quim to make it perfect. It was given, the spanking stopping abruptly as Lucy caught Augusta between the thighs, to cup her quim and rub. Again Augusta cried out, a long moan of pleasure as everything came together for her, and as Lucy at last stopped rubbing and the pleasure began to slowly fade, she felt the hairbrush handle between her cheeks, touching her anus, then inside, pushing past the sweaty little ring and up, deep into the cavity of her bottom, where it was left. She went slowly limp across Lucy's knee, with the hairbrush sticking out between her upturned cheeks.

'Come, come, Augusta, dear,' Lucy chided after a moment. 'Should you not thank me?'

Augusta nodded and slid to the floor, turning to kneel between Lucy's now open knees to embrace her, shivering in her arms. Lucy gave a low purr and hugged Augusta to her chest, stroking her hair, but only for a moment before pushing her back and standing up.

'Down on the floor now, and quickly. Mrs Hawkes is sure to make enquiry if we are in the house too long.'

As ordered, Augusta went down on the carpet, with a brief squeak as she accidentally sat on the hairbrush in her anus and pushed it further up before managing to get on her back. Lucy stood over her, eyes glittering with mischief, and spent a moment re-adjusting August's skirt to bare her quim.

'Pull up your knees!' Lucy ordered. 'And keep them wide, to show your quim, and the hairbrush also.'

Augusta nodded and obeyed, spreading her thighs to leave her quim naked to the cool air with the hairbrush protruding from between her bottom cheeks. Only as Lucy straddled her did she realise that if Hippolyta looked through the keyhole she would have a fine view of her open legs. It was no worse than seeing Lucy's bare bottom go in her face, and she contented herself with a sob as Lucy straddled her, immediately reaching back to throw up her skirts and bare her neatly formed bottom, the cheeks just open enough to hint at the rose-pink pucker between.

Lucy quickly squatted down, and everything was showing, the sweet pink purse of her quim, wet and ready with the little bulge of flesh that blocked her hole plainly visible, the neat curves of her bottom and the tiny hole between. Augusta could only stare, struggling to come to terms with the idea of kissing another girl's bottom hole, yet knowing full when that she no longer had it in her to resist.

She was given no choice. Lucy paused only long enough to allow Augusta to let her fate sink in, then sat down. Augusta gave a muffled squeak as her face was smothered in soft, fleshy bottom, with Lucy's cheeks fully spread so that she could feel the puckered ring of her cousin's anus against her nose, and then her lips.

'Give me a kiss,' Lucy demanded, her voice full of wicked delight. 'Give me a kiss, Augusta darling, on my bottom hole!'

Augusta resisted only for a second and then her lips were puckered up and she had done it, pressing them to Lucy's anus and planting a firm, deliberate kiss. Lucy gave a delighted squeal and wiggled her bottom in Augusta's face as she spoke.

'Delightful! So delightful! You have kissed my bottom hole, Augusta, my bottom hole! Now you are truly mine, and I shall make you do it again, ever so often, and lick me too, between my cheeks and in my bottom hole! My quim too, Augusta. Now do it, my bottom hole again, then you are to lick my quim until I come to rapture!'

Augusta puckered up once more, to kiss Lucy's anus, then to lick as she gave in to her feelings, probing the little rubbery hole with her tongue, lapping at it, probing again, all to the sound of Lucy's pleased moans and delighted laughter. All her resistance was gone, and all her pride. In moments she was licking eagerly and her hands had gone down between her thighs, one to rub, one to ease the hairbrush handle in and out of her own bottom, at which Lucy's laughter grew shrill with delight.

For a while Lucy let Augusta masturbate and lick at her anus, before shifting her weight a little. Augusta's tongue found Lucy's quim, licking in an ecstasy of subservient delight as she rubbed at herself. The thought of how she was and what she was doing was going round and round in her head and her pleasure rose; spanked and made to kiss and lick her cousin's bottom, utterly degraded, deliciously degraded. When Lucy came in her face she only licked the harder, revelling in being made to bring her cousin to ecstasy in such a rude way.

Lucy stayed put, moving only a little, to bring her bottom hole back to Augusta's mouth and giggling as it was immediately kissed. Near her own orgasm, Augusta kept her lips pressed to the tiny hole, the knowledge that she was kissing Lucy's bottom hole raging in her head as her muscles started to tighten, and she was there, the whole exquisite way she had been handled running through her mind as she squirmed and bucked on the floor: spanked and buggered with a hairbrush, her face sat on and made to kiss a bottom hole . . .

Only as Lucy finally climbed off did Augusta realise that the door was open a crack, and that Hippolyta was peering in.

Robert Fairbrother reined his horse in and dismounted, tying his reins to the holding bar outside the Crown in Chagford. He walked inside, ignoring the hostile looks and guilty whispers that followed him from place to place. He ordered a glass of punch, which the landlord brought himself, placing it on the table with a bow that was somewhat obsequious and not at all friendly.

Wearily, Fairbrother spread his map out on the table. It told him nothing he did not already know, and yet still he studied it, trying to find some pattern in what little information he had. He had made enquiries in every town between Ilfracombe and Tavistock, between Launceston and Exeter, and a great many of the villages in the countryside between, and yet his efforts had yielded only rumours, which he had wasted yet more time investigating.

Maintaining the fiction that he was engaged on an excise enquiry had made his task more difficult still. Many people were reluctant to speak to him at all, some refused point blank, while he was sure that more than one had deliberately set him on a false trail. On giving the description of the mummer in Barnstaple he had been directed to a group of players who were said to be lodging in Crediton. They had proved to be dwarves. When he asked in Tiverton it had been suggested that a strange man had been seen dressed in red and white harlequin near Holsworthy, but if such a man had ever existed nobody else had heard of him.

It was beginning to seem likely that the man had left the district altogether, perhaps taking fright, perhaps in the normal course of affairs. What was clear was that the harlinquinade was no part of a professional costume, but a disguise, doubtless intended both to provide a diversion and conceal the man's face. As one route of enquiry after another proved fruitless, he had increasingly turned to his original theory, that the man was one among John Coppinger's gang.

If the harlinquinade was indeed a ruse, then the solution still fitted all the facts, especially the popular reluctance to speak with him. No doubt half the inns and coaching houses he had enquired at purchased their brandy from John Coppinger, and it also seemed clear that his description had been circulated, because the reaction to his arrival varied little whether he was in uniform or not.

As he sipped his punch he pondered the situation, and his life in general. It was less than satisfactory. Being so generally detested stung his feelings, and all the more for his certain knowledge that what he was doing was right. With the exception of his fellow officers, whom he seldom saw, and his men, with whom he had no thought of social acquaintance, he was barely tolerated, save only by the Truscotts without whom he was certain he would have gone mad.

Yet even there all was not well. Lucy's behaviour was maddening, one minute flirtatious, so that he was sure she returned his feelings, the next icy cold, showing a lofty contempt and a barely concealed distaste for his society. By contrast, Octavia was almost worshipful, constantly seeking out his company and hanging on his every word, with her beautiful eyes looking up into his in what he was sure was adoration. Yet to turn his affections to Octavia was a betrayal of Lucy, something which he had agonised over through many a sleepless night, more often than not punctuated by periods of frenzied and guilty masturbation over one girl or the other, frequently both.

His only other comfort, and no less double-edged, was Molly Hynes, with whom he now had regular appointments, on the Monday and Thursday nights. On each occasion he would be racked by guilt beforehand, swearing to himself that he would not go, only to give in at the last moment. He was also racked with guilt afterwards, not so much while he was with Molly, who accepted having her breasts fucked with casual forbearance and good humour, but afterwards, when he was with his fellow Preventative Officers or worse, at Beare or Driscoll's. To watch the gentle innocence of Augusta, the playful vivacity of Lucy, Lydia's demure propriety, or the sweet devotion of Octavia and think back to the grossness of his own behaviour just hours before was enough to make him sick to the stomach for his own wickedness.

Yet neither prayer, any number of patent draughts, nor bathing in cold water made the least difference to his carnal appetite. He still wanted to fuck Lucy, preferably between her breasts, or with her skirts thrown up as she knelt to accept him from behind, also Octavia, and sometimes all four. At worst, after rather too much claret and strong cheese at supper, he had woken from a vivid and erotic dream to jerk himself to a furious and agonisingly guilty climax over the thought of tying all four as Octavia had been tied and taking his time with his cock in their cleavages before at last ejaculating in Octavia's face, to close her beautiful, worshipping eyes with thick blobs of semen.

With Octavia suitably chastised, and Augusta her willing slave, only Lydia remained to be punished by Lucy. She was the hardest of the three, with more pride and determination then her sisters, also less wanton. True, she had gone into raptures under Hippolyta's fingers, but she had been spanked first, and Lucy was sure the pleasure had been purely physical. She was also cautious, fully aware of Lucy's intentions and determined that it would not happen.

Lucy was equally determined that it would, and each day contrived to create a situation in which she would

131

be alone with Lydia long enough to at the very least administer a worthwhile spanking. Worthwhile meant having the time and privacy to get Lydia's bottom bare and make her truly sorry. The best part of a week had gone before an opportunity presented itself. Mr Addiscombe had invited the family over and, as always, had plied them with generous quantities of both food and drink. After the meal Stephen and Caroline had been obliged to return to Beare, and Mrs Hawkes had suggested a walk up the lane which led to the moor.

Before they had reached the valley bottom Lydia had begun to show signs of discomfort, and finally made an embarrassed confession of needing to return to the house. Lucy immediately volunteered to accompany her, and after a moment of clucking by Mrs Hawkes and a few flustered protestations by Lydia it was agreed. Lucy spoke the moment they were out of earshot of the others.

'It would have been wiser, dear Lydia, to avail yourself of the opportunity before we set off.'

'I did not wish to!' Lydia hissed. 'That man Mudge, I am convinced he watches us!'

'In the privy? What nonsense! How could he?'

'I do not know, for certain, but I suspect the air grill in the wall is not all it seems, and more than once I have heard noises in the adjoining room.'

Lucy frowned, not wishing to believe what Lydia was saying, and yet with the blood already rushing to her face at the realisation that it could well be true. If so, something would have to be done, but in due time. For the moment there was the more pressing matter of Lydia's punishment.

'I suggest,' she stated, 'that we go in among the bushes. I will stand guard for you, thus preserving your modesty and purchasing us a little time.'

'Time?' Lydia queried. 'Time for what?'

'You know full well,' Lucy answered. 'I intend to punish you, as I have punished your sisters.'

'No,' Lydia replied. 'I will not tolerate it. Lay a single finger on me and I shall scream. Mrs Hawkes will hear me!'

'Scream and all will become known, including your part in the theft of my clothes, and how Hippolyta spanked you, be sure of it. Which do you fear the most, cousin Lydia, disgrace and your father's belt, or a little time spent across my knee?'

'How would this be? Mrs Hawkes would merely think us playing, somewhat undignified, perhaps, but . . .'

'I would inform her, as indeed I am tempted to do, unless you do as you are told, and promptly. Now come along, all I intend is to spank you, and thus teach you a much needed lesson!'

Lydia's expression grew abruptly more sulky, a determined pout. Picking up her skirts, she began to walk faster. Lucy moved after her, catching one arm. Lydia tried to break Lucy's grip, but slipped in the mud of the lane, to fall back against the high, grassy bank. Immediately Lucy was on top of her, and in an instant Lydia's arm had been twisted cruelly behind her back.

'Up the bank with you!' Lucy ordered, twisting her other hand into Lydia's hair. 'One scream, and I swear I will tell everything.'

Lydia gave an angry sob, but began to scramble up the bank, propelled by Lucy. The top opened to a flat area at the side of a field, shaded by dense thorn scrub and quite invisible from the lane below.

'This will do well enough,' Lucy said, propelling the struggling Lydia towards where a low blackthorn bough made a possible seat.

'Why must you be so beastly!' Lydia protested as Lucy sat down.

Lucy didn't bother to answer, but hauled Lydia down across her knee as best her seat allowed her. With her arm still twisted hard up into the small of her back, Lydia could only squirm uselessly and kick her feet, also sob, all of it in a growing agony of consternation. Lucy was grinning as she stripped her cousin for spanking. The dress came up, then the petticoat, and it was done. Lydia gave a last, bitter sob as the twin globes of her bottom came on show, Lucy a chuckle of satisfaction.

'Legs apart,' Lucy chided, applying a gentle slap to the back of Lydia's tightly closed legs. 'It is important, I think, that a punished girl should be made to show what she has behind. Do you not agree?'

'No!' Lydia responded angrily. 'Is it not undignified enough that I should suffer a spanking, without you having to make it so rude!?'

'To the contrary,' Lucy replied happily. 'I like you to know that I can see your quim – or your cunt, to use the vulgar expression – and your bottom hole too. It amuses me. Now open your legs.'

'No!'

'Open your legs, Lydia Truscott!'

'No!'

'No matter then,' Lucy said airily, 'they will soon start to open when the spanking has begun.'

She adjusted herself a little and set to work, applying a salvo of hard smacks to the naked, squirming bottom stuck high over her legs, before suddenly hooking a foot around Lydia's ankle and jerking it back, to spread her out, virgin quim open to the air, wrinkly pink bottom hole showing between the fleshy cheeks. Lydia let out a howl of frustration and rage, which broke to pain as the spanking began again, Lucy now applying the slaps with her full strength and laughing as she did it.

'There, you see!' she crowed. 'Now you are showing your quim, and I do declare your bottom hole has begun to wink, just like a little pink eye! Could you but see yourself, I am sure you would be amused by how comic you look!'

Lydia went wild, kicking her free leg in a manner Lucy found delightfully ridiculous, also tossing her hair, which had come completely loose, thumping the ground with her balled fists and squealing lustily with every smack. The greater the fuss Lydia made the more Lucy laughed, and the faster she spanked, until Lydia's bottom was a fat red ball, the cheeks bouncing crazily to the slaps and with every secret detail of quim and bottom hole on full, rude display.

Still Lucy spanked, faster and faster, as hard as she could, until at last Lydia's babbling pleas and squeals of pain broke to a cry of utter despair as she lost control of her bladder. Lucy squeaked in alarm, but also delight, as a fountain of pale yellow pee erupted from Lydia's spread quim, to arch high in the air and tinkle down onto the leaf-strewn ground. Lydia did it all, unable to stop herself, sobbing her heart out as she urinated in full view and to the sound of Lucy's joyous laughter as well as the hiss and splash of the piddle. Only with the last few squirts did Lydia at last burst into tears.

'Do not be a baby, Lydia!' Lucy chided, as she laid a hand on her cousin's burning bottom. 'My, you are hot, and I think suitably chastened. Do you?'

'Yes, Lucy,' Lydia mumbled between heartfelt sniffs.

'Good,' Lucy replied. 'Then it only remains for you to kiss my bottom to show that you are truly sorry and we shall be friends again. After all, it is horrid to quarrel, do you not think?'

'Kiss . . . kiss your bottom?' Lydia answered as she was released from Lucy's grip. 'Lucy, you have spanked me! Please, is that not enough to show I am truly sorry!?'

'No. You will kiss my bottom, willingly, and both cheeks, mind. Then I will know you are sorry.'

'Lucy!'

'Say you will kiss my bottom, Lydia.'

'You said you would only spank me!' Lydia wailed, now standing, with her face if anything showing more consternation than before.

'Yes,' Lucy answered, 'before you dared to show fight. Now you must kiss my bottom, and one more word and I will make you do it not on my cheeks, but between them.'

'Lucy!'

'Very well . . .'

'No, no . . . that was not another word! Not at all! I will kiss your bottom!'

Lucy was laughing as she stood up, and Lydia's sulky pout grew more sulky still as she dropped into a squat. Still giggling, Lucy threw up her skirts and pushed out her bare bottom towards Lydia's face. After only a moment Lydia puckered her lips, leant forward and planted a gentle kiss on one bottom cheek, then the other. She stood, still pouting badly as she spoke.

'Are you quite done with me?'

'Quite,' Lucy assured her, 'although one could wish that you were a little more playful. If you were to lick my quim, for example, I would return the compliment, in which there is great pleasure, and . . .'

'Pleasure there is,' a voice growled, and both girls turned in shock.

A man stood looking at them, his face hidden by a rough mask crudely sewn from sackcloth. Coarse, woollen clothing covered the rest of his lanky body, but failed to conceal a large bulge in the front of his breeches. Lydia gave a single, fearful gasp and stood back, only to find her way blocked by the thorn trees. Lucy tilted her chin up, looking down her nose at him.

'How dare you spy upon us, you revolting little man!?' she demanded. 'Get away from us, this moment!'

'That I'll not do,' he answered, his voice low, grating and full of lust.

Lucy's throat went tight as his cock unwound itself in the confines of his breeches, pushing up and to the side to make a long ridge, the implications of which were frighteningly obvious. Steeling herself, she spoke again as he took a step forward.

'I know you, Saul Mudge!' she stated.

'Who's Mudge?' the man grated.

'You!' Lucy answered him, fighting to control her fear as his hands bent like claws, as if to reach out and grasp her. 'I know you . . . by your ways . . . by your voice . . . by . . .'

'What of it then?' he grunted.

'You'll not touch us!' she snapped. 'Do, and . . .'

'And what?' he sneered. 'And you'll tell your Papas? Tell 'em what you gets up to, kissing each other's arses. Sluts.'

'Mere cousinly affection!' Lucy answered back. 'Of no concern to the likes of you, Saul Mudge!'

'Plenty of concern, from where I'm standing, Miss Lucy,' he said, abandoning all pretence. 'Quite the little pair of bob tails, aren't you? Now come, if you're that eager to lick your cousin's cunt, you must be more eager to put your pretty mouth around a man's cock.'

'Absolutely not!' Lucy snapped.

Mudge laughed.

'So you're not, eh? Not so high and mighty with young Jack Gurney up on the moor, were you? Took him all right, didn't you? Swallowed his load and all, didn't you? So what's Jack got that I've not, eh? Now how'd you like your father to know that, Miss Lucy?'

Lydia had gasped at the revelation about Jack Gurney, and gasped again as Mudge abruptly tugged aside the flap of his crude breeches to let out a long, dirty brown penis, already fully erect with the glossy red tip wet, and little bubbles emerging from the tiny slit at the end. He grinned, showing his teeth, some blackened, others merely yellow.

'On your knees, the both of you,' he growled. 'You can use your mouths together, on my cock, and my balls too. You'd be better to do your best and make me spend fast, or I might be tempted to put it up those little cunts of yours. Get back here, you!'

Lydia was trying frantically to get through the thorn trees to where the green of a field could be seen beyond, but her dress was catching and she had begun to panic, clawing at the branches but without the sense to take one at a time. Mudge started after her. Lucy stepped aside, shaking. To her utter horror her quim had begun to twitch in anticipation of the big ugly cock being put in her mouth, but she forced herself to speak calmly as he took hold of Lydia by the scruff of her neck.

'Force us then, and I shall tell my father. Perhaps I shall be whipped, but you, Saul Mudge, you will end up with a rope around your neck outside Okehampton jail, and as you swing in the air, with your feet kicking foolishly beneath you and the life choking out of you, I shall laugh, Saul Mudge! Come, put it in my mouth, but that's the price!'

Lydia was screaming as she was hauled out of the undergrowth, and collapsed among the thorns as Mudge turned on Lucy, his face contorted in hatred and fury, but his cock going slowly limp. Lucy lifted her chin and set her jaw to stop herself trembling, then spoke again.

'Go now, and nothing will be said, you have my word. Touch Lydia again, or myself, and all will become known.'

He was glaring at her, his hand on his cock, tugging frantically at it in a vain effort to restore his erection, his breathing harsh and low. Behind him, Lydia lay limp among the bushes. His mouth came open to speak, but closed again, and with a sudden hiss of anger he was gone, jumping back down to the lane and away. Lucy sat down on the hawthorn bough, her legs suddenly too weak to support her, trembling violently and sick to her stomach.

Eight

Returning to his house, Robert Fairbrother was surprised to see a woman waiting in the doorway, a cowl drawn close around her face. She looked around as he came nearer, her expression agitated, and he hurried to open the door and draw her within, realising that she was likely to be offering information in the hope of a reward.

'What is it?' he asked as he closed the door. 'You have something to tell me, perhaps?'

'More than you are bargaining for, I'll warrant,' she answered as she let her cowl down to reveal a handsome but somewhat weatherworn face framed in thick blonde hair worn loose. 'I am Annie Coppinger.'

Fairbrother felt his pulse rise and he had to struggle to suppress a smile as he ushered her into the main room. He had heard the stories, of how Coppinger beat his wife and let his men use her in reward or merely to keep their spirits up, but he had never imagined she would find the courage to come to him in an effort to end her torment.

'You have done well,' he stated. 'A bold decision, just and right.'

'I come because I must,' she answered, 'and in turn you must rid the district of the monster who is my husband!'

'This is my aim,' Fairbrother stated. 'I know his deeds, and how he holds the coast in fear, but still it is my aim.'

'He is a tyrant!' Annie answered with feeling. 'You cannot begin to imagine how it is to live with him! But quickly, I cannot be seen here!'

Fairbrother nodded.

'What do you have?'

'Enough to bring him to the gallows. In four days, perhaps five, a French boat will come in, but not to shore. Rafts will be sunk, a quarter mile offshore from Welcombe Mouth, and somewhat south, among rocks.'

'You are certain of this? You know the exact location?'

'Certain sure, and how the rafts are to be placed, and brought up. The exact point is known by the position of lanterns on shore. These are in two lines, three lanterns in each line, and where both line up exactly, the rafts lie beneath.'

Fairbrother nodded in response, his excitement rising as he took a chart. Spread out on the table, it showed the coast from Hartland Point south to Tintagel. His finger stabbed at a point in the sea west and south of Welcombe Mouth, where the headland of Marshland Cliff was marked.

'Here?' he demanded. 'Outside Gull Rock?'

Annie nodded.

'Perilous ground,' he remarked. 'Here, one fathom and three, here one and two, here but four feet.'

'A safe channel exists,' Annie assured him, also pointing at the map. 'The cutters which bring in the goods come in so, close to shore, and tack, sailing in with the northern lights in line behind and drop anchor where the two lines cross.'

'So the *Bull* might come in by the same method,' Fairbrother said, speaking to himself as much as to her, 'but it is no easy work.'

He frowned, considering the possibilities the information offered to him. To take the French boat as she unloaded achieved the seizure of the goods and crew, but not Coppinger, while if he waited for Coppinger to lift the rafts he would take both goods and the man who controlled the local trade. Without Coppinger, the Frenchmen would have nobody to trade with, at least for a while. To wait was clearly the better course.

'What is the cargo?' he enquired after a while.

'Three hundred and fifty casks of Cognac,' Annie replied. 'Now I must be back, or I'll be missed.'

Fairbrother nodded.

'You will be rewarded,' he assured her as she made for the door.

'To be rid of my husband is reward enough,' she answered him.

Henry Truscott gazed idly out across the landscape, somewhat bored, and wondered what might be done in the way of amusement. With Eloise and Lucy having gone to Exeter in the coach, driven by James and taking their maids with them, he was without female company – a rare event, and one that left him feeling ill at ease. He had begun to wonder if a visit to Molly Hynes in Bideford might not repay the long ride when a rap at the door drew his attention. The cook was about somewhere, but he went to answer it himself, finding a nondescript man in a worn red coat whom he recognised as an associate of John Coppinger. The man spoke immediately.

'John Coppinger presents his compliments, sir, and asks if you'd kindly provide some spare hands for his crew.'

'Cargo coming in, is there?' Henry responded, brightening immediately. 'Yes, I can help. Tell Coppinger he can have Jack Gurney and my man James. He can send to Mr Addiscombe for Saul Mudge too. You'll be seeing Todd Gurney at the mine, and he has my instruction to help as needed. That should muster a round dozen.'

'Our thanks on that, Mr Truscott, sir,' the man answered.

'He can be sure of my support,' Henry said. 'God knows but I've enough interest in the cargo. When will he need them?'

'Night after tomorrow, sir. There's three hundred and fifty casks in, from Roscoff, which we aim to have stowed in double time. There's a shilling and a bottle for each man down, after the work, double if we've a mill or the excise show, not that it's likely.'

'Time enough, and you may tell him that I'll be inviting a certain Mr Robert Fairbrother to sup with me that evening.'

The man gave a bow and withdrew, but backwards, looking hopeful.

'Go around to the kitchen door,' Henry went on, 'and I dare say cook will have something for you, then if you'd be good enough when you return to the stable, pray tell the boy to saddle Rose up for me.'

After closing the door, he walked back into the house, rubbing his hands together as he made for the stairs. It would be a stiff ride to Bideford, especially on Lucy's pony, but worth it none the less, with the prospect of Molly Hynes and also of playing Robert Fairbrother for a fool one more time.

His good mood continued as he rode north, taking his time to ensure that Rose didn't tire unduly. At Holsworthy he paused to rest and water her while he took a flagon of ale and a meat pie, then moved on, coming into Bideford with the sun still well up in the sky. Intent on the less strenuous task first, he left Rose at a coaching inn and made for the Customs House, only to find Fairbrother out. The *Bull* was at anchor in the stream, but he was not aboard, and after another glass of ale by the quayside he moved into the back alleys and to Molly's.

Her curtains were drawn, to his irritation, but he went up anyway, quietly, for the amusement of listening on the landing as she entertained her visitor. Whoever it was, he proved a man of few words, speaking rarely, and then in a mumbled undertone. Molly responded as always, with giggles and moans, some put on, some real, and from the noises Henry quickly guessed that she was having her breasts fucked. Nodding in silent appreciation of the visitor's taste, he wondered if it might not be an idea to do the same himself, at least as part of his pleasure.

Finally the grunting and moaning rose to a crescendo and stopped. A brief conversation followed, and Henry stood back politely to let the man pass. The door opened, the man backed out, mumbling something about the next visit to Molly, turned, and stopped still, mouth open in horror.

'Mr Truscott!'

'Ah, Mr Fairbrother,' Henry responded. 'I was looking for you this moment.'

'I . . . I . . . I . . .,' Fairbrother babbled, his face white, and then he had fallen to his knees.

Henry looked down, worried and then puzzled as Fairbrother gripped his hand and began to make a long and earnest protestation, so fast as to be unintelligible. Molly appeared from the door, stifling a giggle as she recognised Henry.

'Do get up, Mr Fairbrother,' Henry finally managed.

Fairbrother rose, his face working with guilt and self-pity, but quickly spoke again, more slowly.

'I am ashamed of myself, Mr Truscott, bitterly ashamed, and . . .'

'Whatever for?' Henry demanded.

'Th . . . this!' Fairbrother answered in astonishment, with a sweeping gesture that took in both Molly and her room. 'What must you think of me?'

'My dear fellow,' Henry went on, 'if your tastes are unusual it's no concern of mine. It's not women's clothes, I see, and if you've a mind to have Molly play flaybottomist or make a piss-pot of your mouth, well, I may laugh, and I hold I've a right to, but no more. Besides, I judged you were paying a visit to the dumpling shop, or was I wrong?'

'I . . . I came to make ill use of this poor woman,' Fairbrother responded, looking puzzled.

'Ill use?' Henry queried. 'So whipping's your thing?'

Fairbrother merely looked bemused, but Henry ushered him back into the room and sat down on Molly's bed.

'Truth be told,' he said, 'I had you down as a cold fish, but I see you're not. Molly, run out for a jug of ale and when Mr Fairbrother here has recovered himself we'll row you fore and aft.'

Molly giggled and curtsied, and had left before Fairbrother managed to put his stuttering response into words. Henry lay back against the bolster, folding his hands behind his head as he went on.

'I came up to ask if you'd care to sup with us tomorrow night, in addition to taking a run at Molly, that is. My brood are in Exeter, you know.'

'You . . . you would still wish me at your house, after finding me in this place?' Fairbrother asked.

'Granted you might not wish to confess that the invitation was issued in Molly Hynes' bedroom,' Henry answered, 'leastways, not in front of the ladies, or my brother for that matter. Truth is, I could wish I'd known sooner, as then we might have enlivened our conversations up of an evening, and more. Suki's game, and Hippolyta.'

'The . . . the negro maids?'

'Why certainly, unless you know of another Suki and Hippolyta hereabouts. Damn fine rattles, the pair of 'em, and believe me, if you think young Molly has a fine top hamper you'll change your tune when you've seen Suki stripped down. So you'll come?'

It seemed to take Fairbrother a moment to realise what Henry was talking about, while he sat with his mouth opening and closing like that of a fish, before he managed a reply.

'I . . . I would be delighted, naturally, Mr Truscott, and yes, nothing need be said, and . . . and I thank you, for I know full well that your bluff manner hides a true Christian charity that is rare indeed. Forgiveness is . . . is a rarer virtue than we might hope.'

'True,' Henry admitted thoughtfully, 'although in this case there is nothing to forgive. Indeed, I'd think you damned odd if you'd not fuck Molly's bouncers at a shilling a throw.'

'A shilling? Is the rate not one and three?'

Henry laughed at the slight irritation in Fairbrother's voice.

'One and three is her special rate, no more. But what of yourself? Any news of the mad mummer?'

'No, sir, none whatever,' Fairbrother answered with evident relief at changing the subject, 'but I'll have him, sir, and I'll not take rest until I do, nor . . .'

He stopped, suddenly looking if anything more embarrassed than before. Henry wondered if he'd been going to mention his intentions towards Lucy, but said nothing and Fairbrother went on.

'I still hold he's with Coppinger's men, and there I hope to put an end to one and all.'

'You do?'

'I have Coppinger caught, but on that I'd be glad to speak to you. It's said that Coppinger can muster a hundred men, when there's call, and I can't hope to stand more than two dozen against him. I'd not ask this, not usually, but you've men aplenty, and know who in the county is honest and who not.'

Henry nodded thoughtfully.

'When would this be?'

'Six days. I have information, on how a cargo of goods is to come in, and how it will be transferred to land.'

'In six days' time, you say? Yes, I will be able to help, but you must be certain no word of this gets to Coppinger. He is not a man to be taken lightly.'

'Nor am I, Mr Truscott, nor am I,' Fairbrother replied.

Saul Mudge tightened his grip in Polly's hair as he forced her down across the table. She went with only a mild whimper of pain and protest, a whimper that was repeated as he began to hump her skirt up with his free hand. With her full pink bottom bare and the lips of her quim on ready view between her thighs, he made quick work of extracting his cock from his breeches. His eyes were fixed on Polly's bare bottom, but his mind was full of images of Lucy Truscott in the same position, only begging for mercy as he readied his cock for her virgin cunt.

'Put up some fight, woman!' he growled as his cock began to stiffen in his hand.

Polly gave an angry wriggle in response, but only succeeded in rubbing her bottom against his rapidly expanding cock. He laughed and peeled his foreskin back to push the head between her buttocks, rubbing it on her anus as he came up to full erection. Moving in close, he pushed his shaft into the soft valley between her cheeks, holding her firmly in place despite her continued squirming as he rubbed in her slit. He thought of Lucy, perhaps forced down across the hawthorn bough on which she'd sat to spank Lydia, his cock growing in Polly's bottom crease as she fought to prevent her violation.

Sure he would soon come, he took hold of his cock and put it to Polly's cunt, sliding the full length deep into her body in one easy motion. She was soon groaning as he began to fuck her, taking a moment to enjoy the warm wetness of her cunt and the feel of her bottom against him before turning his thoughts back to

Lucy. Closing his eyes, he let go of Polly's hair and took her by the hips. Her groans changed to a frenzied grunting as he picked up his pace and let his imagination go.

He knew he should have fucked Lucy; once her maidenhead had been burst on his erect cock she would have been far too ashamed to speak out. Really he should have done both of them, and in style. He'd have forced them to strip, stark naked, and to lick each other's cunts and bottoms, to suck his cock and take his balls in their mouths, to kiss his arsehole, to beg for mercy before they were made to kneel side by side, their hands strapped behind their backs to have their cunts fucked. He would do Lydia first, holding his cock to her hole before bursting her so that he could hear her beg, then Lucy, her tight little cunt hole lubricated with her cousin's virgin blood, and the noose tightening around his neck as he stood on the gallows . . .

Suddenly his cock was limp in Polly's hole. Lucy would do it, he knew, for certain. He cursed and spat a gob of phlegm into Polly's hair, then once more began to fuck her, moving his cock slowly in and out as he struggled to rearrange his thoughts. Lucy was a haughty little bitch, and needed fucking, but she was dangerous too. Perhaps Lydia would be better, more afraid certainly, perhaps so afraid she could be forced to his will, made his plaything, to suck his cock, maybe even take it up her dainty arsehole.

He was hard again, and soon had his rhythm back, once more reducing Polly to helpless grunting as her cunt was used. Lydia came into his mind, struggling against the thorns, unable to break free. If only Lucy had run away it would have been so easy. Lydia would have been helpless, helpless to stop her bottom being stripped, her freshly spanked bottom, helpless to stop him feeling her breasts and her belly and legs and her buttocks, helpless to prevent him getting his cock erect, nice and slow, as she squirmed in pain and anguish among the thorns and stinging nettles, helpless to prevent him jamming his erection up her virgin cunt, to burst her maidenhead and fill her bloody hole with spunk, but no more helpless than he would be on the gallows once Lucy had exposed his crime . . .

Again he stopped, panting, his cock almost limp. Gritting his teeth, he gave Polly a few hard slaps on her rump, making her cry out and squirm on his cock as he moved it inside her. His erection began to grow again, and with Polly whimpering softly into the table as she was fucked he once more turned his mind to the girls. If he was to have Lucy his recourse was plain. His mask was not enough. He would need to purchase an old blue coat or, better still, have Polly make the sort of multicoloured garb that mummers wore. That was how the man had been dressed on the moor, so rumour said.

For a moment it occurred to him as odd that Lucy should have been accosted the same day he saw her with Jack Gurney, but he pushed the thought aside in the interests of getting his cock hard in Polly's hole once more. Lucy might suspect, and he would have to do all he could to alter his appearance, and have Polly swear he had been with her. That way he could catch her, somewhere well away from home, catch her and beat her and fuck her, to leave her stripped and bruised in the ditch with her cunt full of spunk and the blood from her torn maidenhead.

She would fight, really fight, clawing and screaming in haughty fury as her clothes were ripped off her body, as her hands were strapped up hard behind her back, as her bottom was beaten, as he put his cock to her virgin cunt hole and pushed, letting her feel the pressure and know, know that her maidenhead was to be taken by force, and by a common man, whom she would surely recognise, him, Saul Mudge, who would just as surely be caught and hanged for his crime come what might . . .

For the third time he stopped, panting with effort. It was no good. Every time he came close to orgasm the consequences of what he wanted to do rose up to break his pleasure. He withdrew, his cock now limp and sore. Polly, assuming he'd come, gave him a single hot glance before going to pour herself a tot of brandy. He sat down, still gasping, but managed to snap his fingers and point to the cask. Polly nodded and passed him the mug she had been going to use, taking another for herself. He swallowed half of what she poured for him at a gulp and set to thinking about what could be done.

Henry Truscott tried to fight down his irritation as he took a sip of his port. The supper party had been dull in the extreme, with Robert Fairbrother and Stephen discussing sectarianism, scientific agriculture and reform, all subjects Henry avoided whenever possible. Caroline had been little better, in a state over the nonexistent fiend. Even Lucy had seemed less vivacious than usual, while Lydia had barely spoken. Neither he nor Eloise had been able to lighten the mood, and when the ladies had at last retired he had been obliged to listen to his brother on the intractability of the locals when it came to growing potatoes as a staple crop, with Fairbrother nodding at intervals and making the occasional ill-informed comment.

Closing his eyes, Henry thought back to previous evenings in more convivial company, teasing the ladies into playing cards for their clothes with his London friends or whipping and buggering Suki as Eloise watched, herself half dressed and masturbating lazily as her maid was used. One such evening had left Suki pregnant and led to the arrival of Hippolyta nine months later. He smiled at the memory of the year that had given him three daughters in succession, first Augusta, although it was just possible she was his brother's, or somebody else's entirely, then Lucy, who was definitely his, and lastly Hippolyta, who again was just possibly Todd Gurney's.

Jack Gurney had been born at about the same time, and Henry quietly cursed the conventions that prevented the boy marrying Lucy. It was an ideal match in every way save status and fortune, while he strongly suspected they had taken to indulging each other's lust. There had certainly been every opportunity, and while Lucy was a flirt by nature, her flushed glances were new. Idly he wondered if they had actually fucked, and if so what the consequences might be, or whether Lucy had the sense to accommodate him in her mouth or up her bottom. He chuckled to himself as he refilled his glass.

'I must say you take these things very lightly,' Stephen remarked, causing Henry to start in surprise before he realised that the remark related not to his daughter's virginity but to social unrest.

'Keep 'em happy,' he remarked, 'that's the answer. Plenty of food, an inn in every village and a brothel in every town and all will be well.'

'You must excuse my brother, Mr Fairbrother,' Stephen stated, colouring slightly. 'He is inclined to be frivolous.'

'It's true,' Henry insisted. 'What fellows like yourself and Young[8] don't realise is that piety and sobriety aren't your friends, they're your enemies. Give a man a pie in his gut, a jack in his hand and his cock in a trollop's mouth and he's content, a piece of advice the French would have done well to take.'

'I believe you are somewhat drunk, Henry,' Stephen remarked with a sigh.

'Moderately so,' Henry admitted. 'Shall we join the ladies?'

'Yes, why not,' Stephen answered, 'as serious conversation is evidently impossible.'

Henry swallowed the contents of his glass and refilled it before returning the decanter to Suki, who had been co-opted as an impromptu butler.

'I trust there is no illness on your estate?' Fairbrother enquired as they moved towards the drawing room.

'Illness?' Henry queried.

'Your man James, and the fellow Gurney . . .'

'Oh, ah . . .,' Henry replied. 'Yes, they are down at the mine, a, er . . . Christening party, I believe.'

Stephen shook his head.

'Too liberal an attitude to one's servants loses their respect, Henry, as I have repeatedly told you.'

Henry merely shrugged. In the drawing room the four girls were gathered around a card table, each with a small pile of pennies in front of her. Lucy was giving an explanation of some invented rule as she dealt. Octavia was eyeing Lucy suspiciously, but all four seemed reasonably composed, unlike their mother, who appeared to be at her wits' end, evoking a stab of sympathy in Henry. Fairbrother was still asking Stephen questions, and Henry sat near to Caroline, giving her a cheerful smile.

'Come, come, my dear, there is no call for gloom. Mr Fairbrother has been searching the county high and low for this fellow, and not so much as a sniff of him. By now he is probably in London, or Scotland even.'

'What if he should return?' Caroline answered.

'Then we shall lay him by his heels in double quick time,' Henry replied, 'but I consider it unlikely. Rogues of his stamp seldom remain in one place for long, for fear of the noose . . . and as a mummer he must move from place to place in any event.'

Caroline responded with a smile, evidently less than convinced. Henry gave her hand a gentle squeeze, and the gratitude of her answering glance immediately filled his head with memories, of her giggling with her breasts popped out of her bodice, of her gasping and shivering as he licked her quim, of her shyly holding her bottom cheeks apart to show off her virgin hole from behind.

He glanced around. Eloise was standing behind Lucy, providing advice on the game. Stephen and Fairbrother were deep in conversation, agriculture once more, and he caught the name Young, signalling that it was unlikely to be short. He turned back to Caroline.

'Perhaps a little air would put the roses back in your cheeks, and the night is warm. Would you care to take a turn in the garden?'

'Thank you, I should be delighted,' she answered, smiling and taking his arm as she rose.

Nobody paid them more than a glance as he led her from the room and out onto the terrace. A half moon bestowed a sheen of dull pewter on the lake, and Henry's eyes gradually picked up detail as he steered Caroline down the steps. His cock had already begun to stiffen, and he surreptitiously moved it to allow his erection to grow unimpeded. Caroline gave a gentle sigh as they started across the lawns, then spoke.

'It is a travail to be a mother, and to have three daughters, and yet I must think myself selfish, when your own son is at the wars.'

'Oh, young John can well take care of himself,' Henry answered, considering how John was more likely to be in a brothel than on a battlefield and thinking of how he might bring the conversation around to more fruitful topics. 'Eloise frets, as is natural, and Lucy, on occasion, but it gains nothing.'

'I could only wish for your insouciance.'

Unable to think of a suitable reply, he slipped his arm from hers to her waist, pulling her close. He caught her scent, and she sighed, laying her head on his shoulder, to bring his cock to full erection in his breeches, so hard it had become uncomfortable to walk.

'Are you quite yourself?' Caroline asked after a moment.

'A slight limp,' Henry admitted through gritted teeth.

'Did you take a fall?'

'No, no fall, it is simply that having you by me has rendered my prick as an iron bar!'

'Henry!'

There was shock in her voice, but a subdued giggle. He took her in his arms, clasping one bottom cheek and one breast as his mouth sought hers. For a brief moment she responded, only to pull back.

'Henry, no! What of Stephen, and of Eloise!'

'What of them?'

'We are in the middle of the lawn! Might they not see?'

'Perhaps . . . perhaps,' Henry admitted and began to steer her towards the shadows beneath the stable walls.

They had no sooner reached safety than she was clinging to him, her kisses as passionate as they had ever been, her hand already on his cock, squeezing it urgently before starting to fumble at the buttons of his breeches. Henry took over, opening the flap and pulling out his erection. Her hand was deliciously cool as it folded around him, and as she began to masturbate him she was giggling with girlish enthusiasm, although her gentle grip and skilled movements showed her maturity.

'Slow,' he urged, 'or I'll spend in your hand!'

Her response was a fresh giggle, and she squatted down, taking his cock in her mouth to suck lovingly at as much of his length as she could get in. Henry closed his eyes and began to stroke her hair, struggling not to let go of himself and waste his spunk in her mouth. Yet she was keen, desperate even, mouthing and licking at his erection with wanton urgency. Henry tried to think of something else, knowing that otherwise he would come at any moment. He tried horses, only each one was ridden by Caroline, naked, with her pretty bottom pushed out from her side-saddle; wheat, only she was making sheaves with her dress turned down to leave her chest naked and glistening with sweat; sheep, only it was a ram, mounted on her back and thrusting vigorously to the sound of her delighted gasps. He pushed her back.

'Stop . . . I must have you, Caroline . . .'

She answered with a delighted giggle and let him lift her. He pressed her to the stable wall, fumbling her gown and petticoats up together, to bare her belly and quim, his rock-hard cock pressed to her flesh. She took it, sighing as she tugged at his shaft, then let go with a delighted squeak as he lifted her by her bottom, legs spread wide and then around his hips as his cock pressed to the wetness of her quim.

'Not there!' she gasped.

'Why not?' Henry answered, and slid his cock deep inside her.

'I . . . I'm a married woman!' Caroline managed.

'All the better!' Henry answered her, cupping the roundness of her bottom as he began to fuck her, easing her up and down on his erection to a slow, even rhythm.

She was moaning immediately, her arms around his neck, then kissing him. He was going to come, at any instant, and pressed her hard to the wall, thrusting into her, only to stop as he realised the implication of what she had said. With a low chuckle he lifted her once more and set her down.

Caroline responded only with a low moan as Henry turned her to face the wall. Her skirts had fallen, but he quickly pulled them up, baring her neatly turned bottom to the dull light. She hung her head, her breathing deep and even as he pushed his cock between her bottom cheeks, rubbing the slippery head on the tight pucker of her anus. Her response was a low sob, then a whimper as he pushed and the tight, muscular ring of her bottom hole began to spread on his cock head. Henry grunted.

'By God, I'll swear you're tighter than when I first had you!'

As he spoke he gave a firm push. Caroline cried out as her anus popped in, and he was up her, the head of his cock embedded in her rectum, followed by more as he slowly and gently eased the full length of his shaft into the warmth of her gut. By the time he was right in she was panting and sobbing to her buggery, and her noises grew louder and more urgent. Henry encircled her waist, fighting to prevent himself giving the last few shoves that would make him come as his hand found the soft bulge of her quim and his fingers delved into the sticky wetness between her lips.

He began to masturbate her, drawing sighs and a gentle squirming of her bottom on his cock as he moved it inside her. Briefly she shifted, tugging the bodice of her gown down to spill out her breasts before bracing herself against the wall, her bottom pushed right out. He rubbed harder and she was moaning and wriggling on his erection, her breasts now swinging bare, then she cried out in ecstasy as her muscles began to tighten. Henry gasped as her anus went into contraction on his cock, and it was simply too much. Clutching her hard to his body, still rubbing at her quim, he began to bugger her with frantic energy, making her anal ring pull in and out and setting her screaming and stamping her feet as she went through her helpless, uncontrollable climax.

She was still coming as Henry hit his own peak, her bumhole twitching on his cock shaft as he buggered her, deep and hard. His erection jerked, he gave a single, harsh grunt and he was doing it, pumping her bottom full of hot spunk as she shivered and squirmed in his grip, begging for it harder and deeper until at last they went limp together.

For a long moment they stayed as they were, moving only for Caroline to twist around so that their mouths could meet in a long, unrestrained kiss, with his cock still firmly wedged up her bottom. Only when she at last broke away did he ease himself out, slowly and carefully. Resisting the urge to simply make her suck his cock clean or wipe it on her petticoats, he walked quickly to the yard pump.

* * *

John Coppinger stood with his massive arms folded across his chest. Lanterns illuminated Welcombe beach, and the cliff behind, either set on rocks or held by the womenfolk among the work team he had assembled. Some way offshore de Cachaliere's boat was hidden in the darkness, the creak of her rigging just audible above the gentle splash and suck of the waves. A longboat was drawn up on the beach, piled high with casks, which men were removing and stacking for transport up the cliff.

There were three hundred and fifty casks of Cognac in the cargo, also a number of bolts of gorgeously coloured silk, pepper and Bordeaux wine, and yet he confidently expected to have every last piece securely cached before dawn. The powerfully built men from the mines of the Tamar Valley worked as if they were on holiday, handling the big casks with little apparent effort. The field labourers, housemen and fishermen were no less keen, each and every one pulling his weight, while de Cachaliere's smugglers were no less eager.

A smaller boat emerged into the light, de Cachaliere himself standing in the bows and waving a greeting. Coppinger returned the gesture in surprise. The Frenchman waited fastidiously until his men had pulled the boat beyond the reach of the sea, then stepped clear, extending his hand. Coppinger shook it as he spoke.

'I'd not expected to see you back this trip!'

'I've business,' de Cachaliere answered, 'but not the sort to concern you. No money in it.'

'A woman?' Coppinger answered. 'Not Lucy Truscott?'

De Cachaliere grinned.

'The devil's luck to you then,' Coppinger answered, 'because you'll need it.'

'I've something better than luck,' de Cachaliere answered, extracting a bottle from the deep pocket of his peacock blue coat.

'Cognac?' Coppinger laughed. 'You plan to make her drunk and have your way?'

'Nothing so crude,' de Cachaliere replied, 'and this is no ordinary Cognac. No, John, I prefer them willing and eager.'

'I also, or at the least wriggling.'

De Cachaliere gave a chuckle before he spoke again, looking at the labouring teams of men.

'How d'you get the fellows to work so hard, mine as well as your own? They were not half so eager loading at Roscoff!'

'No mystery there,' Coppinger replied. 'Any that don't show willing lose the reward I've put on top of their pay. For those that're married and their women-folk here there's two yards of silk, and for those that're not there'll be Molly Hynes and my Annie back at the farm, mouths wide and legs akimbo.'

De Cachaliere gave a full-blooded laugh.

'Now that's a practice I'll have to introduce! One more load in, we're done and my boat's away clean, God willing.'

'I leave nothing to God,' Coppinger answered, 'or leastways, nothing of business. As we speak Fairbrother the excise man lies snoring in a bed at Driscoll's after supping with the Truscotts, dreaming of young Lucy no doubt.'

'A wise precaution. He's an eye for Lucy then?'

'So I hear. An eye, but no hope.'

De Cachaliere nodded.

Molly Hynes eased a lard-smeared finger into her bottom hole and spent a moment fingering herself before withdrawing it and passing the pot to Annie Coppinger.

'Don't stint,' she advised, 'not if they're to spare your cunt.'

Annie nodded and took the pot, grimacing as she pushed a finger into the lard. Rolling her legs high to display her quim and the broad spread of her bottom, she applied the lard to her anus, smearing it around the hole and then up, inserting her finger deep inside. Like Molly, she wore only stockings, half-boots and a pair of ruffled garters borrowed for the occasion. Her body was otherwise nude in the yellow candle light.

'Eighty-four men,' she said nervously, still with her finger well up her bottom.

'Not that,' Molly replied, 'not to yourself. There's eighty-four at work, certain sure, but the half are married men, and some'll likely not get their reward. Twenty to each of us, I'd say.'

'Plenty enough, where they're going,' Annie replied sulkily as she withdrew her finger.

'A good many'll spend in your mouth,' Molly reassured her, 'and elsewhere . . .'

She went quiet at the bang of a door, then they heard John Coppinger's laughter. A moment later he appeared, ducking to enter the bedroom. De Cachaliere was behind him. Molly greeted both with a smile and let one finger brush idly across a nipple.

'It's done,' Coppinger announced as de Cachaliere gave a polite bow towards each woman in turn, 'every cask stowed.'

Beyond him Molly could hear the men streaming into the farmhouse, their voices loud as they boasted of how they had worked and what they now intended to do. She heard the old woman asking if they'd rather have ale or cider, to which a voice replied, raised above the others.

'A flagon of cunt for me, mother, if it's all the same to you!'

There was raucous laughter, and John Coppinger was grinning too as he unbuttoned the flap of his breeches.

'Would you have my Annie, or Molly?' he asked de Cachaliere.

'I abide your preference,' de Cachaliere replied with a bow.

'I'll take my own,' Coppinger said, 'and a crown wager I spend first. Get your arse up, woman!'

Annie hesitated only an instant before obeying, turning over onto her knees to stick her big white bottom up towards her husband as he climbed onto the bed. Coppinger's cock was already half-hard, but he moved to the side, taking Annie firmly by the hair and pushing it into her mouth. She began to suck, cheeks bulging with the effort, even as Molly took de Cachaliere's cock in her hand and guided it into the valley of her cleavage.

In moments he was erect and fucking her breasts. Coppinger wasted no time either, tugging himself into Annie's open mouth until he was hard, then getting behind her and slipping his cock in. Annie took the fucking in silence for a moment, but quickly began to groan and gasp as the big cock worked inside her. Coppinger slapped and pinched at Annie's upturned bottom to encourage her, and was soon going for all he was worth. He mounted her, taking her breasts in her hands and fucking with his hips as if he were a dog in his bitch, which made Molly giggle.

De Cachaliere was also hard, and as he left her cleavage Molly found herself being turned bottom up, into the same rude position as Annie. She was penetrated, sighing as her quim filled with cock and soon her moans and grunts had joined Annie's. She heard the door bang behind her, and laughter, then Coppinger's voice.

'Spend on her arse to show it's done!'

A moment later he grunted, and Molly turned her head to see him whip his cock out of Annie's quim. It began jerking frantically over her bottom, erupting spurt after spurt of come over her cheeks and into her crease. Before he'd finished his grunts of ecstasy had died and he had begun to laugh.

'My game!' he called, and de Cachaliere laughed in turn.

'Your game it is, and no wonder, mine's packed with lard!'

Coppinger laughed louder still and gave Annie a resounding smack on her bottom as he climbed off the bed. Several men were already in the room, one at the end of his bed, with a dark, badly bent erection sticking out above lowered breeches. Coppinger grinned at him and jerked a thumb towards Annie where she knelt with the glistening spunk running slowly down her bottom cheeks and pooling in her well greased anus.

'Take your pleasure, lads, arse or mouth or tits, but if it's cunt you're wanting, stick to Molly, or I'll break your necks.'

He made for the door, not even troubling to look back as the man with the bent cock took Annie by the ears and stuck it in her mouth. Having lost the bet, de Cachaliere was taking his time, easing himself in and out of Molly's quim with his hands locked around her waist. Only as the smuggling crew began to pack into the room did he speed up, tightening his grip and finishing off with a hard flurry of shoves before coming deep inside her.

The instant he was done the men were crowding around Molly. Two cocks were pushed at her face and she took one in hand as she began to suck the other. A man caught her by the quim, masturbating her with a thumb in her hole as he readied his cock. Even as he pushed it up her a third had begun to feel her dangling breasts. Annie gave a pained grunt as her anus was roughly penetrated and the two of them were being fully used, two cocks in each, hands groping at their bodies, the men laughing and joking, the air thick with the smell of cock and cunt, ale and cider, candle wax, salt water, dirt, sweat, and spunk.

Annie was making muffled grunting noises around the cock in her mouth as she was buggered, and gamely trying to keep two men ready in her hands. The man in

Molly's mouth came down her throat, leaving her gagging for an instant before she was able to swallow and take in the man she'd been masturbating. Another, one of the young farm hands who'd been keeping his cock ready, came in her face and across her hair, finishing with a groan of disappointment.

Before she could wipe the come out or her eye her hand had been taken and put on a half-stiff cock. She tried to pull back, to retain at least some control over what she was doing, but she was held firmly in place. A hand twisted into her hair and the man in her mouth jammed his cock deep, blocking her throat and immediately spunking down it. Come exploded from her nose as her muscles went into painful spasms, with her whole body now shaking to the thrusts of the man in her quim. He too came, deep inside her, and the moment he was out she was surrounded by jostling, cursing men, each eager for his share and few willing to wait.

Strong hands took her, lifting her and spinning her about. A man who'd been about to make her suck him cursed in annoyance and growled an oath, even as she was stuck firmly on a cock by a man who had got beneath her. His hands found her breasts, groping as he began to bounce her on his cock. Briefly she caught a glimpse of Annie's bare, open bottom, anus oozing sperm and lard, before her head was twisted around and a fresh cock forced into her mouth. She struggled to pull back, wanting to tell them to calm down and take their turns, but the grip in her hair only tightened and the man begun to fuck her head.

One was trying to mount her bottom, his cock between her cheeks, but he was pushed aside, knocking into a man who was just inserting his cock into Annie's anus. Both men swore and tumbled from the bed, grappling and striking out at each other even as two others took their places at the girls' bottoms. Molly was bouncing on the cock in her quim, but she was taken hard by the hips, and felt a cock put to her slippery anus. A moment later it was forced deep with a shove that made her eyes pop and her teeth lock on the cock in her mouth. The man she was sucking gave an angry grunt and cuffed her head, but kept his cock in, fucking deep in her spunk-filled mouth.

With three cocks in her and her body held hard she could do nothing. Her flesh quivered to the thrusts as she was fucked, faster and harder. A froth of spunk bubbles was sucking in and out of her nose as she struggled for breath. Her skin was slippery with sweat and come and spit, her quim was sore and her jaw ached, and already she had lost all count of how many had finished in her or on her. Another man came in her face, closing her other eye and she was blind as well as gagged. Annie was getting the same, her body groped, her mouth and anus full of cock, her grunts mixing with the fleshy slapping of flesh on flesh.

Beyond those fucking the girls other men were ready, some calling encouragement, others jerking at their cocks or with flagons in their hands, all staring at the fucking, save the two who were fighting on the floor. When the man in Molly's bottom finished himself off with a flurry of hard shoves and withdrew, he was replaced immediately. Her gaping bottom hole was filled and spunked in almost before the man had got his rhythm. Another replaced him. The man in her mouth came, he too was replaced, and Molly was lost in a welter of cock and sweat and spunk, barely conscious as her body was filled over and over.

When it did finish it was sudden, a last man coming in the gaping mouth of her well fucked quim, another in her face as he pulled from her mouth, and no more. She collapsed, unable to see for the spunk coating her face, gasping for breath as she rolled over, and her hands went to her quim, rubbing in the spunk as she took one big breast in hand. A male voice called out in amusement to see that she was masturbating but she ignored him, rubbing herself hard to bring herself to climax within moments, her whole aching body going tense as she cried out in ecstasy, her moans mingling with the gaps and grunts of Annie's final buggering.

Molly collapsed, exhausted. She was slick with sperm, her face a sticky mess, her hair caked, her bottom hole and cunt slack and dribbling. Annie's buggery ended in a final crescendo of male grunts and female cries and it was over. The last man discharged into or over their bodies. The task was done and, in her case, it was money well earned.

Nine

'Ah, Monsieur de Cachaliere!' Henry greeted the Frenchman. 'I had heard you were in the county. You had a good crossing, I trust?'

'Ideal,' de Cachaliere replied, with a sweeping bow that took in Henry, Eloise and Lucy. 'Madame, *demoiselle*, for a mere glance at your radiance I would make a dozen crossings.'

Eloise responded with a measured inclination of her head. Lucy flushed slightly and hid a smile behind her fan. De Cachaliere was in his cherry red coat, and turned again to Henry as he extracted a bottle from within.

'Mr Truscott,' he stated with another bow, 'may I take the liberty of presenting you with a small gift in appreciation of the kindness you have shown me?'

'A generous thought,' Henry replied, resisting the urge to lick his lips just at the deep, bright golden brown of the liquid within the bottle

'The seventeen fifty-two,' de Cachaliere went on, 'forty years in cask before bottling. Not the estate's oldest, it is true, but, as you will find, it is possessed of great finesse and complexity.'

Henry accepted the bottle, to inspect the somewhat damp-eaten label, which showed the vintage, the date of bottling and a single line in description, giving the estate and a name.

'Marquis de la Motte?' he enquired.

'My title,' de Cachaliere confessed, 'although as you will appreciate it is not something I generally remark upon.'

'You are of the *noblesse*?' Eloise asked, her tone full of both surprise and hope.

'I am,' de Cachaliere admitted. '*Noblesse de l'épée*,[9] indeed, although this is a concept which few care for in present times.'

'It is a term dear to my heart,' Eloise answered with feeling. 'As you know, my family is that of de la Tour-Romain, my late father the Comte Saônois.'

'A name more noble still,' de Cachaliere replied with yet another bow.

'I recall the name,' Eloise continued, now wistful, 'and a face. A tall man, of great elegance. I thought him ever so severe, but then I was only a child. It would have been at Chenonceau in 'eighty-five, perhaps 'eighty-six.'

'My father,' de Cachaliere answered, 'sadly a victim of the mob.'

Eloise gave a shiver and her mouth tightened before she answered.

'I present my sympathies, Marquis. I myself would have suffered the same fate had not Mr Truscott brought me free.'

De Cachaliere gave a stiff bow to Henry, then extended his hand. Henry took it with a trace of embarrassment and shook, then gestured towards the drawing room.

'In any event, let us not stand talking in the hall. Pray excuse me while I place your most generous gift in safety.'

He made for the cellar, leaving de Cachaliere with Eloise, only for her to join him as he carefully placed the bottle in a rack.

'What of your guest?' he asked.

'He is speaking with Lucy on the terrace,' she replied in an agitated whisper. 'They must be thrown together at every opportunity, and on no account should you mention your father, nor Wheal Purity, nor money, nor . . .'

'They must?' Henry queried. 'Are you hoping he'll make a declaration to her?'

'That is surely his intention!' Eloise replied. 'Has he not returned, at great risk, with his ship? Why else do this?'

'A dozen reasons! Perhaps he has further business with Coppinger? Perhaps he does not altogether trust his crew? Perhaps he . . .'

'He means to make a declaration to Lucy. I am sure of it.'

'And you hope for her to accept?'

'She must accept. To refuse would be unthinkable.'

'For Lucy? I . . .'

'I shall instruct her at the earliest opportunity, and you must do the same. He is a de la Motte, Henry, a family ennobled before a Capet ever sat on the throne of France. It must be, Henry, it must!'

Henry gave a chuckle for her enthusiasm, earning himself a glare in response as he replied.

'He's a decent enough fellow, I dare say, and a sight less effete than many . . .'

'His manner lacks something of refinement,' Eloise interrupted, 'but when for twenty years and more a man, even of the highest breeding, has had to suffer such . . . such indignity, such barbarity, at the hands of men little more than apes, then this is to be expected!'

'No cause for tantrums, my dear,' Henry laughed. 'I meant only that I'd rather have the fellow as a son-in-law than most. He has spirit at least.'

He had given the neck of the Cognac bottle a tap as he spoke, but his attempt at wit was ignored by Eloise, who went on urgently.

'We must make him our guest. It is unthinkable that a man of his rank should stay in a mere, rude farmhouse.'

'What if Stephen finds out, as he is sure to?'

'This presents no difficulties. We merely state that we have as our guest the Marquis de la Motte, a distinguished gentleman and an *émigré* from his native land.'

Henry nodded, unable to deny Eloise's logic, nor her determination.

John Coppinger looked out into the night. To left and right the faint gleams of the signal lanterns showed, in the fields and among the rough at the cliff tops. Each was suspended on a pole, and while their positions appeared random from where he stood at the summit of Marshland Cliffs, the siting of each was exact to within a foot or less, creating a marker for a point at sea no larger than the space in which a longboat could be conveniently turned. Far below, two more lanterns showed, bobbing to the motion of the old longboat to which they were fixed, fore and aft, and providing only enough light to mark their position.

'The wind is not what it might be,' Henry Truscott's voice sounded from the darkness beside him. 'He'll not come in if there's a risk of a lee shore.'

'South-sou'east is good enough,' Coppinger growled in answer, 'and we've cloud. I'd not ask for more.'

'Fine entertainment in any event,' de Cachaliere remarked, although there was a somewhat hollow ring to his voice.

They fell silent a while before Henry spoke again.

'Before I forget, John, it's two casks to Nat Addiscombe this time.'

'Two?' Coppinger responded. 'Some junket planned, has he?'

'Who knows?' Henry answered. 'He may want to feed it to his damn tulips.'

'And welcome, so long as he pays,' Coppinger said. 'I've yet to collect for the last. Best go myself to be sure of him.'

167

'Oh there's no malice in old Addiscombe,' Henry stated. 'He'll have forgotten, and be full of apology.'

'Mostly they are,' Coppinger answered and chuckled. 'Been a year now, and more, since I had to put my fist in a man's face.'

'Another swallow of Cognac, gentlemen?' de Cachaliere offered.

Coppinger accepted, waiting as Henry took a draught and accepting the flask as it was pressed to his side. The Cognac traced a warm line down his throat, and he took a second swallow before passing it on, then once more cast his gaze around the horizon. A faint light was visible to the north, no more than a glimmer, and barely moving, yet bright enough that when he turned to look to the east it took some moments for his eyes to register the first flush of dawn.

'I do believe our guest is coming after all,' Henry remarked.

'Seems so,' Coppinger answered, rubbing his hands.

The flask was pushed towards him again and he took another swallow before handing it back to Henry. They fell silent save for an occasional bantering remark, with the dawn light slowly building until at last the dark bulk of a ship could be made out against the sea, still some way to the north, but closing. Her sails grew distinct, then the shape of her hull and the white-painted gun ports at her flanks.

'The *Bull*,' Henry stated flatly.

'None other,' Coppinger retorted.

He raised a hand. The lantern on the longboat went out and a moment later she began to swing in the current. The *Bull* tacked, taking a reach that barely filled her sails and put her aimed directly at the open sand of Welcombe Bay. Coppinger nodded, grudgingly impressed by Fairbrother's seamanship as he saw that the line would give the *Bull* the best chance of putting on speed in the final chase.

168

'A shilling wager he runs her straight onto the beach,' Henry offered.

'Taken,' Coppinger growled, de Cachaliere accepting at the same time.

Coppinger's mouth curved up into a cruel grin as the *Bull* tacked a second time, just yards from where the caps of the waves were turning white. As Henry gave a soft curse the *Bull*'s bows swung around, aimed precisely at the moored longboat, in which the shape of casks could now be made out, and the black figures of the two men on board. The crack of canvas reached them, and a groan of rigging, shouts from the *Bull*, triumphant, and then from the men in the longboat, raised in alarm. The *Bull* began to gather pace as the longboat's crew struggled to raise their anchor and fit the sweeps. John Coppinger's fists went tight with joy.

The longboat began to move, swinging clumsily in the current with the anchor still in the water and the man at the oars missing his second stroke, to catch a crab and fall heavily back. Some three hundred yards of open water still separated the longboat from the *Bull*, but there could only be one outcome, with the sloop rapidly gathering pace, water frothing up under her bows as she cut through the waves. Coppinger's fists were clenched, his teeth set, as the gap narrowed, two hundred yards, then one, with the longboat making not for the shore, but for the open sea, and at an angle, as if hoping to outrun the *Bull*.

'He'll notice!' Henry exclaimed.

'Not that one,' Coppinger answered even as Fairbrother's demand for the longboat to heave to rang up from far below. 'Too eager by far.'

The answer from the longboat was a curse, but the *Bull* was just fifty yards short, exactly where the longboat had been anchored, her bows lifting to a wave, crashing down in a spray of water, lifting again, and descending once more, to hit with a terrible splintering crack as her full weight came down on the submerged rock. Coppinger gave a great roar of laughter, clutching his sides as the tension of hours and days came out in a great roar of mirth. De Cachaliere was chuckling quietly, Henry laughing hard and slapping his thighs in glee as the *Bull* settled onto the rock, leaning so sharply for an instant that her crew were left clinging to whatever handholds they could find, only to lift on the next wave.

As the *Bull* came free of the rock, an awful tearing sound reached them mixed with yells and curses and bellowed commands. The wave had pushed her back, into deeper water, and as she settled once more she began to wallow. Another wave hit her, breaking over her bows, and she was turning side on, her sails flapping wildly, men leaping into the water or fighting with the sheets. Fairbrother was visible in the stern, tall and straight in his dark blue coat, screaming at his crew, but his orders had no effect. The *Bull* was clearly doomed, listing badly as she was pushed slowly inshore, but not onto the rocks as Coppinger had hoped, rather towards Welcombe beach. He cursed.

'You were right, Mr Truscott, damn wind's wrong. That'll not drown 'em.'

'You have your boat,' Henry answered cheerfully, 'and the Lord alone knows how long it'll take them to find another, and that some ancient cutter no doubt. Still, I'd not want to be in at your farm when that crew arrive!'

'Certain sure!' Coppinger laughed. 'Though I've a mind they'd be in no state to fight.'

Below them the first of the seamen had begun to reach shore, dragging themselves up onto the shelving rock through the gentle waves. The *Bull* had almost keeled over, with white spume showing in her broken bows as she drifted lazily towards the beach and stopped, stuck fast on a bar some fifty yards from shore.

Coppinger laughed again, watching as the men scrambled off the dying hulk, to stand neck deep in the water. Fairbrother went last, swimming ashore to emerge bedraggled on the beach and sit down heavily in the wet sand.

'I'm for Holsworthy and the Dun Cow,' Coppinger chortled, 'where indeed I've been all night, supping with Alderman Coates and his party, no less. Will you be joining us, gentlemen?'

'Not I,' Henry answered. 'I've a mind for my bed, and Mrs Truscott has promised to show our French friend Brentor church this afternoon.'

'Then we'll bid you farewell,' Coppinger answered, putting his arm around his wife's shoulders as they turned back towards the valley. 'Good work, my Annie!'

Saul Mudge sat sipping beer and toying idly with his cock, the leathery skin still sticky with Polly's spit after yet another failed attempt to come in her mouth. As before, he had grown hard easily enough, but every attempt to turn his imagination to the delights of the Truscott girls had met with failure, making him increasingly angry. Finally he had cuffed Polly off his cock and kicked her bottom for her as she turned away, taking at least some satisfaction in watching her sprawl on the floor and in the large, dirty boot print he had left on her milk-white skin.

He had called for beer and settled down to drink, not only determined that he would come, but obsessed with the thought of bursting Lucy Truscott's maidenhead. So many times he had tried, and so many times had he failed, while the orgasms he had taken over the simple physical pleasure of fucking Polly's throat or arsehole had only made his resentment worse. Now just to think of Lucy made him boil with anger, and her cousins hardly less so.

As he grew slowly more drunk his lust rose, but his cock remained obdurately limp, yet heavy and curiously damp. Only when he heard the grate of carriage wheels on gravel did he put it away, cursing as he rose, then again as he peered from the window to see Stephen Truscott's man Reuben leading the team forward towards the stable. He spat vaguely in Polly's direction.

'Them bob tail bitches again. Best put a new pot in.'

Polly nodded and hurried to her task as he went outside, feeling somewhat unsteady. Reuben greeted him with a measured nod and they began to take the horses out of harness.

'How many're here?' he asked after a while.

'The four of 'em,' Reuben replied as he pulled a buckle loose.

'Little whores,' Saul growled, and caught a surprised look from Reuben.

'Well, they are,' he insisted. 'Flirt with every man jack in the country if he's a few thousand and an acre of land, but will they spare a glance for good honest men? No, not them! Bitches and whores!'

'You're drunk, Saul,' Reuben answered.

'What if I am?'

'Nothing, but I've a tale to tell you.'

'What's that then?'

'Squire Henry and Mrs Truscott, that's Mrs Stephen Truscott.'

'What of it?'

'Fucking behind the stable at Driscoll's, that's what.'

'No!'

'Heard it all, I did, saw some too. Took a flyer, they did, against the stable wall, Madam with her skirts up and her arse stuck out. Put it in where the dirt comes out and all, I reckon.'

'No! The dirty whore!'

'Moaning fit to bust, she was, and after, I saw him wash his prick at the pump.'

172

Saul shook his head, his burning sense of resentment growing stronger still at the thought of Henry Truscott fucking his own sister-in-law.

'Enough to make you spit!' he snarled after a moment.

'Why so?' Reuben asked. 'Got me well ready it did, and I gave Rose one before I went home.'

Saul gave a discontented grunt.

'All we get, eh? Their leavings!'

'Leavings?' Reuben queried.

'What they don't want,' Saul answered. 'Everything else, they take.'

'What's biting you?' Reuben demanded. 'Not jealous are you, not when you've Polly to fuck. Fine girl, Polly.'

Saul nodded, unable to deny it but keen to stoke his sense of resentment. When the horses were loose he led them into the stable while Reuben saw to the carriage. With both horses rubbed down, watered and provided with bags of feed he went back to the kitchen, to find Reuben eating a chunk of bread liberally spread with beef dripping and with a flagon of beer in hand. He filled his own flagon and sat down in the chair by the window he invariable occupied. Polly was setting the fire, the seat of her skirts just within reach of his boot. He kicked out his leg to get her attention.

'Don't go wasting logs, girl. It's not cold.'

'Mr Addiscombe says to keep a fire,' Polly replied. 'Says it keeps the damp from the house.'

Saul answered with a dismissive grunt and gave her another kick for good measure, laughing as she sprawled on the floor. She returned a dirty look, which he chose to ignore and took a swallow of beer. Reuben had laughed to see Polly pushed over, but a little uneasily, and he smiled at her as she got up.

'What's the matter?' Saul snarled. 'Want a piece of her, do you?'

Reuben merely shrugged. Saul laughed.

'Need it, do you? Better'n what you're used to, ain't she?'

Polly had turned back to the fire, and Reuben responded only with an embarrassed grin, but Saul went on, his cock stirring in his trousers at the thought of making Polly perform for the lanky coachman.

'How's this?' he grunted. 'Tuppence and she goes about her work with her top hamper out?'

'That's not a thing to ask of . . .' Reuben began, his face going abruptly pink.

'See yourself!' Saul laughed. 'Colouring like a virgin, you are! Go on, Poll, get your dress down. Let him see the meat!'

Polly continued to work on the fire, ignoring him completely. He lashed out with his foot, but she was ready and moved quickly to the side, causing him to slip in the chair. He had to snatch at the arms to catch himself, dropping his flagon to spill beer out over the slate flags.

'Stupid bitch!' he shouted. 'Look what you've done! Get the mop now, and be quick!'

Polly had already risen, and patiently fetched a mop and bucket. Saul went to refill his flagon, and Rebuen's, who made an attempt at a bluff smile but was still looking uneasy. Feeling well pleased with himself, Saul walked back towards his chair, only to stop as he reached Polly, grab her by the hair and the front of her dress which he pulled hard down, flopping her big breasts out. She gave an angry gasp and tried to put them back, but he caught her arms and pulled them sharply behind her back, holding her with her bare chest thrust out towards Reuben, who gave a nervous laugh.

'Grand, ain't she?' Saul drawled. 'How'd you like to fuck between 'em?'

Reuben had gone pink, and only managed a gurgling noise in response. Saul laughed and pushed Polly down.

'On all fours, girl, so as we can watch your dumplings swing as you scrub.'

For a moment she was struggling, but it only made Reuben redder still as her tits began to bounce. She quickly went down, as ordered, her big breasts hanging beneath her chest and moving to the motion of her body as she scrubbed the beer up with the mop head. Saul laughed to see her, took a swallow of beer and then slowly poured what remained in the mug out over her head and back, to leave her dripping and soiled, her hair a bedraggled mess, with drips hanging from her nose and both nipples.

'Scrub harder,' he ordered, 'you're making more mess than you're bringing up.'

Polly responded with a bitter sob, but did as she was told, making her dangling breasts wobble and slap together. Reuben's eyes were glued to her, full of pity, but also lust, and as he shifted in his chair he gave his cock a quick squeeze. Saul laughed, pleased with himself, for Reuben's reaction, and because his own cock had begun to stiffen.

'Like her, don't you?' he chuckled. 'Like to rub that between those fat dumplings, eh?'

Reuben's answer was a guilty glance and Saul laughed again, enjoying himself and determined to take it further. Taking Polly by the scruff of her neck, he pushed her face down until her nose was touching the floor. She was whimpering, and he could feel her body trembling, which set his cock stiffer still.

'Watch this!' he chuckled, nodding to Reuben. 'Lick it up, you fat bitch!'

Polly resisted, shaking her head and trying to speak, but managing only a choking sob.

'Lick it up!' Saul ordered. 'Lick it up, or I'll take my belt to your arse in front of Reuben here!'

Polly gave another sob, but her tongue came out, licking at the beer wet-slate. Saul laughed and began to move her head as if it was a mop, with her sodden hair trailing on the floor and her breasts squashed out in the

175

dirty puddle beneath her. His cock was rock hard, and he pulled it out, opening his breeches flap one-handed as he rubbed Polly's face on the floor. Reuben looked quickly away.

'You're hard yourself, so don't play the preacher on me!' he laughed. 'Go on with you, show it, and I'll make her suck on it.'

Reuben swallowed hard, but hesitated only a moment before extracting a stubby white cock from his breeches. Saul took a firm grip in Polly's hair and pulled her up to her knees. Her face was filthy, her breasts wet and smeared with dirt where they'd been pressed to the floor. As she saw their erections her eyes went wide. Saul gave her a grin and snapped his fingers, pointing at Reuben's straining penis.

'Go on, girl, get your cock trap around that!'

For a moment her eyes came wider still in a silent plea, but as he reached out to cuff her she drew quickly back and scrambled over to where Reuben was sitting. The coachman's expression was deeply guilty, but he said nothing, and it changed to pleasure as Polly took his cock in her mouth. Saul settled back, nursing his erection as he watched her suck, her face screwed up in misery as her mouth worked on the fat erection. Just from the way his cock felt he knew that this time there would be no difficulty in coming.

'Pull your skirt up, girl,' he growled after a moment, 'let's see that big arse.'

Polly reached back, still sucking, with her tits swinging gently to the bobbing motion of her head as she humped her skirts up onto her back, taking her single, threadbare petticoat with it to expose her broad white bottom. The lips of her cunt were showing between her thighs, pouted and tempting, also the anus, a soft brown star between her ample cheeks. Saul grunted and pulled himself up. The invitation was too good to resist.

'Spread 'em wide,' he ordered, and Polly glanced back, giving a low whimper on her mouthful of cock even as she pulled her bottom wide to make herself available.

Saul squatted down, cock to cunt, and slid himself up her. He began to fuck, setting her body moving between them, back and forth, a cock in each hole and her breasts swinging free.

'Like a hog on a turnspit!' Saul laughed. 'Basted in ale and all!'

Reuben didn't respond, his eyes locked on the junction between Polly's mouth and his erection. Nor did she, accepting her fucking in mute surrender. Wanting some reaction, Saul began to spank her in time to his thrusts. As her broad, wobbling bottom began to pink up, she was soon sobbing on Reuben's cock, encouraging Saul to spank harder. With her bottom going quickly redder she began to grunt and squirm, while her bottom flesh grew hot.

'Warm for you?' he grated, stopping. 'Need to cool off?'

With a grim chuckle he took Reuben's flagon and emptied the contents over Polly's well smacked bottom. Most of the beer ran down her slit, wetting her anus and dripping from his balls, deliciously cool. He began to fuck harder, now urgent, and wanting to come while she still had her mouth full of cock.

He took her tits, bouncing them in his hands and slapping them as he fucked her, faster and deeper, to set her spanked bottom wobbling. She lost her breath on Reuben's cock, but he pulled her head back down, grunting in pleasure as she struggled to suck him. Saul pumped harder still, his hands locked in the soft, fat flesh of her tits, puffing and cursing as he felt his orgasm start to rise. Reuben came, crying out in ecstasy as he filled Polly's throat with spunk. She started to choke, a great mass of spunk and mucus exploded from her nose, and then Saul was there too, filling her cunt with cream, and still pumping, until it had began to squash out

177

around her hole and join the beer still dripping from his balls.

'It is such a shame we are forbidden to visit Meldon Pool,' Lucy Truscott sighed. 'The day is quite perfect for a swim.'

'Meldon Pool,' Octavia answered, 'may be visited at leisure, just so soon as a certain fiend is brought to justice. If you wish to bathe, dispose of the fiend. This should pose no great problem, as you created him.'

'You had your share in it,' Lucy answered, drawing an indignant gasp from Octavia.

'The weather might take a turn for the worse,' Augusta put in, glancing around at the cloudless blue of the sky, 'and besides, we have our duty to Mr Addiscombe.'

'In any event,' Lydia added, 'we could not possibly bathe with your manservant in attendance.'

'I care nothing for Mr Addiscombe,' Lucy replied. 'Once we have taken our meal, and perhaps paid a moment of polite attention to his tulips, we may take ourselves off without fear of giving offence. Besides, Augusta, what if he were to choose this afternoon to make his declaration?'

Augusta grimaced and Lucy went on.

'Jack Gurney will do as I tell him, and we might bathe in privacy, if not at Meldon Pool. Instead, I propose we visit the pools on the East Okement, which are every bit as pretty and secluded, although smaller. I also have a surprise for you.'

'A surprise?' Octavia asked suspiciously.

Lucy laughed.

'You need not fear for your precious posteriors, cousin dearest. I am quite done with you, so long as you remain in your place.'

'We need not concern ourselves, with Mrs Hawkes present,' Lydia added, but Octavia gave a disdainful sniff.

'Precisely,' Lucy said. 'Listen to your big sister, Octavia. With Jack Gurney to guard us and Mrs Hawkes as chaperone, we may have a merry time.'

'I shall not go naked,' Lydia stated firmly. 'And what of that horrible Mudge? He is sure to see us leave. He watches, always.'

'He'd not dare follow with Jack Gurney present,' Lucy answered.

Lydia still looked doubtful, but didn't reply. Mr Addiscombe was coming towards them across the lawn, rubbing his podgy hands, his red face beaming. Mrs Hawkes was with him, and as the two approached she made a quiet remark to Mr Addiscombe, evidently intending that the girls should see it spoken, but not hear what was said. Augusta briefly caught Lucy's eye, looking concerned for an instant before making a polite greeting.

'Our repast is served,' Mr Addiscombe announced, still rubbing his hands together, 'a fine country meal for hungry girls. A dish of boiled cod, not rich, but wholesome, good beef stew with dumplings – ah, how you do love dumplings, eh? Trifle for dessert, always a girl's favourite.'

Lucy managed a polite comment and shared another look with Augusta as they turned to troop into the house. The meal, as always, was huge, far more food offered than she wanted, but with Mr Addiscombe constantly urging them to eat up. By the time the trifle was served her stomach was a rounded, aching ball beneath her dress, and it took all her willpower to be polite when he pressed a second bowl on her. As soon as she was able to leave the table she visited the privy, but it made little difference, while it was impossible to be comfortable after what Lydia had said about the grill.

Even the inevitable tulip inspection was a relief. The broken pot had gone unnoticed, or more likely

179

unremarked, but while there were several of the purple Miss Augusta Truscotts in bloom, nothing else had changed. Mr Addiscombe was full of enthusiasm, certain that the latest round of cross pollination would produce the fabulous black tulip he had sought so long.

Something in his remarks suggested to Lucy that she was more intimately connected with the project than simply having the expected bloom named after her. Only one answer seemed possible: that he intended to propose marriage when he was successful, a thought that brought her a characteristic twinge of indignation, but also some amusement.

The previous evening her mother had spoken to her at length when they had retired to leave her father and Monsieur de Cachaliere, or the Marquis de la Motte as she was supposed to address him, to their port. Marriage had been the subject, and the importance of Lucy making herself agreeable to the Marquis in what her mother saw as the certain hope of a declaration. Lucy, already fascinated by the man's poise and his romantic life, had nodded at all the right moments and made all the right promises.

Underneath there had been a degree of resentment. De Cachaliere had been increasingly gallant in his attentions, but she had been hoping for a romantic, and preferably dramatic proposal, rather than being gently manoeuvred by her mother. She had considered how it might be, perhaps with Saul Mudge making renewed threats, and the Marquis coming upon them. Ideally, she had decided, Mudge's cock would actually be at the mouth of her quim when the Marquis ran him through with a single rapier thrust, although she knew full well that the reality would be too terrifying to bear.

There was also the matter of Jack Gurney, whose cock she had developed a taste for, in her mouth, and on one occasion between her breasts. It seemed a shame to lose him, which she undoubtedly would. She knew she would also miss her cousins, Augusta in particular, as there were plenty of new humiliations she was keen to try out. Hippolyta, at least, would stay with her, guaranteeing the pleasure of having her quim frigged and licked, although it had also occurred to her that the Marquis would doubtless expect Hippolyta to stand in for her while she was bleeding, or pregnant, or simply disinclined, just as Suki did for her mother.

By the time they left the glasshouse her stomach had begun to feel a little less strained. Mr Addiscombe frequently took a nap in the afternoon, leaving them to their own devices, an interlude she had used more than once to punish or humiliate her cousins. At the least he could be certain to retire to his study, where he was known to make long and mysterious entries in an enormous ledger. Judging her moment carefully, she made her suggestion.

'We must not waste this beautiful afternoon. Who will join me in a walk up the valley, perhaps as far as those pretty pools beneath West Mill Tor?'

'A delightful suggestion,' Augusta answered immediately. 'I shall come.'

Mrs Hawkes looked slightly put out, but managed a smile, after which both Lydia and Octavia agreed.

'I shall speak to your man,' Mr Addiscombe stated, 'and yes, I shall come myself. You are right, it is a beautiful afternoon, and a shame to sit indoors. I remember the pools you speak of, and how you used to splash in them as a child. Ah, it seems only yesterday!'

Lucy hid a grimace, but glanced towards the moor, then at Mr Addiscombe's girth and the breadth of Mrs Hawkes' hips.

'I shall have your man bring a hamper,' Mr Addiscombe continued, 'for there is nothing to equal good moorland air to raise the appetite. Polly Mudge has made a cake for us, I believe, with strawberry jam and cream. Will that not be a treat!?'

Lucy managed a wan smile, but he had already turned for the house, rubbing his hands once more. Taking Augusta's arm, she began to walk slowly across the lawn, aiming for the gate which led to the moor lane. Mrs Hawkes and the other two girls held back, and they were soon able to speak without risk of being overheard.

'You say there is a surprise?' Augusta asked carefully. 'If it is anything beastly, please spare my sisters, or at the least poor Lydia. She has not yet recovered from the behaviour of Saul Mudge. Which behaviour, dear Lucy, I still think we should report to our parents, and face the consequences of our actions!'

'You do not wish to be belted, surely?' Lucy answered. 'In any event, you must say nothing. I have given my word on the matter. You are a Truscott, so if you wish revenge, take it yourself.'

Augusta pursed her lips but said nothing. Lucy went on happily.

'No, cousin dearest, my surprise is not beastly, although you may be sure I will be beastly to you, just as beastly as may be, if only the opportunity presents itself.'

'As you wish,' Augusta answered with a shy smile.

They walked on, down into the valley where the banks of the lane rose to nearly twice their height to either side, forming a cool, mossy tunnel even in the full heat of day. Lucy found herself feeling nervous as they passed the place at which Saul Mudge had accosted her and Lydia, and was glad when they reached the river and the lane began to rise towards the open moor.

Where the lane emerged from the woods they stopped to wait for the rest of the party, Lucy taking the opportunity to tease Augusta into a kiss, which quickly became passionate but soon had to be broken. Just a couple of minutes later Lydia and Mrs Hawkes emerged from the lane, arm in arm, then Mr Addiscombe with

Octavia, who looked less than happy. Jack Gurney came last, bent down with a large wicker hamper supported on his brawny shoulders.

Lucy and Augusta moved on, following the river across increasingly steep and difficult ground, and yet to her annoyance both Mr Addiscombe and Mrs Hawkes stayed with them, slow but determined. By the time they reached the lowest of the pools Mr Addiscombe had made his fatigue an excuse to have Lydia and Octavia support him, and both were struggling to keep the sulky expressions from their faces. Determined not to be made to take a turn at the distasteful task, Lucy moved ahead, bunching her skirts up as she jumped from rock to rock and ignoring Mrs Hawkes' gentle admonishments.

By the time she reached the pool by which she had indulged herself with first the puppet stick and then Jack Gurney she was damp with perspiration and breathing hard. The others were far behind, but still coming. She moved on, not wishing to spoil her memories of the pool by visiting it under less special circumstances. Another fifty yards and she was by another pool, larger, if less pretty and less secluded, but above a tumble of granite boulders she was quite sure neither of the older members of the party would be able to negotiate.

They did, puffing and panting, Mr Addiscombe taking every opportunity to put his podgy, sweat-slick hands on the girls, but with a determination Lucy found positively inconsiderate. She drew a sigh as Mr Addiscombe reached a hand up for her to help him over the last bit, and even resisted the temptation to let go when he was off balance. Evidently she was going to have to go to greater lengths to get the privacy she so badly needed.

'Did I not say I would manage it?' Mr Addiscombe remarked as he sat down heavily on a rock, red-faced and puffing. 'As I have, and before your man Gurney, who is not a third my age!'

He beamed cheerfully at the girls as Jack Gurney appeared, barely sweating, the huge hamper still supported on his shoulders. Lucy gave Gurney an admiring glance, and a wink as she went to help him set it down.

'A drink, if you would, my man,' Mr Addiscombe said to Gurney. 'Now, girls, what is it to be? I have brought nothing spirituous, save a nip of Cognac perhaps for myself and the good Mrs Hawkes in case of need, but there is an infusion of birch bark and nettles I consider most invigorating, and milk should you require something wholesome.'

Lucy accepted a mug of the infusion, which tasted so bitter she could barely swallow and it made her throat tingle when she did. Her legs ached a little, and her skin was prickly with sweat, making the cool water of the pool seem deliciously inviting. To have stripped naked and plunged in would have been sheer delight, and all the better for Jack Gurney watching, or in the pool beside her. Even with Mrs Hawkes there she would have done it, ignoring the irritating little clicks of the tongue the woman made when she felt the girls were being unduly boisterous. With Mr Addiscombe present it was out of the question; his piggy eyes followed her even as she chose a patch of dry grass on which to sit.

'Beside me, my dear Lucy,' he said to her horror as he patted the rock beside him, 'and you, dear Augusta, to my other side, that you may perhaps bestow one of those pleasing little intimacies that cost you nothing yet bring such joy to a gentleman's life.'

Lucy gave a little start, wondering if he was going to expect to fondle their bottoms or even demand his cock sucked, but he had withdrawn a slim volume from his pocket, and handed it to Augusta as she came to sit beside him. Relieved, Lucy sat down, only to have his plump arm encircle her waist as Augusta began to read a poem. Desperate to escape, she raised her eyes to the towering bulk of West Mill Tor, a good five hundred feet above them up a steep, rocky slope. When Augusta finished, Lucy jumped up before the book could be passed to her.

'I for one propose to climb the tor,' she said. 'I have not done so since I was little, and the view is magnificent. You shall escort me, Gurney.'

Jack Gurney nodded and stood up from the place he had occupied some little way off among the rocks.

'Have you not had exertion enough?' Mrs Hawkes asked.

'No,' Lucy said firmly, 'not I.'

'But my dearest Lucy!' Mr Addiscombe put in. 'This is sheer foolishness! Come, read to me a little while or, if you seek a more vigorous pastime, you might wish to bathe in this delightful pool.'

'Thank you, no,' Lucy answered. 'The water is cold, and . . .'

'. . . and we have nothing to wear,' Lydia put in indignantly.

'Oh what nonsense you do talk!' Mr Addiscombe exclaimed. 'Go as you were born. Your man may be sent away, and the presence of a gentleman of my age and station in life need hardly concern you.'

'That would not be proper, Mr Addiscombe,' Augusta insisted. 'I shall accompany you, Lucy, if I may.'

'Not proper?' Mr Addiscombe chuckled. 'My dear girl, what harm could there possibly be? Do you really suppose I would be affected by the sight of your little pink bottoms? Come, Lydia, Octavia, you at least are not so vain as to think this?'

Augusta was already standing, and her sisters rose quickly, both hot with blushes. Octavia spoke.

'Thank you, but no, Mr Addiscombe. I am of a mind to climb the tor.'

'I also,' Lydia added quickly.

Lucy was already scrambling up among the boulders on the opposite side of the river, and the others quickly followed. Her heart was fluttering with outrage at the idea of Mr Addiscombe expecting her to go naked in front of him, making her wonder if it would be possible to bring home to him the sheer impossibility of such a thing without causing a scene. Nothing suggested itself, and her sense of chagrin only increased.

Behind her she could hear the others talking as soon as they were out of earshot, in angry whispers. She pushed on, not wanting to talk about it, nor to do anything else that acknowledged her reaction. Yet it stayed in her head, not only that he had dared to suggest she go nude, but that he had shown no shame when she refused, apparently quite unaware of how outrageous a suggestion he was making. Nor had Mrs Hawkes intervened, as if she too felt that having the four of them paraded naked for Mr Addiscombe's gloating inspection were of no consequence.

By the time she had reached the summit of the tor and stood looking out across the full panorama of north Devon and much of Dartmoor, her anger had begun to cool a little. Thinking more clearly, she wondered if a suitable revenge might not be to somehow hint of intimacy between herself and Jack Gurney. Nothing too dramatic, of course, but it might make Mr Addiscombe realise just how inappropriate his suggestion had been if he was made to see that they were less concerned by the presence of a servant. She could perhaps ask him to stand guard over her while she relieved herself, when of course Mr Addiscombe had no idea of what really transpired between her and Jack.

The idea set her smiling, and more determined than ever to enjoy herself with him. For him she would go naked, and more. She would suck his cock, gladly, and let him touch her wherever he wished, favours to which the horrible Mr Addiscombe could never aspire, at any time, or in any circumstances.

She climbed down from the peak, to find the others standing among the rocks, still evidently offended. Jack

Gurney had climbed to the top of a separate mass of rock, but came down as she signalled to him. Moving in a little deeper among the squat masses of granite, she selected an area of flat grass screened in every direction but towards the heart of the moor, in which empty bog stretched to the horizon. Augusta had followed, and seated herself by Lucy's feet.

'What is this surprise you spoke of, Lucy?' Octavia asked cautiously.

'Gurney has it,' Lucy answered as he appeared behind Lydia. 'A bottle of Cognac, from the estate of the Marquis de la Motte, who is currently a guest in *émigré*. A young man, and of the finest manners and appearance, who is quite devoted to me. Gurney, the bottle, if you would.'

Jack Gurney delved into one of the long pockets of his coat, to pull out a bottle of golden liquid, which he held out to Lucy.

'Open it, silly!' she chided. 'Do you think I carry a corkpull?'

She laughed, a sound echoed rather more nervously by Augusta. Lydia was looking doubtful, Octavia relieved. Jack Gurney had produced a large clasp knife from somewhere within his clothes and was working on the wax seal of the bottle. It quickly came loose, and after a moment of concentration he managed to extract the cork, ignoring Lucy's gesture of feigned exasperation to the others.

'I fear we are without glasses, or so much as a mug,' she remarked as she took the bottle. 'A necessary deception, but no matter. What of manners between the four of us?'

As she finished she put the bottle to her mouth and took a swallow. The Cognac was warm and rich and wonderfully smooth, tracing a golden path down her throat to her belly. She smiled and shook her head at a sudden flush, passing the bottle to Augusta, who took a

187

carefully judged sip. As she sat back against the rock she could already feel the warmth flowing through her, and she stretched before speaking.

'Shall we play, then? A game of choices perhaps, which will be greatly enhanced by the presence of a man.'

Lydia gave her a shocked look. Octavia choked on her mouthful of Cognac. Augusta merely looked at the ground.

'Come, come,' Lucy urged. 'Think how angry, and how jealous, Mr Addiscombe would be to know we had misbehaved with a mere servant, especially one so young and so well formed. I wish to, for one. Come, make me choose, and be harsh. Think how often I have spanked your fat sit-upons for you!'

'Lucy!' Lydia exclaimed, her face cherry pink and trying to make a gesture to decline the Cognac bottle even as she spoke. 'Have you no shame?'

'Shame is a greatly exaggerated virtue,' Lucy answered, 'if indeed it is a virtue at all. Come now, or I shall put the three of you in a line and spank you all together, quite bare.'

'You could not!' Lydia answered her. 'Not the three of us at once!'

Lucy shrugged.

'I could have Jack hold you down, and Octavia beside you. Augusta will do as she is told. Now come, what shall it be?'

She took the bottle again, from Jack Gurney, who had emptied a good quarter of it down his throat. None of the girls spoke up, all three blushing and uncertain, but none made a move to leave. With a second draught of Cognac inside her, Lucy looked around.

'Well?'

Lydia looked away pointedly. Augusta gave her a shy glance. Octavia spoke.

'I will make you choose, Lucy Truscott, if I have your word not to pick me.'

'This is the essence of the game!' Lucy retorted. 'You are such muffs, the two of you! Come here!'

She made a dart, not for Octavia, but for Lydia, only not quite fast enough, as she paused to hand Augusta the bottle first. Lydia fled squeaking among the rocks, Lucy laughing as she came in pursuit. Both girls ran with their skirts hitched up, Lucy faster, and almost catching Lydia on a long stretch of open ground, only to stumble and fall, laughing so hard she had difficulty in rising. When she did Lydia was some way off, standing on a low boulder in the bog. Her skirts were hitched high, her boots and stockings smeared with black mud, her face set in a typically sulky expression.

Lucy turned back, still giggling to herself, flushed and happy despite Lydia's cowardice. The other girls had stepped out from among the rock to watch, and Octavia moved away as Lucy approached. Augusta held the Cognac bottle, now barely a third full, and stayed put. Lucy wagged a finger at her cousin as she took it.

'Do not be greedy, Augusta, or I really shall spank you! Where is Jack?'

'Where we had gathered before,' Augusta answered.

'Off we go then,' Lucy answered, gesturing with the bottle before taking another swig, 'for without Jack we cannot do this at all. So how do matters stand?'

'You had threatened to spank me,' Augusta answered.

'So I had,' Lucy answered her, 'and so I shall, or what then would be my worth word . . . my word worth. Get down over my knee, Augusta, and I shall show Jack what a beautiful bottom you have. How will that be?'

Augusta shook her head, but made no move to escape. Lucy took Augusta firmly by the hand, leading her in among the rocks to where Jack Gurney had climbed on a rock to watch the chase. He jumped down as Lucy sat on a low boulder, Augusta blushing and with her head hung low. Octavia appeared between the rocks, staring as her big sister was put into spanking position, then retreated once more. Only as Lucy began to lift her skirts did Augusta protest, reaching back to hold them in place.

'No, not that,' she managed. 'If it must be done, do it upon my clothes!'

'There will be no nonsense!' Lucy chided. 'You must be bare, and you know you must be bare. How else should a girl be spanked?'

'On my clothes!'

'Nonsense!'

'On my petticoat seat then, but not bare, Lucy, I pray you!'

'Bare,' Lucy stated firmly, and took Augusta's arm, twisting it up to get it out of the way and render her helpless.

Augusta squeaked, and Lucy could feel her cousin's body trembling as the skirts were lifted. Her petticoats followed, and Augusta began to struggle, but it made no difference. They were lifted, tucked up under her twisted arm in a matter of fact manner and her bottom was bare, the round little cheeks stuck high, her thighs squirming in her embarrassment as Jack Gurney gave a dry chuckle. Lucy was finding it impossible to restrain her grin as she began to spank, deliberately swatting at Augusta's cheeks to make them part and show off the little pink star between.

Augusta took it gasping and shaking, obviously in an agony of embarrassment, and also pain, with her feet kicking and her head tossing up and down. Lucy only spanked the harder, until Augusta had begun to pump her stocking-clad thighs up and down and shake her head so hard her hair fell loose. By then she had abandoned her efforts at preserving even what tiny speck of modesty might have remained, bucking her bottom up and down to give a full show of her anal charms and also her quim. She was shamefully wet, to

190

Lucy's delight, with the fleshy plug of her maidenhead glistening in its little hole. As Jack Gurney watched, he adjusted his cock in his breeches. Lucy laughed and paused in the spanking, stroking Augusta's bare pink bottom as she spoke.

'Pull out your prick, Jack! I'll suck you, and have her strip naked. How would that be?'

Jack Gurney gave a happy nod, and there was a gasp, but not from Augusta. Lucy looked around, to see Octavia standing in a gap between two great columns of granite, her hand to her mouth as she stared at her sister's naked, reddened bottom. Lucy smiled and beckoned. Octavia shook her head but held her ground. Jack Gurney had also seen, and paused, one button undone to leave the top corner of his breeches flap loose, with his cock making a long, hard bulge beneath the material.

'Pull him out, Jack!' Lucy urged. 'I wish to show the girls how fine you are, and how large, also what should be done with a man who is in a state of excitement. Octavia, you must help him while I warm your sister's tail.'

Still holding Augusta firmly in place, she reached down for the Cognac bottle and put it to her lips, draining a good part of what was left down her throat. Jack Gurney took it for a hearty swig, still fiddling with his breeches flap as he passed it on to Octavia, who swallowed what was left and dropped the bottle as his cock came free. Lucy laughed, delighting in the shock and uncertainty on Octavia's face.

'Take him in your hand!' she urged again. 'He does not bite!'

Octavia shook her head urgently, but her eyes remained fixed on the big cock rearing from Jack's open breeches. Lucy went back to spanking Augusta, who had given in and lay limp, thighs open to show off her quim, with a trickle of white juice running down between the plump little lips. As her bottom began to bounce once more she was crying out, but not so much in pain, and Lucy laughed to see the reaction, calling out, 'See, Octavia, dearest! See what a good spanking does? A few deft touches and she would be in rapture! Is that not worth a sore behind?'

Octavia didn't answer, her gaze flicking between her sister's hot bottom and Jack Gurney's cock. He had began to masturbate in a lazy, casual way, and now pointed his erection at her with a nod and a grunt. Octavia responded with a shocked squeak, shying away as if threatened. Her face was flushed, her mouth a little open, her hands shaking. Lucy clicked her tongue and beckoned to Gurney, once more pausing in Augusta's punishment.

'Watch. No devils will come to fly away with me!'

She opened her mouth to take him in, sucking drunkenly, with as much cock in her mouth as she could get and still breathe properly, and watching Octavia sidelong, whose eyes seemed to be in danger of popping from their sockets. Then she had stepped forward, tentatively, biting her lip before speaking.

'Will . . . do I . . . do I have your word this will go no further?'

'Do not be foolish!' Lucy chided, drawing back from Jack's cock. 'Did I make you walk naked to Meldon village? Did I let Saul Mudge violate your Lydia?'

Octavia shook her head.

'Come,' Lucy urged, 'take him in your hand, gently, like so, and move up and down, thus. You will be married some day, and it can only be to your advantage to know such things.'

She was holding Jack Gurney's cock and masturbating him gently, her hand only just ringing the thick shaft. For a moment Octavia simply stared, only to suddenly reach out and take a firm grasp on the big cock, tugging clumsily. Jack moaned and Lucy gave a delighted peel of laughter.

'There! You have done it!'

Octavia managed a shy, sloppy grin, and then her pretty face had set in an expression of earnest determination as she changed her grip. Lucy let go, returning her hand to Augusta's hot bottom cheeks. She felt rude, her head spinning with drink and the smell of cock, her quim tingly and expectant. Jack Gurney had taken hold of his balls, squeezing gently, his eyes shut in pleasure.

'Not so fast!' Lucy urged. 'He will come, and our pleasure will be spoilt. Men are like bulls, much more than a touch and out it comes.'

Jack Gurney gave a gruff laugh. Octavia was still tugging at his erection as she answered.

'I have never seen a bull! I mean . . . seen a bull so . . .'

'There is little difference,' Lucy said with assurance as she once more began to stroke Augusta's bottom. 'Both grow hard and long, then emit a white stuff, thick and with an odd smell, pleasant enough, but not in taste, all salt and slime . . .'

'You . . . you have let him . . . in your mouth?' Octavia demanded.

Lucy nodded, smiling.

'Shall . . . shall I pull him over Augusta's bottom then?' Octavia asked. 'Or will you want to suck again?'

'I want more,' Lucy answered. 'I want everything. Get up, Augusta, you little trollop, you have had your punishment. Let us suck him together, Octavia, while your sister shows her bottom for his pleasure.'

Octavia nodded urgently and ducked down, hesitating only for a second before taking the big cock into her mouth. Her eyes closed in bliss as she began to suck, and Jack Gurney groaned in pleasure. Lucy allowed Augusta to scramble off her lap before going down on her knees and taking his balls into her mouth, sucking in drunken joy. Augusta was giggling and looking back over her shoulder as she obeyed Lucy, tucking her skirts well up to show off her red bottom, with the wet mouth of her virgin quim on full view to Jack Gurney.

With the taste of man in her mouth and eager for more, Lucy had quickly pushed Octavia to the side so that she could suck Jack's cock herself. Octavia knelt on her haunches, giggling behind her hand for what she had done before rocking forward to take Lucy's place on his balls. Jack began to stroke their hair, gently, but his grip quickly tightening as they sucked. When he began to groan and fuck into her mouth Lucy forced herself to pull back.

'There is more, much more!' she giggled, pushing her bodice down to show her breasts.

Octavia came off Jack's balls, and was tittering in delight as Lucy folded her breasts around his erection. He began to fuck in her cleavage, the head of his cock popping up and down between the soft pink pillows of her breasts, until he was groaning again and Lucy was forced to pull back.

'I must spend soon!' he gasped.

'Be patient!' Lucy admonished him. 'You would like the three of us together, would you not?'

Jack nodded, and Lucy swung around to Octavia, who squeaked as her bodice was tugged down to let her fat little breasts bounce free.

'You do it,' Lucy instructed. 'You have more than I.'

Octavia obeyed, her face aglow with pleasure as she folded his cock into her cleavage.

'Will . . . will he make his white stuff now?' she asked as he began to fuck her breasts.

'Yes!' Jack grunted. 'I . . .'

'No!' Lucy cut in firmly, and pushed Octavia back. 'Not yet! Come, we will show for Jack what the awful Addiscombe wants so strongly. Off with your clothes, both of you, quickly now!'

Octavia had fallen on her bottom, giggling foolishly with her knees up and her breasts still in her hands, while Augusta still held her rude pose, only with her hand between her thighs to stroke her quim. Both began to strip, laughing as they peeled their clothes off, Lucy too, pushing her dress down over her hips and quickly divesting herself of petticoats and chemise. Jack Gurney watched, gently stroking at his erection, until all three girls were in nothing but stockings and boots. Lucy stood, her hands on her hips, head cocked to one side.

'Are we not beautiful?' she teased. 'Do you not want to put that everywhere it will go? With all three of us?'

Jack nodded urgently.

'Come then,' Lucy replied, and took him by the cock, to lead him to where Octavia and Augusta lay curled on the ground.

Augusta was nearest, and got his cock fed into her mouth, sucking in bliss for a moment, eyes shut and stroking her breasts and quim. Octavia came close, crawling, to mouth at his balls, and Lucy clapped her hands in delight to see the two sisters sharing a cock. She began to spank them, turn and turn about, to set both bottoms wobbling.

'You are dirty girls!' she chided playfully. 'Wanton little trollops, the both of you. But stop it now, one more pleasure remains!'

She took them by their hair, pulling both off his cock. Octavia tried to get back on, but Lucy grabbed her and gave her chubby bottom a brisk salvo of slaps, leaving the little fat cheeks flushed pink. Even as she was spanked she was wriggling in Lucy's grip, trying to get back to Jack, but he had sat back, tugging at his cock as he watched her being punished. Lucy stopped and spoke.

'As you are so eager, you may have him, in a way I know will bring you to rapture. Come, Jack, get behind her!'

Lucy had a firm grip on Octavia's waist, and kept it as Jack shuffled quickly around, cock ready in her hand.

The tip was already wet, with a froth of bubbles emerging from the tiny hole. Octavia saw, and spoke as she began to struggle in earnest.

'Not my quim, Lucy, I am virgin!'

'No, not your quim, silly!' Lucy laughed. 'Up your bottom! Go on, Jack, put it in!'

Octavia gave a squeal of alarm, but Lucy had changed her grip, to take hold of her cousin's fleshy bottom cheeks and haul them wide, spreading the little pink star between, and also her virgin cunt mouth, the tiny bump of her maidenhead glistening in the sunlight. Both holes were wet with juice and sweat, her anus winking in what was rapidly becoming panic as she squirmed in Lucy's grip, babbling.

'Lucy, no! It could not fit, not possibly! I beg you, Lucy, no . . .'

'Hush,' Lucy chuckled, and slapped Octavia's bottom, 'and do stop wriggling so. Of course it will go, girls are made to accommodate men, are we not?'

'Not in our bottoms!' Octavia wailed, but Jack Gurney already had his cock head to her anus.

Lucy laughed to see Octavia's bottom hole go into frantic spasms as the big cock pushed at it. Jack grunted, and pushed. Octavia's writhing grew truly desperate, sending Lucy into peals of laughter, and determined to see if a man's cock really could fit up a girl's bottom. Octavia's ring began to spread, only to tighten, and Jack's cock slipped, up into her bottom crease. Lucy took hold of it, putting it back between Octavia's squirming cheeks.

'No, Lucy, please!' Octavia begged. 'Let him do it in my bottom slit, my mouth, anywhere, but . . .'

'Hush, and hold still!' Lucy ordered. 'Come, Jack, push it up.'

'I cannot!' Jack grunted. 'She is as slippery as an eel and tight as a cat!'

'Just push!' Lucy snapped.

Jack grunted. Octavia went wild as her ring began to spread, thrashing her bottom from side to side, but not enough as he took a firm grip on her hips. His cock slipped again, but Lucy took it again, guiding it back to the slippery little bottom hole. Again Jack pushed, again the little ring began to spread. Lucy laughed, high and wild, to see her cousin buggered. Octavia gave a frantic heave, screaming out, and Jack's cock had slipped a third time, downwards, just as he pushed.

Octavia gave a sharp cry as the full, fat bulk of Jack Gurney's cock was jammed up her cunt, bursting her hymen and erupting inside her, spunk squashing from the torn hole as he finished off. Lucy screamed at him, ordering him to stop, but it was already too late. Octavia put her face in the grass, gasping and whimpering as she was fucked with a half dozen hard pushes that set the spunk squirting from around her cock-bloated hole, then silent as Jack sank back, his face set in horror at what he'd done even as his cock left her body. Suddenly all was silent, and Lucy's hand went to her mouth as she watched the white fluid running from Octavia's ruptured hole, with a thread of scarlet where her virgin blood had mingled with Jack Gurney's spunk.

Ten

Lucy put her hand to her stomach as she stepped into the hall. It felt weak, while however many times she visited the privy, she still felt as if she urgently needed to pee. Octavia followed her, and their hands clasped together as they came to stand at the living room door, their need for mutual support overriding all other feelings. Jack Gurney came behind them, silent and abashed. Lucy's head ached.

After a little hair pulling, many angry recriminations, and a great deal of talk, it had been decided that the only possible thing to do was tell her parents what had happened. Octavia did not dare broach the subject to her own family, for fear of her father's belt and her mother's undoubted hysterics. Augusta had agreed quickly, Lydia only after the others had threatened to say that she had been the instigator unless she did as she was told.

'Papa?' Lucy managed, seeing him slumped in a chair, chuckling over a novel he held in one hand.

He turned around.

'Ah, there you are Lucy, and Octavia too, just in time for supper, although your mother and the Marquis are not yet back.'

Lucy opened her mouth to speak again, but no words would come. His expression changed from happy unconcern to puzzlement, but before either of them could speak again a man walked in from the terrace, tall, massively built, his head a bald dome and his face seamed with age, but still full of power and assurance. Behind Lucy, Jack Gurney swore under his breath, then spoke.

'Father.'

Todd Gurney nodded and gave a polite inclination of his head to the girls, then sat down, throwing a sheaf of papers onto the table beside Henry.

'That's for April. Down, but we've had shoring to do. New gallery along under Tucket's, seem so.'

'Excellent . . .' Henry replied, taking the papers.

'Means we'll have to clear low adit,' Todd continued.

'No difficulty there. I'll tell John Coppinger to make his first run of deliveries with those casks.'

Todd gave a grunt of assent.

'Er . . . Papa,' Lucy managed.

'A moment, dearest,' he answered. 'I must run an eye over the mine accounts.'

Lucy went silent, biting her lip, then turned to cast an imploring glance at Jack, who spoke after a moment.

'We've news, father . . . Mr Truscott. Ill news.'

Henry turned again, now looking worried. Todd Gurney looked up, his face grim.

'Nobody's hurt,' Lucy said quickly, 'well, not hurt, not . . .'

She trailed off, unable to meet her father's eyes.

'Whatever is it?' Henry demanded. 'Speak up, girl, you look like a cod!'

Lucy had opened her mouth, but still couldn't speak, quite unable to find the words to express what had happened. Octavia tried too, but only managed an odd gurgling noise, and it was left to Jack Gurney, who stepped forward, his voice formal and slow.

'We have a confession, Mr Truscott. This afternoon, on an excursion to the moor, I grew very drunk.'

'What of it?' Henry laughed, then stopped. 'Not on the Cognac the Marquis brought, because if so, God help . . .'

'No, Papa,' Lucy broke in. 'I was careful to fill a bottle from a cask, as you do.'

Henry nodded, smiling.

'What then?'

Jack Gurney swallowed.

'I . . . I have ruined your niece, Miss Truscott.'

Octavia gave a little whimper and her hand tightened in Lucy's. Jack's father immediately began to go dark with anger, his great fists clenching, but as he made to answer Henry put an arm out to silence him and spoke instead.

'You've had Octavia?'

'Yes, sir,' Jack answered as Octavia burst into tears and ran from the room.

Lucy followed, catching up with her halfway up the stairs and trying to comfort her cousin. At first Octavia tried to push her away, before giving in and burying her face in Lucy's dress, sobbing her heart out. Below them the door banged and Lucy looked down to find Jack Gurney standing in the hall with his hands clasped behind his back, looking sorry for himself. In the living room she could just make out her father's voice, but not the words. Releasing Octavia, she scampered quickly down the stairs to press her ear to the keyhole, just as Todd Gurney began to speak, his voice raised in anger.

'Damn fool puppy! By God he's not too big to feel my belt, he's . . .'

'Calm yourself, Todd,' Henry cut in. 'Here, have a Cognac.'

Todd didn't answer. There was a chink of glasses and the glug of liquid before Henry spoke again.

'No gain in temper, Todd. Too late for that. We must find out what harm is done, and see how best to remedy it.'

'Harm enough and more,' Todd growled. 'She'll be ruined for marriage, no doubt, and like as not there'll be a baby along.'

'We must certainly assume there will be a baby,' Henry answered, his voice serious but nothing more, then suddenly jocular. 'Won't do to wait and see if she starts to swell, will it!?'

He laughed, leaving Lucy torn between anger and relief at his casual attitude. There was a pause, and she tried to peer in, but could only see Todd, seated, his face set and stern, one huge hand gripping the brandy glass as if about to crush it. Henry spoke again.

'We've two options, it seems. It becomes known, and merry hell breaks loose with blame and recrimination in every direction, which is the route my brother would take, devil a doubt. Or it don't, and we make damn sure little Octavia's wed in quick time.'

'Wed to who? There'll be talk if she weds Jack!'

Henry laughed.

'I can see my brother's face, were you to make the suggestion! No, I have just the man – our excise puppy, Fairbrother, who stands high in Stephen's estimation following his rescue of Octavia from the clutches of the fiend, and would seem the ideal man in every respect. Also, he is currently paying court to Lucy, which neither she, nor Mrs Truscott, appreciates. We have a rather bigger fish in mind, the Marquis de la Motte. French fellow you met the other day.'

'He'll ask her, Fairbrother, d'you think?' Todd queried.

'Oh he'll ask her,' Henry replied, 'but we may need to hurry the fellow along a bit. So near as I'm any judge, he can't decide between Octavia and my Lucy, and in any event, he's hell bent on catching the fiend first. That's his game, d'you see, catch the fiend and he'll be a hero. What girl could refuse him?'

'Difficulty there, sir . . .'

'Well, yes, no fiend, but we can at least steer him towards Octavia and away from Lucy. Two weeks, we have, a month at the outside.'

'A month, sir? But . . .'

'Don't concern yourself,' Henry interrupted. 'You think he'll notice when the baby comes early, but he won't. A crown piece to the midwife and she'll say anything we damn well tell her to. Fairbrother and Jack are like enough in height and hair, and he'll be too proud to think foul play if the brat was ginger and came out at a stone and a half.'

Todd gave a doubtful nod. Henry went on.

'Best to try and have her fucked by him just as soon as we are able. I'll have Lucy prime her, but if I know anything, after her first filling of cock she'll be eager for another, protestations regardless. Leastways, if her mother's behaviour is anything to go by!'

'Her mother? Mrs Truscott?'

'Who else?' Henry answered him. 'A fine bob tail Caroline was, still is for the matter of it. I'm damn sure little Augusta's mine, that or Stephen was having her at the same time as I. Then there's Hippolyta, though for the size of the wench I'd think you'd sired her!'

Todd gave an embarrassed cough and Henry went on quickly.

'No great matter, and for that matter Stephen's parentage is known only to God.'

'Your brother's?'

'Yes. Mama was married before, d'you see, to a man named Pargade, and while she was having 'em both by all accounts I'm damned if I can see much of the governor in Stephen.'

Todd Gurney gave a reflective nod and spoke again.

'What of her maidenhead? He'll notice that's gone, certain sure!'

'Fairbrother? I doubt it. He's barely the courage to look a cunt in the eye and say boo, though I don't doubt he'd stand sword to sword with the best, damn fool that he is. Candles dowsed and under the covers is more his style, I'd say, and not the sort to question his lady's virtue. Besides, after Molly Hynes she'll seem tight enough, I don't doubt.'

Henry finished with a coarse laugh.

Robert Fairbrother's fists tightened in anger as he looked down on the cutter sent from Bristol to replace the *Bull*. Even her name, *Canary*, seemed a studied insult, while to judge by her lines, the way she was rigged and the six ancient cannon poking from her ports, she might well have seen service in the Civil War. Yet there was nothing he could do. It had been made abundantly clear that he had only kept his post because of the acute shortage of officers available, while the Commodore at Bristol had suggested he'd have been better drowned with his ship.

The incident had left him in a state of blind fury. Dragging himself up the cliff, he and his men had descended on Welcombe Farm with murder in their hearts, only to find it empty. They had searched every room of the house, and every outhouse, but found nothing, and now faced an action for trespass and damage to property. John Coppinger, his wife and mother-in-law had proved to be at the Dun Cow in Holsworthy, taking their supper with Alderman Coates, and had stayed the night.

All of it had been engineered, he was certain, from start to finish: Annie Coppinger's supposed betrayal of her husband, the signal lights, the longboat loaded with casks, which had since mysteriously disappeared. He had been played for a fool, and it had left him so angry that even the abundant charms of Molly Hynes held no appeal. Lucy Truscott still did; she and her family were the sole light of purity and innocence in a black world, but even they added a final sting to his trouble. He had discovered that a French *émigré* of noble blood and great wealth had come to stay at Driscoll's, a man who was not only sure to turn Lucy's head, but had the advantage of being constantly in attendance.

He turned on his heel, stalking back towards the Customs House with his head full of black thoughts, but also calculation. Beyond doubt a cargo had come in, or was about to. It had to be stored somewhere, and even if Annie Coppinger's statement of three hundred and fifty casks of brandy was an exaggeration, it could not be that easy to conceal. Possibly it was sunk on rafts, or hidden in some deep sea cave along the cliffs. Possibly it was inland already, but what little information he had managed to pry from the locals said nothing of horses moving by night.

Yet he had to act, and fast, to restore his credit, both with the Waterguard and with the local gentry. He had not dared even go to Driscoll's, afraid as much of Henry Truscott's pity as of Lucy's disdain. Nor had any further clue emerged as to the identity of the fiend, making his vow to catch the man ring somewhat hollow. As he approached the house he ground his fist into his hand. Only one course of action stood out as at all worthwhile. He would have to set spies on John Coppinger, perhaps even take a hand himself, a dangerous task by any standards, but one which must eventually bear fruit.

Saul Mudge hacked feverishly at the old bed sheet. At last he had a course of action which he felt he could risk, or rather, which he knew he had to risk. Across the kitchen, Polly was pouting badly as she worked to sew the pieces of cloth together, constructing the red and white mummer's harliquinade like that the fiend was said to wear. At first she had refused, even threatening to go to Mr Addiscombe. Belting and buggering had changed her attitude, and as she worked she occasionally squirmed her thighs uncomfortably for her sore bottom and anus. Saul took no notice of her, save to urge her to work faster.

The party over for the noon meal was entirely female, and unusually small; Mrs Truscott, Augusta Truscott, and Mrs Hawkes. Why Jack Gurney was not in attendance Saul did not know, nor care. Once Mr Addiscombe had retired for his afternoon nap, and with port and cheese on top of a large meal it was inevitable, then he, Saul Mudge, would be the only man on the property. The possibilities were limitless.

Of the women, only Mrs Hawkes failed to excite his desire, and even then he was considering a quick fucking, if only to shame her. Augusta would be easy, a weak spirit easily cowed by fear, so easily she was barely worth the trouble of tying up, but to take her virginity, and spunk in her cunt, would be the grand climax of his scheme. Better still, it would in front of her mother, who would also have been fucked, maybe buggered as well. Unlike Lucy, none would dare to attempt revenge.

It was hard to know exactly what had happened from Reuben's account, but it was clear that Henry Truscott had fucked his sister-in-law, possibly even buggered her. The details were unimportant, although something about a cock being put up such a proud lady's bottom appealed to him. What mattered was that it had happened, and he knew. At heart she was a slut, and would surrender herself with no real fight.

'Work faster, you 'angallus toad!' he snarled at Polly. 'They'll be through eating soon.'

'I'm going as fast as I'm able,' Polly answered. 'I've to serve and all.'

Saul made to retort, but the bell rang, not for the dining room, but the one set to detect when the girls were visiting the privy. He gave a dirty chuckle and moved into the next room to peer in at the spy hole. To his disappointment it was Mrs Hawkes, but he remained watching long enough to watch her expose her colossal buttocks and seat herself. Once she was finished he changed the pot and took her soil out to the dunny pit.

Back in the kitchen Polly was almost done. He cuffed her for being slow anyway, and drew himself another flagon of beer. The hood was finished, and after a couple of swallows he tried it on and went to admire himself in the cracked mirror. It fitted well enough, and Polly's hasty sewing gave it an added air of the grotesque, the lopsided seams creating an impression of deformity he was sure would terrify all three women. Removing it, he placed it carefully beside the girls' dung pots, chuckling to himself as he went back to his beer.

He was growing pleasantly drunk, and his cock pleasantly stiff. The temptation to make Polly suck him was considerable, but he held back, determined to save his spunk for Augusta Truscott's virgin cunt. As the dining room bell rang for Polly to go and clear the table he was imagining how it would feel, how tight she'd be, tighter even than Polly's arsehole, and how she'd scream in fear and despair as her hymen burst. It would be blamed on the fiend, that and everything else. If he was even suspected, Polly would swear he'd been indoors, and Mr Addiscombe would also support him.

As he continued to drink another thought occurred to him, a minor revenge but a good one. Years of carefully saving the four girls' dung, rotting it down in their labelled pots, mixing it with peat he'd cut from the moor and preparing the ill-smelling result for Mr Addiscombe's tulip cultivation programme, had added considerably to his resentment of the world. It was a stupid idea anyway, to suppose that somehow the girl's virtues might be transmitted to the flowers through the soil, but typical of Mr Addiscombe. After all, had it been true, then Lucy Truscott's yield would have been sure to produce a tulip of perfect black at the first attempt.

The girls, he was sure, imagined that Mr Addiscombe hoped to marry one of them, an absurd idea when the inevitable refusal would disrupt the cultivation programme. Possibly they suspected they were watched on the privy, but not for an instant that their dung was collected, nor the purpose to which it was put. He

206

chuckled to himself, imagining their chagrin at the discovery and deciding to go ahead with his idea.

It was an amusing, and fitting, act. He would cut one of Augusta's tulips, which would make a fine detail to his antics as the mad mummer. When he'd fucked her he'd stick it up her cunt and leave it there, the big purple bloom protruding from between her thighs, deep in her hole, eased up in the spunk and blood, showing clearly she was no longer virgin. It was more than fitting, it was perfect – to be fucked and left with a tulip grown in her own shit protruding from her ruined cunt.

He laughed out loud at the thought, and drained the rest of his beer. It was almost time, and he began to run through the plan in his head, and what he'd need. Not for the first time, he considered the matter of gags. It would be good to hear the girls scream and plead, but there had to be a possibility that Mr Addiscombe would wake up, despite his room being on the far side of the house, or again some labourer overhear. They'd be silent enough with his cock in their mouths, it was true, and even gagged they'd still be able to whimper, while it might be amusing to have them trying to beg but unable to get the words out.

Deciding it would be best to use gags after all, he quickly rolled some of the off-cuts of red and white cloth lying on the table into balls, using Polly's needle and thread to bind them loosely together. Polly returned with the plates and cutlery while he was still doing it, and gave him a single dirty look before going back for the next load. When she returned he was ready.

'What of Addiscombe?' he demanded. 'Will he sleep?'

'He's yawning already,' Polly answered.

'Then I'd best be ready,' Saul said.

Polly's mouth was a tight line, and as he rose she spoke, determined, despite her evident fear.

'Won't . . . won't you leave them?' she demanded. 'At

the least Miss Augusta . . . she's no harm, not to you, not to a soul . . .'

'All the better,' Saul chuckled. 'Now shut your cock trap and get on with your plates, and you're to suck my prick hard before I go out.'

'No, Saul, please,' Polly begged. 'Not Miss Augusta, please! Do me, if you must, but . . .'

'You?' he laughed. 'You're past use, you, you great sow.'

Polly's face hardened as she spoke again.

'I'll tell my sister . . .'

Saul spat.

'Tell her, and a lot of good may it do you. She gets the same as you, don't she? A husband's right, no more, that's what he'll say.'

'If it were me, yes, not Miss Augusta . . .'

'Think he cares? He'd laugh, and do the same, if he were able.'

'No. He takes only what is his.'

He laughed at her, and again as he saw the tears filming her eyes as she bent to pick up a pail. Saul took the costume into the adjoining room, stripped and began to dress, his excitement rising fast as he pulled the tight red and white striped breeches up his spindly legs. His cock wasn't going to need much sucking, it was already half stiff in anticipation of Augusta's virgin cunt. As he continued to dress he decided on the last details of what he would do. Once the women were bound and gagged, first would be Mrs Hawkes, for a brief fucking and perhaps a buggering if she proved loose. Not that he'd hurry, because it would be good for the other two to watch, and leave them in no doubt at all of what was coming to them.

With Mrs Hawkes finished he would start on Mrs Truscott, Miss Caroline Cunningham, as she'd been, and still one of the haughtiest little bitches in the district. First he'd slit her bodice and pull out her tits, perhaps put nettles to them as had been done to her daughter. That was a good detail, and one he knew through servants' gossip, so it would go further to pin the blame on the fiend. With her tits stripped and nettled he'd bare her arse for the same treatment, then bugger her, right up her dirty tube, and then make her suck his cock clean before she was fucked, all in front of her daughter.

Last would come Augusta, no doubt already in terror after watching her mother and her guardian used. She'd beg and scream for sure, and struggle, with luck, but it would do her no good. He'd put her through the same regime, her tits stripped and nettled, her arse stripped, nettled and buggered . . .

He squeezed his cock at the thought of Augusta's tight, hot anal tube on his erection. Only the mask remained, and he pulled it quickly on as he added to his scheme. Augusta would need a good buggering, long and hard, so that her virgin arsehole would never be the same again. Then he'd give her a choice, to suck the cock she'd just had up her arse, or have her cunt popped. She'd choose to suck, inevitably, and in would go his cock, steaming and filthy, into her pretty mouth. Not that he'd keep his promise. Just as soon as his cock was nice and shiny clean, it would go up her cunt.

How she'd hate it when she realised she was to be ruined anyway! How she'd fight, her legs kicking wildly before they were caught and hauled apart, to show the neat pink purse of her quim in its nest of hair, her buggered anus, her virgin cunt. How stupid she'd look, and sound, with her pathetic struggles and mumbling for mercy through her gag. How she'd thrash, desperate to save her cunt, but to no avail. He'd fuck her.

She deserved it. She needed it. For every haughty glance and sniff of distaste. For every remark she'd made to her sisters and others. She would get it too, his cock, driven hard up her cunt, to burst her oh so precious maidenhead, to deflower her, to fuck her and spunk up her hole, to leave her dribbling blood and spunk with the tulip that bore her name stuck well up, to shame her utterly, and forever . . .

He was chuckling under his breath as he made for the glasshouse, his cock too hard to need sucking. First the tulip and a ball of twine, then to wait his moment.

Henry smiled happily as he drew in a draught of the sweet scented air. Eloise stood beside him, and the Marquis, the two of them reminiscing of bygone days in France, with Lucy listening attentively. The Marquis had expressed an interest in Mr Addiscombe's attempts to cultivate a black tulip, and they had driven over in the carriages, two groups, his own, and another consisting of Stephen, Lydia and Octavia. The others were still climbing down, and Henry waited until all seven of them were gathered together.

'I trust that Mr Addiscombe will not think this an inconvenience,' Stephen remarked.

'He'll be fast asleep, like as not,' Henry replied, 'but I think the length of our acquaintance would bear us walking around and having a look for ourselves. Besides, Caroline and Augusta are about, somewhere. Mr Addiscombe plans to name the black tulip after Lucy, did you know, Marquis?'

'So I have heard,' de Cachaliere answered. 'A singular honour.'

'My own bloom is very pretty, and a most curious shade,' Octavia remarked, 'while Lydia's is crimson, and Augusta's a wonderful purple, but we shall see.'

They made for the side of the house rather than the door, rounding the bay window of the dining room, to come out onto the lawn, and stop short in their tracks. Ahead of them, on the far side of the lawn within feet of the glasshouse door, was a man, a mummer beyond doubt, masked and in harliquinade, the same red and white harliquinade as Lucy's toy. He was sprawled front down on the grass, his head was snapped back and around at an impossible angle, and blood stained the front of his mask, which was half lifted from his distorted face, but it was not this that had Henry staring open mouthed. The man's breeches were down, his scrawny buttocks naked, and a single specimen of Miss Augusta Truscott had been inserted between them.

Octavia screamed, Lydia sank down, fainting. De Cachaliere swore and started forward, then Stephen as Eloise began to shepherd the girls away. For a moment Henry could only gape in astonishment, before following the other men across the lawn. Stephen reached the body first, and reached down to twitch the mask fully from its head.

'I'll be damned, Saul Mudge!' Henry exclaimed.

'His neck is broken,' Stephen stated.

'So much is plain,' Henry answered, 'and much of his face also.'

'A terrible blow,' de Cachaliere put in, 'yet one only, as I judge it.'

Stephen had stood up again, grim faced and shaking with anger.

'Who would have thought it, a trusted servant, among us for years! As well for him he is dead.'

'Well indeed,' Henry answered, trying to imitate his brother's tone of voice but only succeeding in sounding puzzled.

Somebody called out, and Henry turned. Jack Gurney, who had driven their carriage, was running across the lawn. In the opposite direction, Caroline was coming through the gate from the moor lane, with Mrs Hawkes behind her. Stephen hurried towards his wife, his arms spread wide in an effort to spare her the sight of the corpse. De Cachaliere turned to Henry, speaking in an undertone.

'Did you not say the fiend was a ruse, Mr Truscott? A ruse to distract the excise men, I had understood?'

'It was,' Henry answered with a shrug. 'Saul Mudge was never at Meldon Pool, nor at the folly on Burley Down.'

'What then . . .'

'I don't know,' Henry answered, 'but I've a mind to make the best of it. Jack, ride up to Bideford with the news for Lieutenant Fairbrother.'

Robert Fairbrother reined in his horse. He felt vaguely foolish and something of a fraud, disguised as he was as a dragoon guard in a uniform which would have been out of date before he was born. Yet it was a good disguise. The heavy red cape allowed him to conceal his face and made his frame appear a good deal heavier, while to see a solider riding from place to place was by no means unusual and drew none of the attention accorded his true office. He had passed Henry Truscott's man Gurney outside Holsworthy without recognition. Indeed, Gurney had barely glanced to the side as he thundered past at a full gallop.

Somewhere out among the lanes was John Coppinger and, when he found him, there would be a reckoning. His information was good, he was sure of it, coming as it did from one of the men who had been on the *Bull* with him when she was lured onto the rocks. John Coppinger had left Welcombe Farm early that morning, riding south along the lanes on a heavy plough horse. The horse had been fitted with straps, but had born no load, surely implying that Coppinger aimed to collect something, and very likely casks of Cognac.

He had ridden hard on receiving the message, but while his search of the coast lanes had yielded nothing, another messenger waiting for him outside the Customs House had news of a second sighting. Coppinger had been seen near Okehampton, not two miles from the Beare Estate, riding boldly with a cask strapped to either side of his horse.

It was the proof Fairbrother needed, and he had taken off without delay, praying that his luck would hold, and that he would not only find Coppinger, ideally with the casks, but at the least with the money he'd had for them and a saddle rigged for barrels. Even then he knew that an arrest would only be the start – that was if he troubled to make one.

Coppinger was a violent man, and not one to come easily. He would fight, and if he fought and died, nobody would think to question the word of the preventative officer who had killed him, least of all Mr Stephen Truscott, and it was the word of Mr Stephen Truscott that would matter. Beneath Fairbrother's cape his broad leather belt supported a brace of pistols and a cutlass.

He had reined in above Halwill, at the edge of a great tract of woodland from where he could look out over lower hills and the valleys towards Dartmoor. If Coppinger was making for Welcombe Farm he could hardly fail to pass by, and before too long. There were several possible routes, but the officer was on the most likely, and could see sections of the lane at the valley bottom and another which led along the opposite ridge. He settled down to wait, extracting his telescope from a saddle bag and putting it to his eye.

He scanned both lanes, and for a while followed the progress of a stout labourer in a mud-stained smock as he walked back towards his cottage. No horsemen at all were visible, let alone the giant Coppinger, and after a while he began to scan the further horizons, Dartmoor, the cluster of hills that hid Okehampton from view, then Burley Down where it rose above the Driscoll's Estate. Even as his thoughts turned to Lucy, he saw her, little more than a dot, but her white summer dress and her flame-red hair were unmistakable. She was running, and behind her came a man, a man in a pale blue coat. With a curse he set his spurs into the flanks of his horse.

* * *

Lucy laughed as she ran. All was well with the world, the awkwardness with the invented fiend resolved, Mr Fairbrother sure to propose to Octavia, and the Marquis de la Motte showing an interest which would have been thoroughly improper had he not intended to make a declaration. Not only had he made a point of asking her to walk up to Burley Down with her, and otherwise quite alone, but he had instigated a playful game of chase.

She was determined to be caught, but not easily, dodging around the pillars of the folly. He carried a cane, and used it to attempt to herd her into the folly, making her wonder exactly what would happen when he did catch her, a thought both frightening and delightful. Three times already he had laid a hand on her dress, only to release her, but the fourth time he held on, and hauled her giggling and squeaking into the folly, where she was laid down on the marble floor. He struck a pose, his legs braced apart across her body, his peacock blue cutaway coat casually open, one hand resting lightly on the top of his cane, the other at his chin.

'You present me with a dilemma,' he remarked.

'A dilemma?' Lucy asked, her voice no less teasing than his. 'What dilemma could there possibly be, when you have me at your cruel mercy?'

'The dilemma,' he responded, 'is between mind and body. Should I follow my mind, and make a solemn declaration to you, and then wait before doing what every fibre of my being urges, or should I follow my body, and simply . . .'

'You are mistaken,' Lucy interrupted. 'There is no dilemma. To a man of intelligence and spirit the course of action would be clear.'

De Cachaliere raised an eyebrow, nodded, dropped his cane and sank down on her. Lucy gave a single squeak of feigned shock before she had been taken in his arms. Keen to seem at least a little demure, she

214

resisted briefly before letting her mouth open under his, but her intent began to waver immediately. Their tongues met, and her arms came around his back, his body lithe and hard against her.

They were kissing with a fierce passion as he grappled with her dress, spilling her breasts out of her bodice, to take one in each hand. His thumbs found her nipples, bringing both quickly erect, then his mouth, suckling on her as she closed her eyes in bliss. With her breasts bare and her nipples stiff, her show of reluctance vanished. Pulling free, she twisted herself around. He gave a little noise of surprise as her hand burrowed for the flap of his breeches, then delight as his cock came free, straight into her mouth. She began to suck eagerly, stroking his balls as she mouthed on his rapidly swelling cock, just as Jack Gurney had taught her.

With his cock growing in her mouth there was no doubt left as to her surrender. Her dress was quickly tugged up, her bottom bared, then her quim as she lifted her hips to make it easier for him. She felt his face as he nuzzled into her belly, then his tongue was between the lips of her quim and he was licking her, one leg held up, his face buried between her thighs, lapping at her quim, her bottom cheeks, burrowing into the shallow pit of her virgin hole, kissing at her anus and, lastly, between her lips.

His cock was a rigid pole in her mouth, full and hard, at once utterly delightful and terrifying, yet her need far overrode her fear, save that in his urgency he might come in her mouth. Still she sucked, not wanting to let go, but to taste him while she came under his tongue, and knowing she would be in rapture at any moment. A finger found her bottom hole, wiggling inside her, and she wondered if she was to be buggered instead. The thought set her thighs tight, her quim into spasm, and she was there, in rapture as she imagined the big penis in her mouth being pushed up her tiny hole, to fill her bottom with spunk even after her virginity had been taken.

She was still in orgasm as he abruptly stopped licking. Her hands went straight to her quim, rubbing to finish herself off. She sighed in disappointment as his finger was eased from her bottom hole, but she was still squirming in ecstasy as he mounted her, his cock pushed to her quim, and her orgasm hit a new peak as she realised that the moment had come a tiny instant before her hymen ruptured and the full, thick length of his cock was jammed deep up her body.

Lucy screamed at the sudden, sharp pain, but only once. Her teeth were gritted against the pain as he began to fuck her, but she was determined not to show it. Clinging tightly to him, her thighs as far up and as far open as they would go, her ecstasy soon began to rise again. Their mouths met, kissing with bruising passion. His thrusts grew harder, deeper, and her bliss was only a fraction less than climax when the real thing hit her again at the perfect moment. His cock erupted deep inside her, to mix his come with her virgin blood, and he was panting as he spoke the words she longed to hear.

'I have ravished you, Miss Lucy Truscott. Now you must be mine.'

She nodded, cuddling close to him, only to break away at the sound of pounding hooves from outside the temple. De Cachaliere laughed, and eased his still-hard cock deep one more time, only to twist around at a scream of wordless fury from behind them. Robert Fairbrother stood in the entrance to the folly, a notched cutlass in one hand, his face a mask of murderous hate.

'You devil!' he yelled. 'For that, you die!'

He hurled himself forward and de Cachaliere rolled frantically to the side, snatching his cane just in time to parry Fairbrother's first wild slash. Lucy screamed, thinking the cane cut through and her lover's body also, but the wood merely splintered to reveal the long steel of the blade hidden within. Fairbrother gave a grunt of anger and sprang in again. Steel rang on steel and they were locked in combat, as Lucy stepped quickly back out of the way and fled the folly, only to find the men coming after her, de Cachaliere giving back in a series of desperate parries.

Fairbrother fought with fury, courage and speed, his face set in grim determination as he launched one furious, slashing assault after another. De Cachaliere defended himself with both skill and panache, a vision of swordsmanship somewhat marred by his cock waving wildly in the air, yet there was no doubt whatever of the outcome.

Lucy could only stare, but fought to regain her nerve as she backed against Fairbrother's horse. Something long and hard bumped her back, a brass naval telescope, and she hesitated only a moment, before snatching it free and bringing it down on the back of Lieutenant Fairbrother's head with all her force.

Eleven

Robert Fairbrother returned to consciousness slowly. A beautiful face was close to his own, somewhat fuzzy at the edges. For a moment he imagined himself in Heaven, which came as a shock sufficient to bring him fully round and to recognise the blonde curls and delicate features of Octavia Truscott. Memory came flooding back.

'The fiend! Lucy!' he exclaimed, jerking upright in bed, then collapsing as a bolt of red pain shot through the back of his skull.

'Lie back, do not exert yourself!' Octavia urged.

Henry Truscott's voice sounded from somewhere off to the side.

'No, no, do exert yourself, at least a little. I am fascinated to know why you assaulted my daughter's intended with such violence?'

Fairbrother turned his head, to stare at Henry in astonishment.

'Lucy? Lucy is to marry the fiend?'

'His mind is plainly feverish,' Octavia put in. 'Leave him to recover his wits, uncle Henry.'

'Damned if I will,' Henry answered. 'What in hell's name are you blathering about, man? The fiend is dead. Did not Jack Gurney tell you this?'

Fairbrother shook his head weakly.

'Not dead, no . . . on Burley Down . . . I caught him,

in . . . in the very act of violating poor Lucy! Oh God, is she . . .'

'She is quite well, thank you,' Henry broke in, 'having brained you with your telescope in order to prevent you from skewering her intended, the Marquis de la Motte.'

Fairbrother groaned, yet still it made no sense. He recalled the man's frantic, obscene humping motions, Lucy's spread thighs and pained face, the pale blue coat-tails flapping as she was fucked, his bloodstained cock as he withdrew.

'But . . .' he began.

'You supposed the Marquis to be the fiend?' Octavia asked gently. 'Why so?'

'He . . . he was in the act of violating Lucy!' Fairbrother exclaimed. 'And his coat, pale blue, you said so yourself, Miss Octavia!'

Henry sighed.

'Many men wear pale blue coats, Mr Fairbrother, and while it may be somewhat unconventional to consummate a marriage before it has taken place, I venture to suggest that it is not unusual. Am I to assume that Jack Gurney never reached you with the news?'

Fairbrother managed a weak nod of his head as the full implications of what he had done began to sink in. Henry went on.

'The fiend is dead by an unknown hand, Mr Fairbrother, and he was no stranger, but the manservant of Mr Nathaniel Addiscombe, a respectable gentleman horticulturist and a man of means, neighbour to my brother at Beare. You have met him on occasion, I believe?'

Again Fairbrother nodded. Octavia pressed him back against the pillows as Henry went on.

'Mudge was in full harliquinade, red and white, just as Lucy described, and clearly intent on some foul deed, a deed he never accomplished. As near as we can judge, his neck was snapped by a single ferocious blow to his

219

head – the kick of a horse, I'd have said, had there been a horse convenient to hand. Indeed, I have already persuaded both my brother and Mr Addiscombe that we should adopt the horse explanation in order to avoid scandal.'

After a moment of shock Fairbrother responded.

'I see . . . a wise choice, for certain, but what of the murderer?'

Henry shrugged.

'My brother is torn between the demands of his conscience for justice and natural gratitude as a husband and father. There seems no doubt that whatever Mudge intended, his victims would have been Mrs Truscott and Miss Augusta, although had it come to the clinch my money would have been on Mrs Hawkes. Speaking of justice, there is also the matter of the assault upon and attempted murder of the Marquis de la Motte, a French *émigré* and guest in our country, also my house.'

Fairbrother could only stare, his mouth coming slowly open as Henry continued.

'I had imagined that your attack was a murderous assault on a rival in love, but from what you say it is clear that I am mistaken. Lucy herself defends you, stating that to her certain knowledge your affections have never been directed towards her, but to another. My brother may take a little more convincing. For all his reforming zeal I fear he has rather been inclined to hang first and examine his conscience at leisure.'

Robert Fairbrother felt the blood drain from his face.

'Then there is the Marquis himself,' Henry went on blithely, 'who speaks of calling you out, and might perhaps prove a more able swordsman without his breeches half down and his . . .'

'Uncle Henry!' Octavia protested.

Henry rose, tousled Octavia's hair in an affectionate manner, gave a polite bow to Fairbrother and made for the door, speaking only as he reached it.

'Naturally, were I to convince my brother that your intentions were honourable, indeed, valiant, matters would be somewhat different. My advice would be to act promptly.'

Henry smiled as Octavia applied a damp flannel to Robert Fairbrother's head. As the officer's senses cleared the full horror of his situation began to sink in. Unless Henry spoke for him, he would stand accused of attempting the murder of a French Marquis, a man who was furthermore engaged to marry Lucy. Henry's meaning was obvious. He must accept the Frenchman's challenge, thus allowing honour to be satisfied. Only then would Henry Truscott speak for him. He made to rise, but Octavia pushed him gently down onto the bed, speaking as she did so.

'You must rest, Mr Fairbrother.'

'No . . .'

She put her finger to her lips.

'Hush. The door is locked in any event.'

'Locked? But . . . No, Miss Octavia, I beg you . . .'

He broke off, his mouth open in shock, then ecstasy. She had pulled the bed clothes down, casually exposing his naked body, and after only an instant of hesitation took his cock into her mouth. The sheer bliss of having his penis sucked made it impossible for him to resist, for all his raging emotions. He simply lay back, letting himself grow in her mouth, with his lust rising to push aside all his doubts. She was the woman for him, without question. Henry Truscott, as generous and as understanding as ever, had not meant that he should accept the Marquis' challenge, but that he should declare himself to Octavia, who was without doubt in love with him.

'Be . . . be mine,' he managed, just as his cock came to full erection in her mouth.

For a moment she continued to suck, as if having his cock in her mouth was more important than any other

221

consideration, even marriage. Then she had taken him in hand instead, tugging gently at his shaft as she came up to kiss him. He faltered a moment at the taste of his own cock in her mouth, but their tongues were soon entwined and his arms around her. When at last she broke away, her voice was full of vitality and need.

'Take me, Robert, here and now. Show me what it means to be a woman!'

He swallowed hard as she swung herself up onto the bed, straddling his body, her own warm and soft through her light summer dress, her full breasts pressing to him, so round, so firm, ideal to fold around his straining cock . . .

'But, my darling, we are not wed!' he managed, forcing himself to say what was right.

'We will be soon, my dearest,' she urged, 'very soon. Do not deny me, Robert, I could not bear it if you were to deny me!'

Again he swallowed. His cock was rock hard and trapped in a froth of lace from her petticoat, his head full of her beguiling scent, his heart hammering. He knew that if he didn't have her he would erupt anyway, soiling her clothes, and likely as not losing her love and her respect both, then and there. What mattered was to have her, to accept her, marry her.

Briefly it occurred to him that with the money Octavia brought to the marriage he would be able to resign his commission and be rid of the burden of acting as a preventative officer. He pushed the unworthy thought aside and, with a brief prayer for forgiveness, he gave in to his lust, tugging at her dress to haul it high, stripping her bottom and taking the plump little cheeks in his hands as their mouths met in an urgent, clumsy kiss.

He felt her shiver as she sat down on him, cock to quim, the head of his erection slipping in the moist folds, and then at her hole, painfully tight as she let her weight settle. She gave a little cry as she opened to him, letting herself be penetrated and he knew that her maidenhead was gone. Yet even as the full length of his erection filled her she was sighing in bliss and clinging to him, her pain clearly nothing beside the rapture of their congress as he began to fuck her.

Sat at her mirror in nothing but her undergarments of a light chemise, stockings and a single petticoat, Lucy admired her reflection in the mirror as Hippolyta brushed out her hair. In a few days she would be married, her belly was already beginning to feel a little tight, and she felt more pleased with herself than ever. Far above all other considerations, she would shortly to be married to a man of fine appearance, wealth, style and rank, a match that perfectly reflected her own self opinion. She had even come to terms with her surrender to him. It had taken a man among men to make her feel the way Augusta did, yielding her body to another's pleasure, but she had. There was still a little chagrin, but knowing that Augusta was her half-sister had made it far easier to accept. It was evidently her nature.

In addition, Mr Robert Fairbrother and Octavia had announced that they were engaged, and would marry the following weekend, which was also ideal. He was suitable, and yet far inferior to her own choice. The money Octavia brought to the union had also allowed him to declare his intention of resigning his commission in the Preventative Waterguard, much to her father's satisfaction.

All that remained were the decisions as to who should live where, decisions made complicated by the situation in France. She herself preferred to remain in Devon, and was sure that with the careful application of her wiles she could persuade de Cachaliere to purchase an estate in one of the pretty valleys where the rivers ran north from Dartmoor. Possibly he might even be tempted by the opportunity of watching her enjoy Augusta; spanking her in front of him, making her drink her own piddle, even surrendering her bottom hole to him.

It was an amusing thought, but it was clearly necessary for her to stay firmly in charge save as far as her husband was concerned. Augusta would do as she was told, but Hippolyta was a different matter, altogether too wilful, especially for a mere maid. Hippolyta would have to learn proper deference, deference such as Suki showed to Eloise, and only then might de Cachaliere be allowed slake his lust with her when the occasion demanded. Many other aspects of Hippolyta's attitude would also have to be discussed, and without delay.

'Now that I am to be a Marquise,' she remarked, 'you must show me more deference. For one, it will no longer do to refer to me as Lucy, even in the privacy of my chambers. I am not certain of the correct address . . .'

Hippolyta laughed.

'It'll always be Lucy to me, in private.'

'No longer,' Lucy insisted, and was about to go on when Hippolyta spoke again, in a high, mocking tone.

'Beg pardon, Madame la Marquise, but how should I address you when you're licking at my cunt?'

'That is another matter which needs discussion,' Lucy answered sternly. 'Not that I wish to break off our liaisons, but I think it better if you lick my quim and manipulate your own, which is more fitting. Also, I may well have to spank you on occasion, whip you even, if only, you appreciate, for the sake of form.'

'You try,' Hippolyta chuckled, 'and we'll see who gets her sit-upon smacked!'

'No, no,' Lucy insisted, struggling to assert herself, 'you do not understand. I have always been gentle to you, and frankly far too lenient. In my new role as Marquise, you must be properly obedient and respectful, and that may well mean you have to be chastised on occasion.'

Hippolyta merely laughed.

'I will carry out my intentions,' Lucy warned her, 'with a dog whip if need be.'

'How would you do that?' Hippolyta answered.

'I shall have you held down,' Lucy threatened, 'perhaps by the Marquis' stable lads, of whom there are sure to be plenty.'

In the mirror Hippolyta had at last begun to look worried, biting her lips and frowning. Her confidence returning, and starting to enjoy herself, Lucy went on.

'I think I shall have to. Not, you understand, from any sense of malice, but merely to be certain that you understand your place, and that I mean what I say.'

Hippolyta nodded, took as large a handful of Lucy's curls in hand as she could manage, and spoke as she began to brush.

'I don't suppose I'll be able to stop it, not with men to hold me down. So it seems I'd better do you now, while I've the chance.'

Her voice was soft, compliant, and it took Lucy an instant to realise what she meant, an instant too long. Suddenly Hippolyta's grip had tightened in her hair and she was being forced to her feet, squealing in pain and protest, but finding her voice as she realised she really was to be put across her maid's knee, and undoubtedly spanked.

'No! Not me! Not me, Hippolyta! You cannot! You cannot! I am not spanked! I am not spanked, not ever!'

'Over you go!' Hippolyta snapped, twisting to seat herself on the stool even as she began to force Lucy around.

The next instant Lucy was down, still fighting, but unable to do more than kick and scratch against Hippolyta's strength, hauled into spanking position across her own maid's knee, bottom up with a hand twisted hard into her hair. Her head was burning in unbearable humiliation as she realised that she really was to be spanked, and that there was nothing whatso-ever she could do about it. She lost control. Her protests gave way to wordless howls and pig-like squeals, her struggles increased to a wild, uncontrolled thrashing, which grew more violent still as Hippolyta began to lift her petticoat. Her bottom was to be bared first, making the spanking a thousand times worse, and she forced herself to speak, babbling out her words.

'No, Hippolyta, please! I am sorry! I am most sorry! I did not mean to suggest . . . I would not . . . No! No, Hippolyta, you are not to bare me . . . you are not! I order you! No!'

She finished in a long wail of utter shame as her bottom came bare, her round little cheeks nude and split to show her anal charms and the pouted lips of her quim in the same rude pose she had held others in so often. Hippolyta didn't even pause to gloat over Lucy's nudity, but laid in, applying firm smacks to the pale, wriggling little cheeks, to set them dancing and quickly bring a red flush to the surface. Lucy went wild, wilder than before, kicking and lashing out, screaming and begging, but it was too late. She was being spanked, and even if Hippolyta did stop, she would still have been spanked.

Hippolyta didn't stop, but clung on tight as she used the hairbrush with a will, belabouring Lucy's bottom with all her force, in silence, until at last the comic sight of bouncing bottom cheeks and winking anus became too much for her and she started to laugh. Lucy's struggles became more furious still, but they only made Hippolyta laugh all the louder, and spank all the harder. Soon Lucy's breasts had tumbled out of her chemise, and began to bounce and jiggle beneath her chest as the punishment went on, adding one more awful detail to her shame. Still she fought, knowing full well how her quim would react to being given a hot bottom, and how helpless she would be to stop it.

Only at the sudden creak of the door did the spanking stop. A shame yet more agonising than before filled Lucy as she twisted her head around, to find her intended standing watching her, in surprise, but also amusement. She tried an angry demand to be released, but it came out as a croak.

'I . . . I had expected some such tableau,' de Cachaliere remarked, 'to judge by the noise, but I had assumed it would be Hippolyta who had earned a beating. Is it then the custom, in England, for the maid to discipline the mistress?'

'No,' Lucy answered sulkily. 'It is not! Let me up, Hippolyta, or it will be the worse for you!'

Hippolyta released her and she stood up, quickly smoothing her petticoat down and returning her breasts to her chemise. De Cachaliere said nothing, but his face registered both arousal and amusement. Lucy maintained an angry silence, burning with shame and unwilling to confess to her own arousal. De Cachaliere squeezed at his crotch. Lucy forced her temper down, realising that to argue with him would gain nothing, for all her pique at being seen in such a humiliating condition. It was too late. She was now a spanked girl, yet the opportunity for revenge was irresistible.

'I had remarked to my maid,' she said, with an icy glance to Hippolyta, 'that in the future it might be necessary to whip her . . .'

'It is, I find, the best way to maintain domestic discipline,' de Cachaliere admitted.

'Absolutely,' Lucy agreed, 'but rather than accept so right a judgement, she . . . she said that if she was to be whipped in future, she would take her opportunity for revenge in advance!'

'And so she spanked you?'

'Yes!'

227

De Cachaliere tried to hide a chuckle. Lucy stamped her foot.

'Intolerable insolence,' he stated, struggling not to laugh, 'and yet, your discipline is a subject perhaps better tackled sooner rather than later.'

'My discipline!?' Lucy demanded.

'Absolutely. What sort of man would not discipline his wife?'

Lucy made a face, but could find no answer, thinking of her contempt for weak-willed men, and her feelings for him. De Cachaliere went on happily.

'I am not a cruel man, by any means, and detest the use of sticks, heavy straps and other such implements, all suited only to the hard skin of peasant girls. I shall use my hand only, save perhaps for a light whip, which I have always felt is an implement suited to Ladies. Hippolyta, in addition, may use her hand or her hairbrush.'

'Hippolyta!?' Lucy demanded. 'Hippolyta must not discipline me! I am not spa . . . not usually!'

'Somebody must, my dearest,' he responded, 'and it would be most inappropriate for me to choose a man. Surely your maid is an ideal choice? She is familiar with your ways, also sympathetic and loyal, should you commit any little indiscretions during your punishment. Who else would you wish to witness the indignities associated with being spanked?'

'Nobody at all!' Lucy answered hotly.

'Precisely my point.'

'That is not what I meant! I . . .'

She trailed off. Her whole body was trembling, her quim urgent for his touch, or better, his cock. She knew she was pouting badly, but was unable to stop herself, thinking of Augusta, her own sister, and what they so evidently shared.

'It is clearly for the best,' he went on. 'Now, off with your chemise and petticoat.'

Lucy gave Hippolyta a sullen look and did nothing.

'Come, come,' de Cachaliere urged a little less gently, 'or must you be beaten again, so soon?'

Lucy shook her head, unable to fight for all that a part of her was raging at her own surrender. Nevertheless, her hands went to her chemise, opening the strings a little before pulling it off. With her breasts bare she felt more aroused still, and available in a way only he had ever made her. Her petticoat followed and she was nude but for her stockings, and very conscious of both her bare flesh and her small size compared to both de Cachaliere and Hippolyta. Lifting her chin with what pride she could muster, she placed her hands on her hips, showing off her body.

'You are beautiful indeed,' de Cachaliere sighed. 'Do you have rouge?'

'Rouge?' Lucy queried, surprised. 'Why, certainly. Do I seem unduly wan?'

'Not at all, rather flushed, if anything, but if you would apply a little to your teats it will provide a wonderful effect.'

Hippolyta had already found the pot of rouge and was holding it out, grinning. Lucy gave her a dirty look but took it. Her hands were shaking badly as she dipped her finger into the pot, to rub it onto her nipples, which left both little buds bright red and prominent against the white of her skin, also stiff. De Cachaliere gave an appreciative cough.

'And your cunt, if you would.'

'I . . . I am somewhat hirsute,' Lucy admitted, blushing.

'Not below, nor around your charming anus,' he answered. 'Hippolyta might, perhaps, apply the rouge to better effect.'

Hippolyta stepped towards her, grinning more broadly than ever, and throwing Lucy into confusion.

'I . . . no . . .,' she managed. 'I shall do it myself.'

She lay back on the bed, rolling her legs up to make what she knew was a thoroughly indelicate display of both her quim and her bottom, including the little hole at the centre. Her emotions were a jumble as she took more rouge and applied it gently to the lower lips of her quim. What he was doing to her was providing so much pleasure, and making her want to yield utterly. For all her pride, she knew she could not resist, no more than Augusta could. A second fingerful went onto her anus, painting a circle of red around the little dimple, and she had done it, rouged her own cunt and anus, painting herself for fucking, for buggery. Both de Cachaliere and Hippolyta had watched, and with her body painted to his instructions Lucy found herself shaking harder than ever, wanton and eager for his cock.

'Stand up,' he instructed, 'and show me your bottom.'

Lucy stood, her voice breaking as she spoke.

'You may leave us, Hippolyta.'

'How cruel,' de Cachaliere chided, 'to deprive your maid of such a charming sight. Come, push your bottom out and hold your cheeks open.'

Lucy hesitated, full of chagrin, also anger at her own feelings. Hippolyta stayed put and, with a last petulant glance at her, Lucy turned, to hold open her bottom for de Cachaliere's inspection of her well rouged anus. He squeezed his cock as his eyes fixed on her. She saw that he was nearly erect, and her urge to take him in her mouth and then up between the painted lips of her quim grew stronger still. She swallowed, feeling slightly foolish and a little put upon with her rouged nipples, quim and bottom hole, as if she were some sort of erotic clown, and wondering why it was impossible to resist him.

He freed his cock, quickly unbuttoning the flap of his breeches to extract it. At the sight she gave in. Turning to sit back on the bed, she opened her mouth, allowing it to be fed to her. Hippolyta had sat back on the stool, watching hungrily as Lucy sucked on her lover's penis.

Suddenly being fucked in front of her maid was what Lucy wanted more than anything, and as de Cachaliere came to full erection in her mouth her feelings for the spanking changed from outrage to gratitude. De Cachaliere was right. She would need spanking when he was gone, and Hippolyta was the only person who could possibly do it.

She lay back, spreading her thighs in welcome, acutely aware of her painted cunt, her nipples and anus too. De Cachaliere's eyes were full of lust as he knelt on the bed, putting his cock to her quim, rubbing, and then slipping it deep up the slippery hole. Lucy took her breasts in hand as he began to fuck her, smearing rouge over her white skin as she stroked her nipples. Her exposure no longer mattered, nor the rude show she was making of herself. She was his, to be used as he pleased. He took her thighs, rolling her legs up and holding her by them as he fucked her, harder and faster, until she was whimpering on the bed.

'Come, Hippolyta,' he grunted suddenly. 'Make a seat of your Mistress' face.'

'No ...,' Lucy managed, in a last feeble attempt to retain at least some dignity, but she knew she didn't mean it, and Hippolyta was already scrambling onto the bed.

A long, lean leg was cocked over Lucy's body as the pace of her fucking increased. As Hippolyta's muscular, coffee-coloured bottom settled over her face, Lucy wondered if Augusta felt the same way, full of shame, yet with an overwhelming need to further humiliate herself. Hippolyta's thighs were already wide, her dark, furry quim damp and wet over Lucy's chin, her anus a dun-coloured star between the meaty bottom cheeks.

'Kiss my bottom,' Hippolyta demanded, 'on the hole.'

She had reached back, to spread herself in Lucy's face, her anal star winking slowly in anticipation of a kiss. Lucy heard her own whimper, and for a moment she was trying to fight, wriggling in futile desperation on de Cachaliere's cock, but still with her eyes fixed in horror on Hippolyta's tight black bottom hole.

'Kiss her!' he laughed. 'Lick her too, and well!'

Again Lucy whimpered, a sound of utter surrender, but she puckered her lips to plant a neat, gentle kiss on Hippolyta's anus. It was done, her mouth put to her maid's bottom hole, and her humiliation was complete, her pride lost completely. She poked her tongue, licking the puckered star of flesh gently, then harder. Hippolyta was laughing in delight, and she wiggled her bottom onto Lucy's face as she sat down more firmly. Lucy's mouth was open against Hippolyta bottom hole, licking and kissing as her body shook to the motion of her fucking. De Cachaliere grew faster still and she realised she was to be spunked in, only for the motion to stop.

'Now,' he stated, 'let us see if you cannot accommodate me up your bottom.'

Lucy groaned against her mouthful of black bottom hole. His cock touched between her cheeks, slipping in the thickly applied rouge, briefly in up her cunt again, then back to her anus. Hippolyta lifted her bottom a few inches, leaving her spit-wet, slightly open anus just above Lucy's mouth. Lucy's bottom hole began to push in to de Cachaliere's cock. Her eyes popped wide, but then the little ring began to spread and she was gasping as her bowel opened. His cock head popped inside, and she was gasping louder still, and panting, and clutching onto Hippolyta's hips as inch after inch of thick, greasy cock shaft was forced up into her reluctant back passage. Only when his balls met the tuck of her bottom did he stop, with a deep, ecstatic sigh.

'Ah . . . but you bugger like an angel, my darling, and now, if you would be good enough to take your seat once more, Hippolyta.'

Hippolyta sat down in Lucy's face once more. As de Cachaliere began to bugger her, she was licking the maids bottom hole without having to be told. Hippolyta shifted a little, reaching down to manipulate Lucy's cunt. Lucy pulled her head up, feeding on her maid's bottom hole, wanton and eager. De Cachaliere began to push harder, deep up Lucy's bottom, her hole already tightening to the skilled touches on her bump. She cried out, coming into rapture, her bottom hole in spasm on its load of erect penis. De Cachaliere grunted and jammed himself deep. Lucy knew he had come in her rectum even as her own body locked in climax and her tongue drove as deep as it would go up her maid's bottom, the perfect climax to her surrender.

Epilogue

De Cachaliere chuckled as he poured himself a measure of Cognac. Leaning to the side, he filled John Coppinger's glass. At their feet knelt their wives, Lucy and Annie, both naked but for their stockings, both with their bottoms flushed pink from recently administered spankings, both with their cheeks bulged out as they sucked their husbands' cocks. Lucy also had her nipples, cunt and anus well rouged. They had been made to strip, serve the Cognac naked, spank each other and kiss each other's bottoms before going down to suck. Now, with both men fully erect, they were working eagerly to take what was about to be done in their mouths and show it off and thus see who was made to lick the other to ecstasy. Neither man seemed in any great hurry, sipping their Cognac and conversing on this topic or that as they were sucked. Hippolyta stood to one side, also in just her stockings, but with a dog whip in one hand, for use in case either of the girls should falter or fail to give satisfaction.

'She is a good little pet, now she is trained,' de Cachaliere stated, reaching down to tousle Lucy's copper-coloured curls.

She came off his cock just long enough to snap playfully at his fingers, but giggled before returning to her task. De Cachaliere laughed and signalled to Hippolyta, who quickly snapped the whip across Lucy's already well reddened bottom. For all his pretence of calm, he knew he was going to come soon, and as Lucy began to nibble on the head of his cock he realised that he could hold back no more. His mouth came open in a sigh of ecstasy, he pushed her head firmly down, and came as his cock jammed into her windpipe. She struggled to swallow as gush after gush of spunk erupted into her throat, failed and ended up coughing it up onto the floor between his boots, with more hanging from her nose.

John Coppinger laughed to see the state Lucy was in, and took his cock, quickly finishing off in Annie's mouth, and, like de Cachaliere, pushing deep at the last moment to make the spunk explode from her nose and leaving her gagging on the floor.

'A fine pair!' he chuckled. 'Up you get, Annie, and when we come in I want to find you with your face in Lucy's cunt ... no, beneath her arse, with her mounted on you, cunt to tits and your nose to Robby Douglas!'

'See it's done, Hippolyta,' de Cachaliere added as the girls climbed unsteadily to their feet.

Hippolyta took both Annie and Lucy around their waists and led them off towards the bedroom, both still snuffling spunk, and Lucy at least also giggling. De Cachaliere sighed and adjusted his cock, speaking.

'Matters are easier, then, with Fairbrother gone?'

'Easier by far,' Coppinger agreed. 'I already have the new fellow in my pay, and not a soul to oppose me.'

'Excellent. And Annie's sister is to marry, I hear?'

'To Nat Addiscombe himself no less. Parlour maid to Mistress of the house, a good step.'

De Cachaliere nodded.

'Though not one to meet with local approval,' Coppinger went on, 'and already she's giving herself airs. I don't suppose old Nat'll even have the sense to keep her arse whipped.'

'Likely not!' de Cachaliere laughed. 'Not after how you served her last husband.'

'Saul?' Coppinger queried. 'Oh no . . .'

'Come, come, John, there is no cause for pretence. You were there, and who else in these parts can snap a man's neck with one blow?'

'One or two,' Coppinger admitted, 'but it was me, yes. Strange tale there. I came to the kitchen with Nat Addiscombe's casks, and there's little Polly Mudge crying her eyes out with some story of how Saul's gone out to have his way with Miss Augusta, Mrs Truscott, and old Mrs Hawkes to boot. Couldn't make out the half of what she was saying, I couldn't, for her sobbing, but I went out to tell the daft bastard to keep his cock to himself. I'm just by the glasshouse when this harlequin fellow comes out from among the bushes with a knife in one hand and a tulip in the other. Shock of my life he gave me. I hit him.'

De Cachaliere laughed.

'Only found out it was Saul when I lifted the mask,' Coppinger continued. 'Stone dead, he was. There were sure to be questions, so I took off.'

'Leaving him with the tulip stuck up his arse!' de Cachaliere laughed.

There was a moment's pause.

'Up his arse?' Coppinger asked.

'Up his arse,' de Cachaliere confirmed.

'Not I,' Coppinger answered. 'You'd not find me sticking anything in Saul Mudge's arse.'

'When he was found, he had a tulip up his arse,' de Cachaliere insisted, 'a purple one, named for Augusta Truscott.'

Coppinger shrugged, and after a moment spoke again.

'Don't tell my Annie how it was, mind you. She thinks it was for Polly's sake I did it. Since then, nothing's too good for me, so far as she's concerned.'

'You have my word on it,' de Cachaliere promised, 'and doubly so for what you know of me.'

Coppinger gave a low, cruel laugh.

'You're safe there, no question. Who then was de la Motte?'

'A Marquis, as I said. The daughter of the Comte Saônois would not be fooled by a mere invention. He was the owner of the estates I purchased when the noble lands were auctioned off in 'ninety. I had been his reeve, and had managed to embezzle a significant fortune, he being forever at court.'

Coppinger laughed loudly.

'The distinction is trivial in any case,' de Cachaliere went on. 'His family won their lands and title by right of conquest, and I have taken them in turn. I also suspect I am his bastard, if all were made plain, as he was certainly exercising his rights upon my mother.'

'And he went to the guillotine?'

'I watched him die. One more sup of Cognac and I'll be ready for another gallop. Shall we exchange trollops? I've a mind to bugger your Annie, if you'd care to see how you fit up Lucy's arse.'

Notes

1. Preventative Waterguard, a force created in 1809 and amalgamated with the general excise service in 1822. Naval officers were appointed to patrol sections of coast with the intent of preventing smuggling, also to ride the coastline and generally investigate anything suspicious. With much of the local populace firmly on the smugglers' side, it was both a frustrating and hazardous task

2. Cruel Coppinger. There was a notorious smuggler by the name of Coppinger, who operated from the coasts of Northern Cornwall and Devon in the late eighteenth and early nineteenth centuries, but the facts of his life have become obscured by legend, at least some of which is exaggerated. He was probably Irish, but of West Country ancestry, and is said to have been the sole survivor of a shipwreck at Welcombe, where the border between Devon and Cornwall meets the sea. His ship had apparently been driven onto the shore, and the local populace had come down to the strand to plunder whatever was available when a gigantic man emerged from the sea and casually took possession of a woman, Anne Hamlyn (or Dinah according to some sources), and her horse, returning to her father's farm to demand shelter and sustenance. His subsequent career is said to have involved smuggling, especially of silk and

brandy, which he stored in a cave accessible only by rope ladder, also orgies and assorted mayhem. In this period he earned the nickname Cruel Coppinger, and is said to have made a habit of flogging his wife, the same woman he carried off from the shore, so as to extort the family savings from his mother-in-law. While he disappears from history, and legend, in around 1807, his wife survived him and is buried alongside her mother in Hartland church.

3. Wild carrots are white, and early domestic varieties white, purple or yellow. The orange carrot was a mutation selected by the patriotic Dutch and did not become widespread until the eighteenth century.

4. One hundred and fifteen of the Cherokee Class sloops were built for the Royal Navy, starting in or around 1807. When fitted for active service, these were of around 300 tonnes displacement and carried ten guns, but the design continued in use well into the Victorian period for a wide range of purposes. HMS *Beagle*, famous for Charles Darwin's voyage of discovery, was a Cherokee Class sloop.

5. On 11th April 1812 Sir Stapleton Cotton defeated the French under Marshal Soult at Llerena in Estremadura.

6. Sinking rafts laden with contraband was a common technique among West Country smugglers, especially after the dramatic increase in excise activity that followed the end of the Napoleonic wars. By taking bearings on shore an exact point on the seabed could be used so that the smugglers' ships did not have to approach too close to shore and the goods could then be retrieved by apparently innocent fishing vessels.

7. 'Canting Crew' was a slang term employed to cover all those who used vulgar slang as a regular means of communication and certain slang terms in order to avoid being understood by others. In practice this might have embraced a range of diverse and even

mutually antagonistic groups, but was used much as the modern media use the term 'underclass'.

8. Arthur Young, a noted agriculturist of the late eighteenth and early nineteenth centuries, also something of a puritan, at least so far as the behaviour of the labouring classes was concerned.

9. *Noblesse de l'épée*, the old French nobility, consisting of those families whose noble status dated back to medieval times and in some cases to the dark ages. By the time of the French Revolution these formed a small proportion of the French nobility and had the reputation of being so proud as to be ineffectual in modern life.

NEXUS NEW BOOKS

To be published in May 2005

ABANDONED ALICE
Adriana Arden

The Cheshire Cat travels from Underland to warn Alice her friends are threatened by the mad Queen of Hearts and need her help to liberate themselves from sexual slavery. Accompanied by her attractive and surprisingly perverse college tutor, Alice finally finds her proper place in Underland. The perverse and capricious animals to be found in this strange place – where humans are sexual slaves and second-class citizens – consign her once again to 'girling' status and take every opportunity to abuse her for their own pleasures. Nonetheless, Alice still has plenty to fear from the unpredictable, sadistic Red Queen. A delightfully perverse retelling of a classic tale, by the author of *The Obedient Alice* and *Alice in Chains*.

£6.99   0 352 33969 1

IN HER SERVICE
Lindsay Gordon

In the Saviour State, women have achieved a peak of dominance and glamour while men are conditioned to please. Young, innocent Franklin is initiated into a forbidden style of bondage by his cruel, beautiful and insatiable mentor – a process not without its own unusual pleasures.

£6.99   0 352 33968 3

TIGHT WHITE COTTON
Penny Birch

Thirteen girls relate their filthy experiences with spanking fanatic Percy Ottershaw, from his headmaster's daughter to Penny herself. From 1950 to 2000, his life was dedicated to getting his girlfriends across his knee, pulling down their tight white cotton knickers and spanking their bare bottoms. Otherwise, he is polite, considerate and every bit the gentleman, always willing to indulge the girls' own fantasies, from wetting their knickers in the street to being tarred and feathered.

£6.99   0 352 33970 5

If you would like more information about Nexus titles, please visit our website at www.nexus-books.co.uk, or send a stamped addressed envelope to:
  Nexus, Thames Wharf Studios,
  Rainville Road, London W6 9HA

NEXUS BACKLIST

This information is correct at time of printing. For up-to-date
information, please visit our website at www.nexus-books.co.uk

All books are priced at £6.99 unless another price is given.

------ ✂ -------------------------

Please send me the books I have ticked above.

Name   ....

Address   ....

            ....

            ....

            .... Post code ....

Send to: Virgin Books Cash Sales, Thames Wharf Studios, Rainville Road, London W6 9HA

US customers: for prices and details of how to order books for delivery by mail, call 1-800-343-4499.

Please enclose a cheque or postal order, made payable to **Nexus Books Ltd**, to the value of the books you have ordered plus postage and packing costs as follows:

UK and BFPO – £1.00 for the first book, 50p for each subsequent book.

Overseas (including Republic of Ireland) – £2.00 for the first book, £1.00 for each subsequent book.

If you would prefer to pay by VISA, ACCESS/MASTERCARD, AMEX, DINERS CLUB or SWITCH, please write your card number and expiry date here:

....

Please allow up to 28 days for delivery.

Signature ....

Our privacy policy

We will not disclose information you supply us to any other parties. We will not disclose any information which identifies you personally to any person without your express consent.

From time to time we may send out information about Nexus books and special offers. Please tick here if you do *not* wish to receive Nexus information.   ☐

------ ✂ -------------------------